"LOOK TO THE HORIZON"

The king's head snapped back as he gazed into the far sky. Then his mouth dropped open in shock.

What he saw froze him with fear. Winging toward the palace-fortress, in numbers sufficient that they blotted out a good eighth of the sky, were hideous flying lizards. The ugly beasts were a good twenty feet long, though half of that was tail. Mounted on each of the creatures was either a wizard of the League of the Black Wing, or an armored man-at-arms, complete with lance and great helm. Onward toward the palace the armada of airborne warriors flew, until they passed by within a few feet of the king's window.

"Power from the skies," Valdaimon said, "to aid your conquering armies on the ground. At their mere appearance many foes will break and flee." The wizard smiled a hideous smile that revealed his few remaining yellowed teeth. "What price would you consider fair, your Majesty, for the display of power you see?"

DRAGONSPAWN

MARK ACRES

AVON BOOKS • NEW YORK

DRAGONSPAWN is an original publication of Avon Books. This work has never before appeared in book form. This work is a novel. Any similarity to actual persons or events is purely coincidental.

AVON BOOKS
A division of
The Hearst Corporation
1350 Avenue of the Americas
New York, New York 10019

Copyright © 1994 by Bill Fawcett and Associates
Cover art by Duane Myers
Published by arrangement with the author
Library of Congress Catalog Card Number: 93-91660
ISBN: 0-380-77295-7

First AvoNova Printing: February 1994

AVONOVA TRADEMARK REG. U.S. PAT. OFF. AND IN OTHER COUNTRIES, MARCA REGISTRADA, HECHO EN U.S.A.

Printed in the U.S.A.

RA 10 9 8 7 6 5 4 3 2 1

Prologue

THE ANCIENT ONE could retreat no farther. She had neither the strength nor the will. She lay along a snow- and ice-covered ledge near the summit of her secret place, a great mountain in the northeast of the world. Her battered scales no longer glowed their ruddy hue; already the transformations of death were overcoming her. The pale sun was a ball of haze in the gray, frozen sky; it offered her no warmth. The mountain face that rose behind her was a final barrier both to her passage—for her wings hung in useless shreds at her side—and to her foe's. Above her giant head a shelf of ice extended almost to the end of the ledge.

The Ancient One stared with her one remaining eye at the hated elf who had vanquished her. Arrogant hatchling, she thought. He couldn't be more than seven hundred years old, yet he had defeated an entire race of creatures who had terrorized the world from time immemorial.

Steam rising from her pooling blood clouded the Ancient One's vision. But she could still see him, his feet spread wide and planted firmly on the granite beneath the snow and ice that crowned the mountain. He stood not ten feet in front of her, the sheer precipice to the abyss below at his back. His armor—there was a filthy elven trick! His reddish black armor, covered with great gouts of her blood, had been fashioned from the very scales of her own offspring. Time and again it had protected him from the fiery blasts of her breath, and it also insulated him from the numbing cold of the icy wind that howled around her final, secret aerie. How many centuries had it taken, she wondered, for elven hands to fashion that armor, gathering the scales one by one, shaping them, stitching them to a soft leather backing, forming them into this impenetrable suit and great helm that now confronted her? Even the boots were covered with dragon scales; only the eyes of her foe could be seen.

A bolt of pain shot through the Ancient One's body from the great gash in her belly. She moaned involuntarily, a great, near-final death moan that began as a rumbling bass sound and soared upward in pitch and volume like the death shriek of a mighty race. The wail caused the very rock of the mountain beneath her to vibrate in response. Snow and ice loosened their grip on the craggy granite face behind her and tumbled down on her back and legs. But the elf neither flinched nor trembled. His black eyes remained locked on her eye, unblinking, unforgiving, unyielding.

The mother of dragonkind refused to die in front of this enemy. She closed her eye, the better to focus her mind. Wounded, aching muscles contracted. Claws stronger than steel bit into the icy surface beneath her sinuous, prone body. With tremendous effort, she pushed back with her powerful hind legs. Her bulk began to rise.

The elf watched carefully as his lungs gulped down the freezing air in huge gasps. He saw the dragon slowly rise once again. Incredible, he thought, that any creature, even one as powerful as this, could still be alive. He had chased her across a hundred leagues or more, pummeling her with half the spells known to elvenkind. He had pursued her for two days up the sides of this mountain in a land known to the elves only in legends and songs. Then, on the sides of this mountain, clad in armor made from the scales of her own race, he had attacked, wielding an enchanted blade proof against the fire of dragon breath. Again and again he had hacked away at the sides and belly of the great beast, darting in, striking, darting out—all the while dodging the blows of her lethal claws. One hit would have stunned him, perhaps ripped him in half. The next instant he would have died between her powerful jaws—jaws that reputedly had once snapped around the sacred oak of the Homeland Wood, destroying the Birth Tree with one bite. He had plunged his enchanted blade into the left eye of the beast and with a flick ripped it from its socket. The dragon had fought on as though it hardly noticed the loss. But at last his moment of opportunity had come when the great beast reared on her back legs. The elf had lunged, stabbing deep, then yanked his great sword upward, ripping open the old dragon's tawny belly. Her roar had nearly deafened him, and he had feared it would bring down an avalanche upon him. The old worm had spilled blood and innards in great gouts then, but still had the strength to retreat higher up the mountain to this ledge. The elf had followed carefully, for he knew that though victory was near, so was the end of his own strength.

Now she was rising again. The elf began to doubt that she would ever die. Perhaps, despite his years of preparation for this moment, it would be he that met death on the dragon's mountain. But it would never do to show fear. He kept his eyes locked on her and watched, watched for the sign that another potentially fatal blow was about to be launched by this tireless creature that had lived longer than the elves could tell even in legend.

First, the dragon's hind legs tensed. Then slowly the body rose, the great crippled wings hanging like dead skin from the arched, scaly back. Then the horrid neck began to tremble. He could see the muscles straining, almost beyond their ability, beneath the covering of nearly impregnable armored scales. Finally, the head lifted from the bloodied snow, lolling to one side. The horrid mouth opened. The elf braced himself, raising his shield, expecting once more the fiery breath that had slain so many of his ancestors. But no fire came forth from the dragon's mouth. Instead, the narrow, slimy tongue flicked against the huge teeth, forming the sounds of elven speech!

The Ancient One hated the sounds the elves made. They were like the sounds of icicles clattering against rocks when they melted and fell in the spring or like the sounds of singing finches in the forest trees at night. They were not the wholesome, gravelly, guttural tones of honest dragon speech, but rather a rippling, flowing, rising and falling series of tinkling notes, repulsive to her ear. Nonetheless, duty to her race, to the world, to the future, demanded that she now use the hated tongue. She must have some tribute before dying.

"Stay your deathblow, elf, long enough to tell me the name of the one who slays me."

The elf staggered backward in surprise. He had heard dragons speak before—he head even heard them casting spells. But never had he heard a dragon speak the elven tongue. And this dragon spoke it perfectly. Quickly he steeled himself again—this could be a trick.

"You are dead, Ancient One. Ask no questions," he replied. "It is best you submit quietly. I will make the deathblow swift. You will not suffer more."

"You do not know what suffering is, elf," the old mother of her race replied. "To see your entire race die, that is suffering. To see all the children of your nest destroyed by lesser things that mutilate even the words of magic, that is suffering. Be just. My death is certain. Tell me your name."

The dragon's head rolled up and back as another wave of pain coursed through the length of her body. Her tail thrashed from side to side, pounding the snow. The sound of the blows echoed from the nearby peaks while the elf pondered her words.

To tell her his name would be dangerous, he reasoned. This dragon knew magic—almost as much magic as the elves. To give any mage one's true name was to risk destruction—for a great part of magic consisted in knowing the true names of things, their names in the language of magic. On the other hand, elven custom demanded that when one elf slew another, the killer reveal his own true name. The giving of the name was a kind of equivalent to the giving of one's own life—a life for a life. The dragon, the elf reasoned, was wise to base her demand on a custom he would normally respect.

"I see you know our elven ways," he retorted. "Then know this: you are not an elf or a creature that elves must respect. You are a beast to be destroyed. I am under no obligation to you."

Rage shot through the dragon, rage even greater than all

her pain. She tilted back her head once more and roared her anger at his insufferable arrogance.

The elf darted to one side as more than a thousand pounds of snow and ice, suddenly loosened from the mountainside above, fell toward his head. Then he ran forward, toward the beast, his sword held level, the point aimed at the already gashed belly of the lizardlike horror. If he was to die buried in the ice of the ages atop this timeless rock, the beast would die with him.

The dragon, ignoring the avalanche crashing down atop her, raised one huge forepaw and struck. Her blow caught the elf squarely on the back. He plunged downward, headfirst, face flat in the snow.

"Fool!" the Ancient One rumbled, as his body and her foot were buried in the slide. "Do you think me ignorant of you or your kind? You would slay me, but you will not show respect to me? You kill my entire race and dare to call me a beast? Then know this: your name is already known to me. It is Lelolan, though you are commonly called Elrond. And this, Lelolan, is your fate: you shall live to see the disappearance of the last of your kind at the hands of lesser beings. Now, be wounded but live—to suffer." The dragon raised her forepaw from Elrond's back, shaking off the mounds of snow and ice as though they were weightless. Then she stamped down again with all her remaining strength. The elf, still barely conscious, heard his ribs crack and his backbone pop. Pain drew his stomach up toward his lungs, but before he could be sick in the snow, blackness overwhelmed him.

The old serpent saw her prey grow still. Without another word she turned and slithered away over the face of the rock she had called home since the early days of the world, her great foreclaws tossing aside the mounds of ice and snow. She had one task left to perform—and just enough strength, she believed, to perform it.

Unerringly the tired, wounded creature drew herself along the ledge until she came to a narrow crevice cut into the mountainside. The crevice sloped sharply down toward the bottom of a small crater hidden in the timeless rock. Her muscles could no longer hold her bulk; she slithered and slid down the icy crevice, tumbling in a painful heap onto the crater floor.

There she lay while time stood still. How long she rested, dying, she did not know. The evening stars were blazing against the clear, freezing night sky when her consciousness returned. She looked for one last time upon their light, then spoke a single word in the dragon tongue, a word unknown to elves and men then as now. The bottom of the crater rumbled and quivered. In the side of the crater wall a new crevice opened, a crevice that led down into thick blackness below. Into this crevice the beast hurled her body.

The rocky sides of the passageway tore at her scales and ate into her wounded belly as she half crawled, half fell farther and farther down into the interior of mountain. Driblets of gore marked her passage, but she did not care. She knew the way behind her would be sealed forever at the moment of her death. Onward she went and downward into the blackness, guided by the dimming sight of her remaining eye that could see, even in the darkness, the tiny spots of heat that marked the outlines of the jagged, twisting tunnel.

At length her head emerged into a great chamber where an underground lake, fed by a warm spring, offered her both drink and comfort for her death wound. She let herself glide into the water, luxuriating in its warmth. Then she kicked with her rear legs and swam, as she had countless times before, to the far side of the underground pool. She dragged herself out on the granite shore to lie by the side of a great heap of gold, silver, gems, and jewelry, a heap so large it dwarfed even her own great body, stretching more than sixty feet along that hidden shore.

She closed her eye and began to dream. She could see them clearly now—the countless thousands of her kind that she had mothered. She could see them, hundreds strong, in great flights that blackened the sky as they soared beneath the shining sun, their scales gleaming crimson, and the earth beneath them erupting in flames as they passed. Whole forests would disappear to appease their malicious anger; countless elves would burst into flames like tiny torches at the touch of their breath. They were a great armada in the sky, destruction on the wing—invincible, invulnerable masters of the world.

But then the elves had learned. Had some god taught them magic? Had some foe of the creator of dragonkind guided their detestable tongues and their nimble little hands? The Ancient One did not know. But their learning was a terror. She saw the endless fights that had turned dragon against dragon, maneuvered by the clever elves with their magic and their lies. She saw the horrid battles in which fiery breath and physical might were turned to naught by magic; then dragon after dragon was slain by creatures barely strong enough to hold their swords. It had taken centuries, but the elves had won. Now she was dying, the last of her kind, while her killer slept in the snow far overhead.

She dreamt of Scatch, her mate, a magnificent dragon twice her size but with less strength of will. How they had frolicked in the early days of the earth when the gods who had made them were still young themselves! What joy they had had in populating the world with their own kind—and what sorrow she had the day Scratch had fallen, giving himself to save three of their sons cornered by a pack of elves. That had been just two short years ago—she and Scratch had had a final frolic just the day before.

The Ancient One's head shot upward with a jerk, her eye wide open. Two years—two years ago to the day! It was the time. It was the time. That was why she had dragged herself here. She must remain awake, must not let the death sleep come just yet. One great task remained to be done.

The great worm curled her tail up beneath her body. She clamped shut her jaws and strained, fighting back the pain that came afresh from her death wound. The great lizard trembled all over for a moment like a dead leaf in a gentle breeze. Then her body relaxed, went limp. The great jaws opened and the dragon gasped.

Slowly she uncurled herself and crawled toward the heap of gold. On the rocky shore behind her, beneath the spot where she had lain, were two large, leathery eggs.

Their dull brown outer cover was tough but flexible. From base to crown each egg was a little over three feet long. They rested side by side, motionless, pregnant with the hopes of a slain race.

The Ancient One reared herself up and cast her fiery breath upon the heap of gold. Flame shot from her mouth in a cone more than ninety feet long, engulfing most of the treasure, the remains of the accumulated wealth of dragonkind. The gold softened. She breathed again, and rivulets of molten gold began to flow down from the pile toward the edge of the underground lake.

Lovingly, with great care, the Ancient One picked up the first egg and turned it slowly in the glowing river of gold, coating it carefully. When the shell was fully covered with more than an inch thickness of the molten metal, she turned and plunged it into the water of the lake. Steam rose as the metal quickly cooled, and the golden egg sank away, out of sight, into the darkness of the deep water far beneath the mountain. The dragon grunted her approval. Then she repeated the process with the second egg. She watched it, too, drop into the black water until even the glow of the heat of its golden shell was lost to her sight. Again, she grunted her approval.

Now it was her time.

The Ancient One dragged herself back to the heap of treasure, which was cooling slowly into a bizarre lump of gold and jewels, as the metal rehardened. Her eye raced quickly over the trove, finding a trace of the item she sought. She extended a foreleg, and a huge claw plunged into the soft metal, grabbed the corner of a great tome, and plucked it from its metallic tomb.

Once again the dragon rose and staggered to the lake-shore. She held the great fireproof volume in one set of foreclaws, while a single razorlike claw carefully turned the ancient vellum pages between the worn silver binding. At length she found the page she sought.

She reared herself to her full height and began intoning the words of dragon magic—words that drifted out over the lake and up into the tunnel through which she had come, weaving their way to the outside air miles above, and threading their way through eons of time, carrying with them the final spell of the mother of all dragons.

She cursed Lelolan, called Elrond, and all his race. She called upon the powers of all the gods and all the spirits of all the gods had made to avenge her race upon Elrond's. She blessed her eggs and consecrated them to the final battle for the fate of dragonkind. And then with magic known only to herself and to no other creature—neither man nor elf nor god—she set the time for their hatching. But whether her hatchlings would live to rule or to serve, not even the dragon's magic could preordain.

The Ancient One closed the great tome and tossed it into the lake. She drew her head full back and sucked in all the air her dying body could contain. And with that final breath, she let out her death cry, the death cry of an entire race of creatures so powerful, so awesome, and so terrible that their very name would be a byword for horror and fear long after their actual existence was forgotten. Again the mountain trembled in sympathetic vibration with her cry, but this time the trembling of the mountain did not stop. It spread and spread through the countless tons of granite until the entire mountain rumbled. Cracks appeared in the rocky ceiling above the underground lake, and sheer slabs of granite broke loose to plunge into it, sinking toward its depths. More slabs fell after them; more cracks appeared. Boulders began to tumble from the sides of the great cavern until the entire interior of the mountain collapsed. The Ancient One pitched forward into the water, and the mountain itself fell in upon her to serve her as a tomb.

But the words of her curse, her blessing, and the incantation of hatching wove their way unheard through the magical fabric of time, until their faint, faint echo was heard five thousand years after the Ancient One's body was pressed into the rock of her mountain.

➤1➤

A Thief's Time Stolen

Bagsby stood with his rear to the roaring fire and rubbed his hands briskly on the backs of his soft leather breeches. He lived in an age five thousand years from the death of the Ancient One; he neither knew nor cared about dragons. He did care for money. His quick eyes darted about surveying the tavern room as he worked the damp, early spring chill from his bones. The dive looked like a good place to make a fresh start—there were plenty of easy marks loitering in their cups, and the tavern keeper kept loose coins in the pocket of his apron.

His backside warmed, Bagsby turned toward the popping fire, extending his arms to warm his hands. He listened intently to the babble of a dozen conversations coming from the tables and benches behind him and to the clatter of bottles and pans from the busy back room. As warmth returned to Bagsby's body, his stomach began to rebel against its long neglect and growled at him, demanding satisfaction.

"Tavern keeper!" Bagsby bellowed over the din. "What's in that great black pot over this fire? Is it fit to eat?"

Laughter erupted from the tables behind him. "We always come here for the fine food," one drunk shouted, thoroughly taken by his own wit.

"Better wash it down with some ale," a second friendly voice chimed in. "In fact, better have the ale first—and skip that poison!"

"All right, all right, that's enough from the likes of you," the burly tavern keeper shouted from behind the crude wooden counter that served as bar, serving counter, and focal point for the cramped room. "It's venison stew, and it'll cost you threepence to find out if you like it."

"Bring us a bowl, then, and plenty of ale to wash it down," Bagsby shouted. The short man, warmed all over at last, turned from the fire and strode to the nearest long table. He wedged his brown boot between the backsides of two drunks whose heads were already hanging stupidly over their mugs and shoved one aside. The drowsy fellow landed on the stone floor with a thud. Bagsby snickered and took the seat, grabbing the unfortunate's mug of ale and pouring it over the man's face.

"Time to go home, old friend," he said, letting a broad, friendly smile form on his pudgy, square face. "Come along now, there's a good fellow."

The other drunks at the table stared stupidly for a moment, then broke into laughter again. But William Clayborne, the tavern keeper, failed to see the humor. He didn't like this little loudmouth who was pushing around his regular drunks without so much as a bit of respect. He angrily slopped a ladle of the stew into a wooden bowl and stomped up to Bagsby.

"Look here, you apologize to this man and get your own seat. Don't be coming in here raising—"

Bagsby flinched at the tavern keeper's words and jumped up in alarm, being careful to drive his elbow up under the bowl of stew so that it landed, steaming hot, on the fat tavern keeper's face.

"Ooowww!" Clayborne howled, letting the bowl clatter to the floor and grabbing at his apron to wipe the scalding liquid from his eyes.

"Oh, oh, I'm sorry," Bagsby clamored. "Let me help you!" The little man grabbed at the apron and tried to swipe at the tavern keeper's face with the dirty rag. By now, gales of laughter had erupted from every table in the room. And, of course, Bagsby had successfully removed all but two of the coins from Clayborne's apron pocket.

"Get away from me, you loudmouthed little dunce!" Clayborne shouted, shoving the short thief away. Bagsby staggered backward and then tumbled over, exaggerating the force of the push he'd received. He contrived to fall squarely onto three other customers at a nearby bench; they were only too eager to help him to his feet and shove him again toward the enraged Clayborne, who by now had the stew wiped from his eyes. Bagsby stumbled forward, shouting, "No! No! Oh, my!" and staggered past Clayborne into yet another bench full of laughing onlookers.

"That does it," Clayborne shouted. "Out you go! Out, I say!" The man's fat fingers closed on the back of Bagsby's cloak—which he had been careful not to remove—and yanked the little man up until his feet dangled above the floor. "I'll put you out like a damned cat, I will!" Clayborne declared, racing with his kicking, pleading burden toward the tavern door.

"Oh, no!" Bagsby shouted. "No! Please! Not out into the cold! I only wanted—"

Bagsby felt Clayborne's free hand close on the back of his breeches, and before he could finish his cry of protest he was flying face first through the tavern door. He landed nimbly in the slop and mud of the filthy, dark back street and was up and running, still protesting, before Clayborne had slammed the door of the tavern.

Bagsby kept running; he wanted to be well out of this section of the city within minutes. As long as he stayed in this neighborhood, with its collection of brothels, cheap sleeping rooms, sharpster merchants, gambling houses, and dives, he was in danger. That was the risk of the method he'd used: recognition. He'd attracted a lot of attention. On the other hand, he'd relieved one tavern keeper and eight patrons of the bulk of the cash they were carrying. If his estimate was correct, he'd have more than enough for a good night's entertainment in a classy place with a higher grade of personnel. By tomorrow night, at this rate, he'd be hobnobbing with the rich in this fine city of . . .

Bagsby paused for a moment to catch his breath and remember the name of the city. Clairton—that was it. Clairton, in the central lands of the minor kingdom of Argolia. Well, by tomorrow night he'd be hobnobbing with the rich of Clairton. The thief glanced back down the dark, narrow street. He saw nothing unusual. He took time to check his soft leather breeches, his fine gray linen tunic, and his heavy black cloak for damage. Nothing serious, he noted, brushing some mud and dung from the cloak. Nothing that couldn't be cleaned by a good lackey when he had enough money to hire one.

There was no alarm coming from down the street—those louts must be really drunk, Bagsby thought. His confidence rising and good cheer beckoning to him, Bagsby sauntered down the street, his hand working beneath his cloak to note the shape and size of the coins he'd stolen. Ah, he thought, this is good. This is better than I'd thought. He counted copper and silver coins, an amount equivalent to at least two gold crowns. More than enough for his purposes tonight. Bagsby began to whistle as he made his way out of the rowdy neighborhood into a more genteel district. He was so pleased with himself that he didn't notice the slim, short, boyish figure, wrapped in a too long cheap black cloak, that darted from a doorway to follow him down the street.

Shulana worked her way cautiously down the street. At times it was difficult for her to believe she wasn't noticed; as an elf who'd had little exposure to humans, she was not yet accustomed to the fact that humans could not see well in the dark. The narrow alley was filthy and crowded with a variety of humans, none of whom seemed appealing. There were the obvious prostitutes, the obvious thieves who eyed anyone who passed, looking for a poorly guarded coin purse, and a large number of drunks who loitered against the walls, urinated in the street, or fell down to sleep, passed out cold, only to be stepped on by others who staggered over and past them. Yet out of this mass of humanity, none paid the slightest attention to Shulana. That, of course, was what she wanted.

Still, the area made her feel uncomfortable. How could humans live in such filth? How could any creature with intelligence—and humans had intelligence, there was no denying that, even though they lacked any semblance of wisdom—how could any creature of intelligence live like this? What malicious joke of some god made them so destructive of themselves and anyone and everyone else?

Shulana shook off these questions and refocused on her mission. The little thief had stopped, brushed off his clothes, and obviously counted the money hidden beneath his cloak. So, as she had assumed, he had, as his kind said, "worked" the dive. He'd never had any intention of spending a long time there. Just as well. She wished he'd hurry up and get to some other section of the city, a section where the Covenant would be respected should her true identity be discovered. The scum in this section of the city would have no second thoughts about killing an elf just for the pleasure of the deed. That was another concept Shulana found strange—killing for pleasure.

No matter. Her quarry was moving again now. She couldn't believe her ears—he was whistling! Why didn't he just light a torch and carry it down the middle of street, shouting out "Notice me!" As she trudged along carefully, staying out of sight well behind him, she wondered if she'd made the right choice.

True, she had inquired of the seers on the Elven Council, and they had been unanimous. Every portent of their magic, every gift of foresight pointed to this Bagsby as the one she must choose. And she had studied his operations in Kala and been impressed by his skills, even though his behavior was abominable by elven standards. In that city he had managed to swindle the entire cabal of thieves that controlled most illegal operations there. He had netted himself a fortune—and an enemy for life in the person of Nebuchar, the leader of the Kala cabal.

But then success had made Bagsby careless, in Shulana's judgment. He had journeyed north through one city after another, always just a few days ahead of Nebuchar's hired assassins, never even bothering to check for signs of their presence. He ate to excess, drank even more, and squandered a fortune on low-class women in high-class gambling houses. He didn't even bother to steal to replace his losses. Shulana could not understand this behavior. And now, when he knew—or should know—that within moments an angry mob of drunks would be racing up the street searching for him, he was whistling! What kind of thief was this Bagsby? How could she trust him?

Bagsby saw torchlight ahead. Cheerfully, he quickened his pace. The narrow street opened on to a small square, bustling even though it was well past sunset and the stars could be seen clearly in the cool night sky. The buildings here were kept cleaner than those in the narrow street, and some rose three stories high. Young swains paraded in their colorful, fancy clothes around the fountain in the center of the square. Bagsby stopped and watched for a while. One youth in particular caught his eye. He was tall, lean, muscular—probably sixteen or seventeen years old. He took great pains to keep his cloak pulled back behind his shoulders, revealing his red- and black-striped blouse with huge padded shoulders and ruffled sleeves, topped by a large, white full-ruffled collar. His breeches were full-length, tight, purple with black vertical stripes right down to the finely polished black leather boots that rose to just above his ankles. He wore a soft felt hat with a huge, drooping brim in the rear and a spray of large purple and yellow feathers on the side. Quite the young suitor, Bagsby decided. And a gentleman, because he chose his jewelry well. Even across the square the trained eye of the thief could catch the gleam of gold rings on three of the youth's fingers and the glint of tiny gemstones set in the hilt of his rapier.

Bagsby watched as the young man walked conspicuously from one side of the square to the other, stopping now to talk with one group, then with another, all the while casting surreptitious glances at a particular balcony where three young ladies, dressed equally lavishly, tittered and chattered as they watched the male displays below.

Across the square, horse-drawn carriages of persons of modest wealth came and went with some regularity in front of a guarded and well-lit doorway. No doubt a fine gambling house, Bagsby decided, and the place where those young men who failed to attract a lady friend—as well as some who did—would end up passing the evening. Bagsby smiled broadly and strode across the square, eager to ply his trade in this new, more pleasant setting. Perhaps he would gain riches this evening. Perhaps he would even fight a duel, cheat, win, and be toasted and feted. One could never tell where the gods of fortune would lead one, Bagsby thought.

Bagsby drew an inquisitive glance from one of the two rough-looking halberdiers who stood by the open doorway of the hall, but the man made no attempt to stop him. Bagsby passed inside, and his eyes widened with delight. The crowd was largely made up of young men, most under twenty-five, although there were a few men in their thirties and forties to be seen in the great hall. The hall itself was filled with gaming tables of all types—dice and card games were most common, though Bagsby saw one prestidigitator running a shell game with an eager throng egging on the current player to wager once again. Another was running a mousehole game, one of the oldest cons known to the gaming hall business. Smaller tables were scattered throughout the room for those guests who chose to drink or eat and hang on to their money a bit longer. The serving wenches were buxom, scantily clad, and beautiful in a cheap sort of way. Bagsby sighed with contented joy. This was his kind of place.

A backward glance at the square showed that fortune was indeed smiling on Bagsby tonight, for the young swain he had scrutinized so carefully was sitting dejectedly on the side of the fountain, talking with a friend. The balcony, on which he had lavished so much time and attention, was now empty, as empty as the wealthy youth's heart and head would be while he suffered the pangs of lovesickness.

Bagsby made his way to a small table, plopped down, propped his feet up, and sang out to a serving girl, whom he promptly and affectionately patted on her ample rear while ordering a mug of mulled, spiced wine. Content, he watched the dice game at a nearby table and waited. Strangely, he paid no attention to the slight, short, boyish figure wrapped in the long black cloak who quietly entered the hall.

Shulana kept her head lowered and made her way

quickly and quietly to the rear, selecting a tiny table near the darkest corner of the room. She knew she was taking a great risk, coming inside this human place. She had considered waiting outside, where it would be easy to hide in a dark doorway or even in the mouth of the narrow street that led back to the rough part of the city. But her curiosity and her doubts had driven her. Before she could approach this Bagsby, she had to be sure in her own mind that he was, in fact, the right one.

Neither she nor Bagsby had long to wait. As Bagsby sipped his mulled wine, he saw the youth he'd spotted earlier walk despondently into the hall. He gave polite nods to several tables and seemed about to join some companions at a card game, when Bagsby made his move.

The little man sprang from his seat and came up behind the young stranger, suddenly all shyness, with his face cast down toward the floor. He walked slowly forward in this posture until he literally bumped into the young man.

"What? Who's that? What are you doing?" the youth snapped at Bagsby.

"Oh, my!" Bagsby exclaimed, feigning shock, surprise, and embarrassment. "Oh my, I do beg your pardon, good sir. I assure you, I meant no offense."

"Well, then, watch where you're going," the young man said curtly.

"Oh, certainly, certainly," Bagsby mumbled. "I'm sorry. It's just so hard, being a stranger in this city, having the problems I have, not knowing anyone of, well, better birth, if you know what I mean, a person I can trust."

At her table in the dark corner, Shulana reached into the recesses of her cloak and withdrew a tiny vial of fine, dark gray powder, almost like ash. She sprinkled a tiny amount in the palm of her left hand, raised her hand to her lips, and softly blew the powder in the general direction of Bagsby. Then she quickly and softly muttered a brief chant and lowered her head again. She could now hear clearly every word of Bagsby's conversation.

"What are you going on about?" the young man demanded. "This has been an irritating evening for me, and you're certainly not making it any better."

"Come on, Reynaldo," called one of the youth's friends. "We're delaying the next hand for you."

"I apologize, good sir," Bagsby said, shaking his head in despair. "I cannot burden you with my problems. Oh, but if you stood to loose the profits I could reap this very night, you too would be despondent and distracted. Indeed, sir, I am quite beside myself."

"A moment, Bertrand," the youth called back to his friend. The young man's eyebrows moved closer together, and his eyes narrowed as he studied the person before him more carefully. He was a short man with close-cropped dark brown hair with just the slightest hint of gray near the temples. He was pudgy. His clothes were tasteful but not rich or fancy. His hands—Reynaldo's gaze focused on the man's hands. By some strange coincidence, the man was alternately wringing his hands and then opening them, making it easy to take them in at a glance. The fingers were fat and soft looking, almost sensitive, while the palms were callused, like those of a laborer. Probably, Reynaldo thought, a gentleman who had fallen on hard times and who may now have a way to recover a part of his fortune.

"I cannot be responsible for your business problems," Reynaldo said haughtily. "But I am curious. What business are you in, and what profit could you reap?"

"No, no, I've detained you too long," Bagsby insisted. "Please, go on with your game with your friends. I must have drunk too much. I really should not discuss this kind of lucrative business with someone I don't know at all, even a fine young gentleman like yourself. Ah me. There's no one I can trust. And a profit of two thousand gold crowns gone to waste."

"Shhh," Reynaldo cautioned. "You're right about one thing—you shouldn't be discussing this kind of thing here in the open. Come, let's sit."

Bagsby's face lit up with joy. "Oh, my! You mean, you'd join me for a bit? I would like that. It's so difficult, being a stranger, having no companions with whom to share even a mug of wine. Here, I have a table right here." Bagsby practically pranced his way back to his table.

"I understand your problem," Reynaldo said, taking the seat indicated by the suddenly bouncy Bagsby. "It is tough being a stranger, particularly when you're in business." Reynaldo leaned forward and stared hard into Bagsby's eyes. "Now, what is the nature of your business?" he asked.

Perfect, Bagsby secretly thought. He's hooked. The only question is for how much. Young men like this always need more money to finance their expensive romances and the extravagant clothes they wore. They also often had access to family funds that they wouldn't dare spend on themselves but might invest on the sly in a sure, fast, profit-making venture.

"Well," Bagsby said, leaning forward himself and looking around carefully to make sure no one was listening, "I'm in the . . . Wait a minute. I don't even know you."

"I am Reynaldo Pendargon, son of Alfonso Pendargon, the richest wine merchant in Clairton," Reynaldo said. "Both my father and I are well known, and our characters are unimpeachable. Ask anyone. And you, sir?"

"I am Leonardo Rondini, a dealer in rare specialty items who has fallen into the worst of luck," Bagsby said, sighing. "Thieved and swindled, that's what I've been."

"Oh," Reynaldo said, his interest growing cold.

"And yet," Bagsby quickly added, lowering his voice to a whisper and shoving his own face up close to Reynaldo's, "a mere four hundred crowns could net me a profit of over two thousand tonight."

"How is that possible?" Reynaldo asked, skepticism in his voice.

"You know that cabal of thieves that operates not far from this very place, down that narrow filthy street just across this square?" Bagsby asked. "Oh, of course you do. Anyone in business here in Clairton is certainly onto them."

"Well, of course we know about them," Reynaldo said uncertainly.

"They bribed my guards!" Bagsby lamented. "I was transporting a priceless piece of rare jewelry from the far north to a customer here in Clairton. The wretches bribed my guards, who delivered the piece to them along with all my operating cash. My customer expected delivery tonight and is waiting to pay me four thousand crowns for the piece. My expenses are only two thousand, so the profit is two thousand clear."

Reynaldo leaned forward again, his eyes involuntarily growing a little wide. "But how would four hundred crowns help? Why not just go to the magistrate, whom I know personally, I might add, and—"

"No, no, that's no good," Bagsby interrupted. "It would take too long. The thieves intend to sell the piece tonight. By the time the magistrate takes action, the piece will be long since gone. Besides, I want my profit, not revenge on these thieves, no matter how sweet that would be. The thing is, you see, they don't know what they've really got. They're willing to sell it back to me for only four hundred crowns. Of course, that would cut my profit down to sixteen hundred, but sixteen hundred crowns is better than nothing. It would still make the trip worthwhile."

"Reynaldo! Come on! We need your money in the game!" Bertrand called.

Reynaldo hastily looked around the crowded hall, irritation on his face. "A moment, friends. I have important business." He turned back to Bagsby and began to whisper. "You mean to say, if you had four hundred crowns, you could retrieve this piece, then collect four thousand for it this very night?"

"Why, yes," Bagsby replied innocently.

"And your profit would then be sixteen hundred crowns?"

"Yes, yes, that's right. Why? What difference could it possibly make now?"

"Well," Reynaldo said, drawing himself upright in his chair. "I will tell you, sir. I will lend you the four hundred crowns in exchange for eight hundred after the transaction is completed."

Bagsby let his mouth drop open. He hoped his pupils widened to register genuine shock. "You would lend me the funds?"

"In exchange for eight hundred, tonight, when the deal

is done," Reynaldo affirmed, his head bobbing up and down eagerly.

"Well," Bagsby said thoughtfully, "I don't know. I am not in the habit of borrowing from men I hardly know. And the cut in my profits is most severe."

"A profit of eight hundred crowns is better than no profit at all. And I am not in the habit of lending to men I hardly know. The high return is fair, considering the risk I'm taking."

"Yes, yes," Bagsby quickly agreed. Anything to get the mark's mind off his risk. "But I need to think about this. And there is time to consider. You surely don't have such funds on your person."

"I will meet you within the hour in that alley, and we shall confront this band of thieves together," Reynaldo said eagerly.

"No, no, no!" Bagsby stood up in alarm. He glanced quickly around the room, catching himself, then sat down again and leaned to whisper to Reynaldo. "You cannot take such risk to your person. These thieves know they already have all that is mine; there is no profit for them in harming or holding me. But you, sir, that is another matter. Surely you don't want to risk being kidnapped."

"Gad, that is thoughtful of you," Reynaldo said, sudden revelation and relief showing on his eager young face. "You're right. I'll bring the money here, and you will return here when the transaction is done."

"Well . . ." Bagsby shook his head.

"Sir," Reynaldo said, standing and extending his hand, "I insist. It is the least the business community of Clairton can do to extend its welcome to a fellow businessman and to show solidarity against these scoundrels who would rob us all blind."

Bagsby reluctantly stood. He pursed his lips, looked at the floor, then swung his concerned gaze around the room. Finally he let his eyes meet Reynaldo's and stared into them intently for several seconds. "All right," he finally said, taking Reynaldo's extended hand. "I guess I can trust you."

"You won't regret this," Reynaldo said, stepping eagerly

away toward the door. "Wait here. I'll be back shortly."
The youth practically ran from the gambling house into the
night, visions of a four-hundred-crown profit dancing in
his head, his mind's eye already picturing the new clothes
that would surely win the heart of his beloved.

In the far dark corner of the hall, Shulana nodded her
head. The council must have been right. For all his faults,
this Bagsby would steal from anyone and could charm
even the undead with his acting ability and his tongue. Her
choice was finally made.

Shulana stood in the dark street outside the palatial city
dwelling of the Viscount Marco D'Alonzo. It was well
past the middle of the night; the sun would dawn over the
city in less than four hours, by human reckoning. The elf
pondered her next move. The question was how to approach Bagsby.

Inside the mansion, Bagsby was sleeping soundly, having been befriended by the viscount after managing to
carefully loose one hundred crowns to him in a dice game
at one of the more exclusive gambling halls in Clairton.
The Pendargon family would not think of contacting the
viscount about a minor matter of swindling—the embarrassment would be too great. Nor were they of sufficient
social standing to be guests at his splendid home. Bagsby,
on the other hand, as the recently robbed son of the Count
of Nordingham in the kingdom of Pantania, many hundreds of leagues distant, was more than welcome to spend
the night. The Pendargons were wasting the time of their
own retainers trying vainly to find the so-called Leonardo.

Shulana thought deeply on her problem. She could not
tell Bagsby the truth; he would merely take her information and then use it for his own profit and the advantage
of her enemy. She glanced up at the great mansion, where
torchlight lit up the carefully sculpted front gardens by
night, and where armed men patrolled the grounds at irregular intervals to foil the plans of thieves. What weakness
did this Bagsby have that she could play on?

Greed, she thought: greed, a fondness for what the humans considered high living, and a total lack of any values

other than the satisfaction of his own desires. Bagsby would do what she wanted as long as he thought he was serving himself. He would respond to the promise of wealth, if the promise were credible, or to the threat of losing what he had—which was very little, other than his wits and his life. And there was his vanity. She had learned that it was a mistake to underestimate the power of human vanity.

Shulana drew her cloak tightly around her and raised its cowl over her head. She resolved upon her course of action. Touching her cloak, she made a hasty gesture, muttering the words of an elven spell. Had anyone been watching, they would have seen her virtually disappear, as her cloak took on the coloration of its immediate background.

Thus protected, Shulana walked boldly into the street and approached the front gardens of the mansion. A convenient fig tree extended its branches upward toward the second-story balcony; the climb was easy. From there, she opened the great glass doors onto the hall leading to the guest rooms. Even in the dark, her elven vision enabled her to quickly spot Bagsby's chamber; it was the only one in use, and its door handle glowed with the recent heat of contact with a living being. The door was unlocked; the wealthy trusted their hirelings to protect them. She turned the knob and slipped inside quietly.

The room was quite large—fully thirty feet across and almost square. A fine oak wardrobe, a marble washstand, a small, polished oak table and chair, a great mahogany bookcase filled with hand-copied and carefully bound volumes of works currently in vogue with humans, a great tapestry depicting one of the countless battles from the human-elven wars, and three fine paintings, presumably of relatives of the viscount adorned the chamber. In the center stood the great canopied bed. The frame was made of solid polished cherry wood; the canopy was satin to match the bedclothes, and the whole enclosed with fine lace curtains. Fresh-cut flowers trembled in finely turned clay vase next to the head of the bed.

Bagsby lay in the center of the bed on his back, his head

raised by several soft pillows, snoring loudly. The satin sheets and a fine woolen blanket were pulled up tightly under his chin.

Shulana stood silently, surveying the scene, drinking in every detail. Only when she was satisfied that no weapons were visible and that therefore her only danger came from Bagsby himself, did she make her next move.

First, with a gesture and a touch to her cloak, she removed the chameleon spell from it. She did not want Bagsby to awaken, only to see what looked like a disembodied elven face looming over him! Then, once again her hand went to the pouch on her belt, and once again she removed a tiny vial. In the vial was pure melted snow. She opened the stopper, stuck in her little finger, and obtained one drop of the fluid. Then, softly whispering a magical incantation, she walked swiftly but silently to Bagsby's bed, drew back the curtains, and touched the drop to his lips.

Bagsby sat bolt upright, his mouth wide open. His left arm raised the covers as he sat up; by the time he was fully up his right arm was already swinging, attempting to slash the figure leaning over him with the dagger in his hand. Shulana had expected this move—she had watched Bagsby for months—and the dagger slash slid harmlessly off her magical cloak.

"Be still, Bagsby," she said in her most commanding voice, standing erect and glaring at him from beneath her cowl.

Bagsby's lips moved and his mouth opened wide and shut several times, but no sound emerged from him.

"Call out all you want; it will do you no good. You are magically silenced. You can make no sound no matter what you do," Shulana said sternly.

Bagsby scowled, glanced about wildly, and then hurled his dagger with all his might at the glass window of his room. The glass shattered noiselessly, and the dagger sailed out into the night. Bagsby watched in amazement as the shards of glass fell silently to the floor. He turned his head and looked at Shulana, his brow furrowed, his dark brown eyes wide, his mouth formed into a small "O".

"You see that what I say is true," Shulana said severely. "Now know this, Bagsby, thief, con man, and scoundrel. I mean you no harm. If you will not betray my presence, I will release you from silence so that we may talk. But you must guarantee that you will take no action against me. If you do, the penalties will be severe. You can see that I am a mage of some power. Do not think I come to this interview unprotected. What is your answer?"

Bagsby thought quickly even as the voice was speaking. His eyes were still adjusting to the dark; he had no idea who or even what this assailant might be. His immediate fear was an assassin sent by Nebuchar; he quickly dismissed that idea. If the intruder were an assassin, he would already be dead. In any event, his word was virtually meaningless, and his word to an intruder was certainly not binding. He had nothing to lose by agreeing and everything to gain. Bagsby nodded his assent to the intruder's terms.

Shulana made a subtle gesture with one hand, and Bagsby found his power of speech returned.

"Who are you, and what do you want of me?" he asked. His eyes squinted, straining against the darkness to see the face that confronted him.

"My name is of no concern to you, thief. What is of concern is what I want," Shulana said simply.

"Fine," Bagsby said, shrugging. "Mind if I get up?" Without waiting for a reply he threw the blankets off his legs and swung his feet to the floor. He leaned over and dug through the pile of clothes by the side of the bed.

"No, I don't mind if you rise. But if you're searching for another dagger, it will be the last thing you ever find."

Bagsby's hand froze. He looked up at the face which was now becoming more clear as his eyes adjusted, and grinned broadly.

"Do you blame me for trying?" he asked, chuckling.

"No. I expected it. I hope you understand that it is pointless to resist me."

"I understand for the moment. Now, about what you wanted."

"Just this. To make you rich," Shulana said. A cold

shudder ran through her body as she spoke the words; it was totally against her nature to lie, even to a swine like this thief.

"Well, then, welcome, friend. Leave the riches as you leave the room, won't you?" Bagsby retorted.

"You must work for this wealth," Shulana said briskly. "I want you to steal something."

"A contract job?"

"Precisely."

"What is the item you want stolen?" Bagsby asked. He could see the face now, and he carefully controlled his own face so as not to betray his deep shock and surprise. At first he thought perhaps his eyes were mistaken, but as he gazed at the face, there could be no doubt. The high cheekbones, the narrow, pointed nose, the short cropped dark hair, the narrow elongated eyes, and the deliberate attempt to hide the ears, all these could mean only one thing. The intruder was an elf. Whether male or female Bagsby could not yet tell, but there was no doubting the species. Bagsby had only seen two elves before in his life, and one of them was dead at the time.

"Yes, I am an elf. A female, to answer your real question," Shulana said casually.

Bagsby cursed silently. He had been trying to control his reaction. Maybe the old tales were true. Bagsby had heard many stories from old thieves about how elves could read a human's thoughts by the expression on the face, even when the human was deliberately dissembling. How the elves could do this, when they understood so little about humans, was a mystery. Bagsby decided that a temporary surrender was the best approach.

"So, I see there is no point in trying to deceive you," he acknowledged. "What is the item you want stolen? At what risk to me and of what value to you?"

"I want you to steal the Golden Eggs of Parona," Shulana stated bluntly. His reaction was exactly what she had expected. Bagsby burst into laughter.

"Oh, my! Oh, my!" he exclaimed between belly laughs. "For a moment I thought you were serious. Who sent you? Who are you? What manner of prank is this? Did old

Sixfingers send you?" Bagsby stood and pulled on his breeches. He caught his tunic on his big toe and kicked it up into his hands. "Come on, now, you've had your fun. Tell me. Who sent you?"

"No one sent me," Shulana replied honestly. "I came of my own accord on my own initiative. This idea is entirely my own."

"Come on now," Bagsby said, pulling on his tunic. "Enough is enough. You'd better get out of here before the servants hear our chatter."

"I came to hire you for a job, and I intend to see that you do it," Shulana said.

"What job?" Bagsby snapped. He was getting worried now. It wouldn't do at all for the viscount to hear of him entertaining an elf under the viscount's own roof. Bagsby had great plans for his newfound friendship with the young noble.

"I told you. I want you to steal the Golden Eggs of Parona," Shulana replied patiently. She had known Bagsby would not believe her at first. It was one of the things that made dealing with humans so difficult; they were so suspicious, because they were so untrustworthy. Although in this case, she reminded herself, Bagsby's suspicions were entirely justified.

"I see," Bagsby said, bustling about the room now as he finished dressing. "By the way, my other dagger's there on the floor," he added, pointing to the weapon. The elf did not glance down at the place he indicated; she already knew where the dagger was, Bagsby concluded. "So," he continued, "let me get this straight. An elf, who refuses to tell me her name, breaks into my room in the dead of night and wishes to hire me to steal the most closely guarded and famous treasure in the world. Is that about right?"

"Yes," Shulana replied.

"And why," Bagsby asked, "should I not call out right now and summon the servants and the guards and have you put out of here and out of my life?"

"Because if you do," Shulana answered, "I will help Nebuchar's assassins find you. I have followed you for the last several months. I can tell you every word that passed between you and Nebuchar. I can tell you how you squandered the fortune you obtained from him. I can tell you how much you stole from those louts in the first tavern you visited tonight. I know how you duped young Pendargon out of four hundred crowns. And I know how you plan to use the viscount to gratify your own greed. Have me thrown out and I will stick to you like glue until Nebuchar has his way with you."

"I see," Bagsby said. "And if I do steal this treasure for you, which is patently impossible, what reward is there for me?"

"Name your price."

"The Golden Eggs of Parona are worth at least several hundreds of thousands of crowns. But only if one could sell them. Of course, they could be melted down, and the gemstones pried out, and so on. But that would reduce the value by more than half. How can you sell something that the entire world will know is stolen?"

"What I do with the Golden Eggs once you have stolen them is my affair and mine alone," Shulana said.

"Show me the money you will pay me, then," Bagsby demanded.

"I cannot. You have not yet said how much your services would cost."

"Let's say, just for sake of argument, two hundred thousand crowns."

"I agree to your price."

"Show me the money."

"I cannot," Shulana said honestly.

"Of course you can't, because you don't have it," Bagsby crowed.

"You are correct," Shulana said, nodding.

"What! You admit it?"

"Of course. What would be the point of denying it? Most of the kings of the human world could not raise two hundred thousand gold crowns in cash. I certainly cannot."

"So your offer is a fraud."

"No. If you succeed, the Elven Council will present to you its entire treasure, which is easily worth the amount you demand," Shulana said. In fact, this was the truth. Despite the reports of their own seers, which seemed to favor Bagsby, the Elven Council had agreed that, if Shulana could engage a thief who actually did procure and turn over to them the Golden Eggs, the entire treasure of the council could be given as payment to that thief. This they did because in their hearts they did not believe the thing could be done. Even then, they were in no danger of losing their treasure, for Shulana had no intention of allowing Bagsby to live once his task was completed.

"Even if that were true, and I don't think it is," Bagsby said, "why should I even think about accepting such a contract? The eggs are more closely guarded than the lives of kings."

"Because," Shulana said patiently, "the Golden Eggs have been purchased from the King of Parona by the Black Prince of Heilesheim. Even now they are being transported from Parona in the north to Heilesheim in the south. The route of the transport passes through this city."

Bagsby sat down on the edge of the bed, hardly daring to believe what the elf said. If it were true, if it were true, such a theft just might be possible.

"How many troops?" Bagsby demanded quickly.

"An escort of five hundred men guards the treasure. These were furnished by Heilesheim."

"Well"—Bagsby shrugged—"maybe, there might be some way. . . ."

Shulana smiled. Despite Bagsby's better judgment, she had him hooked, and she knew it.

⇒2⇐

Preparations

THE SUN WAS not yet up when fat Marta awoke, her slumber broken by the clamor and clanking on the far bank of the river. With an angry grunt she threw back the thick quilts and hoisted her bulk from the fine goose-feather mattress. Two short shivering steps brought her to the wooden shutters of the bedroom window. She threw them open and stared into the night, her anger rising as goose bumps crept along her cold flesh. Strangers across the river—a lot of them by the sound of it. And, that worthless, lazy, skinny dullard she'd married had let the bedroom fire burn out as well.

"Albert!" she squawked. "Wake up, you lout! The fire's cold, and there's a large party at the river ford." Without waiting for Albert's response, Marta opened her large oak wardrobe and drew out a heavy woolen shawl. Tossing it about her shoulders atop her thick blue sleeping gown, she stooped, grabbed the fire irons, and began a futile effort to poke life from the dead embers. "I said, wake up, you slothful nobody!" she shouted, sharply stirring the crumbling, burned logs.

Albert, who had awakened at her first call, gave a dull grunt in response. "Go back to bed, cow," he muttered, pulling the covers up tightly about his head. As the commander of the Count of Dunsford's Yeoman Border Guards at Shallowford and the highest official in that tiny village, Albert owed loyalty and obedience to the count. He neither deserved nor took lightly the abuse of his spouse, who enjoyed—thanks to his industriousness, boot-licking, and embezzling—this fine wooden house, a man- and maidservant, and a status far above that to which she was born. So, Albert thought, let the old cow bellow. He'd sleep till sunup, and if her ass was cold, she could make the fire herself.

"Are you deaf?" Marta screeched. "Can't you hear that clatter across the river? There must a hundred or more men over there—and you'd better see what it's about. I don't intend to have you lose the position I've worked so hard to get you into just because you're too lazy to roust yourself out of that soft bed." Having failed to find life in the ashes, Marta turned the irons and her attention to the blankets under which her husband's legs were curled. Three sharp whacks brought him howling to his feet, hopping first on one foot, then the other. As he continued his dance of pain, he massaged the spots on his shins where bruises were already forming.

"You cursed old swine," he shouted. "What devil has seized your brain to treat me thus in the middle of the night?" Albert gave up his dance and flopped over backward atop the bed, drawing up his legs and rubbing both shins at once. "You might have broken—"

His whining was cut short by the sound of a loud shout in the distance—a shout that clearly came from a huge number of men.

"Great gods of Dunsford, Marta, what is that?" Albert exclaimed, forgetting his pain and sitting bolt upright.

"I've been telling you—there's a great crowd down there across the river," Marta said, looking at him with a sort of fondness. Once awake, he was still a handsome rogue, she thought, even if he did owe every achievement of his life to her nagging. "Go on, see what the matter is. Do your duty, and I'll be waiting here when you get back. If you don't vex me further, I'll see you have breakfast on your return."

Albert rummaged through the wardrobe until he found his favorite pair of warm, purple velvet breeches. He pulled these on quickly, along with a clean white linen shirt. With Marta's help and much grunting and straining, he managed to squeeze his gouty feet into his fine, shiny black boots. From the table by his bedside he lifted the gold necklace that bore his seal of office and placed it around his neck. Marta brought him his best thick woolen cloak and fastened it by the gold clasp that bore the count's emblem.

"Get that breakfast ready," Albert grumbled as he strode down the stairs of his fine house. His steps clicked sharply on the cobblestones of the village's one paved street as he stomped his way to the shack that served as a border station by the river ford. No doubt this was some bunch of deuced nonsense, he thought. Probably some hunting party on the Heilesheim side of the river, with a dozen drunken lords and their attendants, raising a ruckus, rousing his wife, and dragging him out of bed in the wee hours of the morning for absolutely nothing.

Albert heard the splash of hoofs in the shallow water as his own steps brought him nearer the water's edge and the border guards' shack. His eyes were barely adjusted to the darkness; it took him several seconds to see the corpse of old Athelston lying on its back with a crossbow bolt sticking straight up from its chest.

"What, ho!" Albert shouted, suddenly alarmed. He whirled to face the ford and saw the first of several horses coming toward him, now at full gallop.

"In the name of the Count of Dunsford, halt and say who goes there!" Albert called at the onrushing form. His eyes grew wide with terror as the moon passed from behind a cloud and its white light glinted off the flawless, polished armor of fully armed knight, charging directly at him. The warrior's left hand loosely gripped the reins of his lumbering, barded horse; his right held the haft of a great morning star, a ball of iron with protruding spikes, that whirled in the air at the end of a length of chain. Emblazoned on the man's white tunic was the form of a great black lizard with wings, the Dragon of Heilesheim, as the Black Prince was wont to call it.

Duty conquered fear in Albert's brain long enough for him to scream out, "To arms! To arms!"

"The sport begins!" came the answering cry from the charging form, whose steed closed the gap to the river shore. The whirling morning star struck Albert square in the face with such force the shouting man's head was ripped from his body, impaled on the swinging ball.

"Hah!" The knight laughed aloud, swinging his gruesome trophy for the following horde to see. He reared his horse up on its hind legs, pointing with the morning star toward the hapless village, where, the few burghers and several dozen families of peasants were just rousing from their slumbers, wakened by Albert's call. "Death and flames," the knight cried. "Put it to the torch and slaughter all!"

With a great shout, a dozen mounted knights charged down the cobblestoned street, followed by more than a hundred men-at-arms on foot. The knights clustered about the three finer houses, breaking down the doors and entering to kill and pillage. The foot soldiers contented themselves with setting fire to the more than two dozen thatched huts that housed the village's peasantry and practicing their archery as the hapless occupants staggered into the fire-lit, smokey streets.

The knight who had slain Albert laughed as he watched the scene of blood and chaos. Tossing his weapon with its grisly trophy to the ground, he raised his beaver and then lifted off the great helm, decorated with spread dragon wings of thin gold-plated steel. This he handed to the young squire who had come to stand at attention beside his mount.

"My lord," an ancient voice called from the river ford, "is the battle already won?" The touch of irony in the question was lost on the young man, who laughed aloud again as two of his foot soldiers stamped to death a young peasant who had tried to flee down the village street.

"Come, Valdaimon, see how easily we tread on old Dunford's lands and what sport we have!" the youth called.

"My lord is in good spirits after his victory, I see," Valdaimon commented, carefully threading his way across the last portion of the ford and stepping gingerly onto the riverbank beside the leader's mount. "An easy victory. May all your battles be won so easily, Black Prince."

The young man turned and looked down at the old wizard who had tutored him through his youth, carefully teaching him the fine arts of government, war, and refined cruelty. "Don't patronize me, old man," the Black Prince snapped. His dark eyes blazed with a cold fire, and his long black hair snapped in the dawn breeze as he tossed his head arrogantly. "This was no battle, and you know it. Killing helpless peasants is mere sport. I was testing my men for their hardness, nothing more."

"As you say, my lord," the old man replied calmly. "In any event, a clear signal to Dunsford that he has little choice but to accommodate your larger designs." The old wizard leaned on the great staff that towered over his head. A smile creased his leathery, narrow, hideously wrinkled face, revealing the gaps between his few remaining teeth. The Black Prince wondered if the old man was smiling at the ease with which the village was sacked, at the continuing cruelties visible in the village streets, or at the fact that he had positioned himself upwind of his ward and the stench of his filthy body was causing the young man's nostrils to flare in disgust.

"Back off, Valdaimon," the prince ordered. "The stink of your potions and filth offends our person."

"May my lord's enemies be so offended soon," Valdaimon replied, lifting his staff and slowly hobbling back toward the ford. "There is no need for me here. I will await your presence and your pleasure at your palace. No doubt we shall talk tonight."

"No doubt," the prince called after the old man. Someday, he thought, someday he would no longer need the meddling old crocodile's counsel. Then he would be rid of his stinking carcass once and for all. But until that time, Valdaimon would be safe. His wisdom and his magic were both necessary for the great plan that was hatching in the prince's mind.

"Lord!" a knight called, galloping up with a fat, screaming wench in tow by her hair. "This is the last—I saved her for you to slay yourself."

The knight released his grip on the woman's hair, and fat Marta flopped to the ground. Her blue nightclothes were a mass of filth and blood, and she trembled and wept for the fate of her village, her home, and her life. Then she spied the head impaled on the morning star that lay in the mud beside her and shrieked her grief to the uncaring heavens.

"Hmmm," the Black Prince grunted. "This must be the wife of the leader of this village. I've a good idea. We'll spare this fat pig to do our will elsewhere. Bring me a torch and hand me your shield."

Puzzled the knight grabbed a torch from a passing man-at-arms and handed it to the Black Prince. Then he removed his great shield, with the sign of the dragon raised in metal upon it.

Laughing, the prince put the torch to the front of the shield, heating the dragon form until it glowed a dull red.

"Bring that fat wench here and bare her back," he commanded.

The knight dismounted and grabbed fat Marta under both her arms. He slung her against the side of his horse, and with his dagger, ripped down the back of what was left of her nightdress. The Black Prince dismounted and stood behind Marta.

"What is your name, wench?" he bellowed.

"Marta, Marta, wife of Albert, the highman of this village, whom you have slain," Marta answered, hatred in her voice despite her tears.

"Well, Marta, I'm going to let you live," the prince said grandly. "I want you to go to Dunsford and tell him all that has happened here. Tell him that what happened here will happen to his entire realm unless he gives fealty to me and complies with my wishes in every regard. Do you understand?"

Marta nodded her head against the sweaty flanks of the knight's horse. There was no point in fighting now—she would live to oppose this young bastard devil's son another day.

"Good," the Black Prince said. "And now, just so old Dunsford will know that everything that is his is now mine . . ." The young man pressed the red-hot front of the shield against the flesh of Marta's back, branding her like an animal with the dragon insignia. Marta screamed and fainted.

The Black Prince tossed the shield to the ground and re-mounted his horse. "Leave her," he ordered. "Re-form the men and return the bulk, leaving a small guard. Send a bridge party here at once. I'd have a bridge built here in two days' time."

"Yes, sire," the knight replied.

Laughing again with his high-pitched, whining laugh, the Black Prince rode off across the ford. Today was going to be a very busy day. He was glad it had started so well.

Baron Manfred Culdus whirled around, his face contorted with rage, and hurled his dagger full force at the form of the wizard who had just materialized behind him and called his name.

"Curse you, Valdaimon!" he shouted. "Leave your wizard's tricks behind when you come calling on me. Knock on my door like any normal man."

Valdaimon casually turned his head as the dagger passed harmlessly through his shriveled body. He watched with feigned interest as the deadly missile flew on across the large, octagonal room to impale itself in a thick wooden beam next to the heavy, ten-foot-high door. "Accurate, as always," he commented. "But, Baron, futile rage hardly becomes a military leader. You must learn self-control. Besides, your door is much too heavy for one of my frail strength to open, and to knock would have torn you away from your studies." With a grand gesture, Valdaimon indicated the huge oak table on which were unfurled more than a score of parchment maps.

Culdus snorted. "I don't like you, wizard," he said plainly. He drew himself up to his full height of six feet three inches. Clad as he was in his chain mail and battle tunic, with a great bastard sword strapped to his side, his great helm and mailed gloves lying beside him on the pile of maps, the baron cut an impressive figure, even at the age of forty-eight. "I don't like your magic or your ways or that stench that hangs about you like a cloud. I don't even know what you really are."

"All true, Baron," Valdaimon said, smiling and chuckling. "All true." Valdaimon fully appreciated the lethal nature of this man. He was a perfect warrior, in the wizard's opinion: a strapping, cunning hulk bred and trained to obey and to kill. But he could be dangerous if given too much freedom of action. "And you don't know how to kill me, either," Valdaimon subtly reminded this perfect tool of war.

Culdus scowled, and his great salt-and-pepper mustaches drooped down around his chin. "Well might you pray that I never learn how," he muttered.

"Prayers are for priests, dear Baron," Valdaimon said calmly, approaching the table and gazing over the maps. "My profession has little to do with religion, although at times we invoke powers that mere mortals might well consider divine."

"Enough," Culdus said curtly. "You are here for a reason. What is it?"

"To report to you, what else?" Valdaimon smiled broadly again, raised his arms, and shrugged his shoulders in a gesture of innocent inquiry. His tattered, filth-covered robes swirled as he did so, and the wizard watched carefully to see the baron's nose wrinkle as the odor assaulted him.

Culdus turned and strode to the far end of the table, his eyes glued to the maps as though there were some important point he was pondering. "Then report. And remember that despite our personal feelings, we are still allies. Be accurate."

"Certainly, friend Baron, certainly." Valdaimon beamed. "Here, let me show you on this chart." The old wizard rushed to Culdus's side and began flipping through the piles of maps. Culdus recoiled from the smell. He strode quickly across the room, away from the table, and hurled his muscled bulk into one of the high-backed wooden chairs scattered through the spacious chamber.

"Stay there, damn you, and say what you have to say!" Culdus roared.

"Ah, I've offended and had no intention of doing so," Valdaimon said with mock sadness. "What a pity—to always offend those one admires, respects, and works with toward common goals."

Culdus suppressed his urge to rush the old wizard, grab his scrawny neck, and snatch the life from him with one, solid, satisfying snap. Patience, Culdus counseled himself. "If you please, Valdaimon, I have urgent work before our lord returns," he said between clenched teeth. "I beg you, report."

Valdaimon leaned forward, his eyes locking intently on Culdus's face. His own lean visage grew suddenly serious; his foggy green eyes suddenly bright.

"We raided Shallowford this morning. Our young lord prince tested the cruelty of the twelve and the hundred. I believe he was pleased with the results," the wizard said.

"Good!" Culdus leapt to his feet, suddenly enthusiastic. "Were there any signs of pity? Any displays of mercy?"

"None."

"All were slaughtered without distinction?"

"All save one whom our lord prince branded and sent to Dunsford as a sign."

"Good! There is no place for pity in an officer of the kind of army we will lead."

"True, good Baron," Valdaimon agreed. Even the old mage was caught up in the joy of the moment.

"Then we have them—the twelve commanders for our twelve legions. And a hundred or more experienced men-at-arms with innocent blood on their hands. They will make fine leaders of hundreds."

"It is as you say," Valdaimon agreed.

"Then we should strike now! Any delay gives Dunsford time to raise allies, prepare defenses. . . ."

"Do not concern yourself, Baron," Valdaimon reassured the Black Prince's chief military advisor. "Even as we speak a great bridge is being built at Shallowford. On the third morning hence, the young lord shall give the order and our legions will march."

Culdus began pacing in his excitement. "That will be a grand day," he began. "Never has the world seen an army such as the one I have trained. Never have such tactics been perfected. Never before has—"

"Never before has the world seen such troops as I, too, shall supply," Valdaimon interrupted.

Culdus wheeled and stared at the wizard. "Keep those cursed things of yours under control, wizard. I trust them even less than I trust you, and you know well that is not much. And I do know how to kill them."

Valdaimon nodded in mock obedience. "As you command, great leader. But in all things, I must obey the prince, as must you."

Culdus snorted again. Little did Valdaimon know that once his usefulness had ended, his prince would turn Culdus loose on the old reprobate. Culdus might not know how to kill Valdaimon, but he would certainly enjoy the many experiments it would take to find out.

Prince Ruprecht of Heilesheim, commonly dubbed the Black Prince, drained his third mug of hot spiced wine, wiped the goose grease from his fingers on his scraggly attempt at a black beard, and belched. It had been an excellent day, capped by an excellent dinner and excellent entertainment. In one day he had sacked a village, gotten construction underway on the bridge over which his armies would pass on their route to conquest, executed prisoners by a variety of ingenious means taught him by Valdaimon, tortured the old elf kept in the deep dungeon for just that purpose, lopped the head and hands off the emissary sent by Count Dunsford with a protest note and sent them back to the count in a plain cloth bag, and eaten his fill of the best food available anywhere in the world. The young lord felt happy and heady. Now it was time to attend with enthusiasm to serious business.

The Black Prince swept his legs across the table, sending platters and goblets flying. "Clear this away!" he bellowed at the cowering servants. "And fetch me Valdaimon and Culdus. Then leave us alone."

The tall, pale, thin youth rose and went to the high window at the end of the long dining hall while servants scuttled and scurried to carry out his bidding. He gazed through the dusk haze at the mighty River Rigel far below, flowing in its eternal course westward toward the Great

Ocean Sea. Barges still plied the waters, those laden with grain from the fertile lands to the north making for the great port of Hamblen, which this very palace-fortress protected, those laden with bolts of cloth, furs, precious woods, and finely handmade goods and devices of every sort beginning their journey east and north to those same lands, which bought most of their goods from Heilesheim, at great price. Soon, Ruprecht thought, the price would be even greater. Once his armies had swept the northern lands, bringing their feuding lords into subjugation, he would bleed them dry.

"My lord, the Baron Manfred Culdus and Valdaimon the Great attend you."

Ruprecht turned around and dismissed the page with a wave of his hand. "Gentlemen. It is time for me to approve the details of our plan. Please, be seated." With a grand wave of his arm, the Black Prince indicated the two great chairs that had been set near the head of the table, one to the left of his own and one to the right. "I assume all is in readiness for our . . . discussions?"

"It is, my lord," said Culdus, stepping briskly to the chair on the prince's right and laying his pile of maps on the table. "I have here the final attack plans for your approval."

Valdaimon, grinning as usual, hobbled to the seat at the prince's left and placed before him on the table a large ball of clear crystal mounted on round black metallic base. "I too have some things to show my lord relative to our plans," he said in his best obsequious voice.

"*My* plans, Valdaimon," the youth snapped. "Never forget you are my instrument, not co-owner of my ideas nor co-ruler of my realm. You have served me well in the past, but do not presume upon my favor to tolerate your impertinence." The Black Prince hopped into his huge, leather-padded wooden seat, threw his feet up on the table atop Culdus's pile of maps, and smiled, first at Culdus, then at Valdaimon. "But enough of reproaches. Show me how my plans that will bring the fulfillment of my prophesied destiny. And, by the way, I've heard quite enough of this 'my lord' business. We all know my doddering, drooling older brother is never going to recover from his unfortunate lack of intelligence. As of today, I have decided to end my regency and assume the throne in my own right. Valdaimon, you will see to the publication of the appropriate decrees."

Both men rose quickly and bowed deeply from the waist. This pup is ready, Valdaimon thought. Culdus, for his part, sighed with relief. It is fitting to have done with the charade, he thought. A kingdom needs a king. Especially a kingdom about to become a great empire.

Culdus straightened to his full height. "Your Majesty," he began, tugging at his pile of maps. "Uh, er, if Your Majesty please . . ."

The Black Prince laughed his high-pitched laugh and lifted his legs, allowing the discomfited soldier to retrieve his pile of parchment. Culdus unfolded the largest of the maps and spread it over the surface of the great table. There laid before Ruprecht was a general plan of the known world, from Heilesheim in the southwest to the Five Ports of the Rhanguilds in the northwest, from the Southern Desert at the eastern boundary of Heilesheim to the spine of the Great Mountains that stretched away to the Kingdom of Parona in the far north. What lay beyond the mountains to the east neither men nor elves knew. In the center of the great map was the real prize: the patchwork quilt of duchies and baronies, provinces and minor kingdoms between the rivers Rigel and Pragal—practically a world unto itself—that contained the most fertile lands in all the earth and more than three score cities richer than any others save those of Heilesheim itself.

By themselves none of the cities, baronies, duchies, or kingdoms of the Land Between the Rivers (so it was called) was a great military force. What might they did have was often squandered in the endless series of wars, blood feuds, and border disputes that made every map of the area obsolete by the time the cartographer's hand had finished it. But these many score of petty states did have a loose confederation, termed the Holy Alliance, by means of which they had in the past repelled invasion from without and suppressed any one of their number who grew too powerful within. It was to the conquest of the Holy Alliance that Ruprecht was about to turn his hand.

"As Your Majesty knows," Culdus said, finally able to begin his presentation, "I have, at your command, trained an army divided into twelve legions, each legion in itself a kind of miniature army, able to withstand attack by a much superior foe for a day or more on its own, able to maneuver swiftly, and able to attack with all arms as occasion presents itself. By swiftly moving, combining, and recombining these legions, Your Majesty can create an army of precisely the desired size and strength at any point on the field of campaign."

Ruprecht waved his hand in the air, signaling Culdus to get on with it. He had heard this theory of the legion of all arms and of their superiority over the large but clumsy field armies likely to be raised by his opponents from the old warrior countless times.

"Yes, sire, I shall attempt to be brief," Culdus acknowledged. He noticed with satisfaction, though, that Valdaimon was hanging on every word. The wizard, too, was familiar with the military theory behind Culdus's plan, but he never tired of hearing it again and again. Why this should be, Culdus did not know. But the warrior took satisfaction in knowing that a . . . creature as intelligent as Valdaimon obviously thought Culdus's thinking worthy of his deepest attention.

"Ten of Your Majesty's legions are concentrating, even as we speak, on the south side of the River Rigel opposite Shallowford, where Your Majesty today began construction of a great bridge to ease their crossing. The eleventh legion is here," Culdus said, pointing to the map, "opposite the twin fortresses of Vladstok and Grullheim. It will remain here to guard our eastern frontier and prevent a descent down the River Rigel on our rear. The twelfth legion, of course, is here at Hamblen, to guard against a descent by sea and to serve as a strategic reserve."

"Do you think it likely, Culdus," the prince—now a self-proclaimed king—asked, "that a coalition of the Rhanguilds will attempt a seaborne landing on our shores?"

"No, Your Majesty," Valdaimon answered. "The political situation in the Rhanguild lands does not favor swift or coordinated action."

"Just so," Culdus affirmed, casting a dark glance at Valdaimon. "Nevertheless, we must leave at least one legion in Hamblen to discourage even the remote possibility of such a landing."

"I see," the king said, nodding. "Go on."

Culdus drew his dagger and pointed on the map to Shallowford. "The attack will begin here. We cross the river at Shallowford, aided by the bridge. Four legions will penetrate into Dunsford's lands about four leagues, then turn westward and march on Fortress Alban from the landward side. Two legions will forge ahead and fan out to crush resistance in Dunford's barony, while the remaining four turn east, cross the unguarded frontier into Kala, and swing south, to assault the Tower of Asbel on the north bank of the river. Once Alban and Asbel are secured, the entire force will move northward on a broad front, conquering all the lands up to the Elven Preserve on the east bank of the Pragal and through the Kingdom of Argolia. That will leave only Vladstok and Grullheim on our right as possible bases of operation against us. They will be completely flanked, easily cut off, and will fall rapidly to our siege."

Culdus stepped back, looking thoughtful and pleased as he studied the maps a final time. "Your Majesty approves?" he asked.

"We are moderately pleased," the Black Prince responded. "We suppose this will suffice for the first phase of operations. However, you will see to it that once the twin fortresses have fallen our forces are quickly positioned to continue their thrust northward. The Elven Preserve must be taken, and the ultimate strategic objective must be the conquest of Parona."

Culdus frowned and glanced at Valdaimon, seeking aid from the old wizard. "Your Majesty's wishes are my command," he said. "But Your Majesty must remember that our armies will need time to accomplish what I have outlined. Even moving with lightning speed, to do what I have described is the work of a full campaign season. After that, we will need rest and, above all, reinforcement. Also, there is the matter of the political consolidation of the conquered—"

"That need not detain the legions," Valdaimon chimed in. "His Majesty has wisely delegated political responsibility to the League of the Black Wing. We will have the territories organized sufficiently to support your continued northward drive."

Culdus scowled deeply and felt the first pangs of fear clutch at his warrior's heart. This damnable wizard would talk the king into a program that would lead to disaster!

"I appreciate that the army is not involved in political matters and am certain that the efforts of the league will be . . . successful," Culdus stammered, almost choking on the last word. "But I beg Your Majesty to consider that time, supplies, and above all numbers are against an extended campaign this year. Once we attack the Elven Preserve, the terms of the Covenant will be invoked. Parona will enter the war long before we are ready to strike at her with lightning blows, and we cannot expect—"

"We cannot expect anything less than victory because of certain matters of which you are not aware," the young king interrupted. A smile formed on the king's thin lips as Culdus's face began to grow white with apprehension. "Relax, Culdus," he said, leaning forward and patting the old warrior on the forearm. "You have done well. But Valdaimon should now enlighten you concerning certain additional forces that will be at your disposal."

"*No!*" the baron thundered, slamming his fist on the table so that the sound of both his shout and the blow echoed in the vastness of the great hall. "Your Majesty, with all respect, you know I am your loyal servant and will obey your commands, whatever they may be. But in conscience, I would not be doing my duty if I did not protest and beg you to reconsider this rash and dangerous course."

The old man began pacing the length of the hall, turning and jabbing at the air to emphasize his points. "I have trained for you the mightiest army—not in numbers but in tactics, skill, and sheer cruelty—that this world has ever seen. You think I do not know of this wizard's surprises, but I do. Yes. And I say there is no need to add the forces of dead, stinking things to those of the fine army I have provided you. What warrior would willingly march next to zombies, wights, and other obscene things of the night? I'd sooner die in battle, fighting honorably, than wrest victory from my foes by using the dead hands this villain would animate."

"Then," Valdaimon said, smiling his hideous smile that revealed his few remaining yellowed teeth, "you will no doubt be uncomfortable in command of such forces."

"Aye, that I would," Culdus stormed, falling into the trap. "I beg Your Majesty to—"

"I have already given this matter much thought, Culdus," the young king said, rising to emphasize his point. "You will command our human forces. Valdaimon himself will support you with his . . . special forces. As for your fears about the elves and Parona—Valdaimon, you will address these points."

The old wizard hoisted himself slowly from his seat. "Your Majesty is well aware of the terms of the Covenant that ended the elf-human wars some three hundred years ago and that have been honored without notable breach since that time. The elves, reduced in numbers to a mere handful, nevertheless held it in their power to wreak magical destruction upon the human powers on such a scale that a settlement seemed advisable to all the human rulers. Under the terms of that Covenant, all human rulers of the time pledged that any attack upon the Elven Preserve, defined in that treaty, would be considered an attack upon all human powers. In short, if we attack the elves, all mankind is pledged to come to their aid."

"Yes, yes," the king said impatiently. "Come to the point, for Culdus's sake."

"This was all predicated upon the powers of magic then held by the elves," the wizard explained. "Now, through means we need not discuss, the League of the Black Wing has come into possession of certain items and certain facts, the which taken together will nullify the magical power of the elves. Indeed, as soon the eggs arrive—"

"Eggs?" Culdus interrupted. "What eggs?"

"Surely you know what is common knowledge in the marketplace." The king smirked. "I have purchased from the King of Parona the famed Golden Eggs of Parona, reputedly the greatest treasure on the face of the earth. Even as we speak, a guard of five hundred hand-picked troops is escorting that treasure from the northlands here."

"What? What drain on the royal treasury was caused by this purchase?" Culdus demanded, his incredulity causing him to forget his place.

"Yes," the king said. "Tell me, Valdaimon, what payment have we made to obtain this treasure?"

"The price is not the point, Culdus," Valdaimon replied. "And Your Majesty told me to spare no expense to guarantee the success of Your Majesty's plans. Now, once the eggs are in hand—"

"How much?" the young king demanded.

Culdus smiled. Now it was the wizard's turn to squirm.

The stinking old man moved out from behind the table and, aided by his giant staff, hobbled across the room toward the high window. He threw the window open and gazed out into the darkening sky. On the horizon, he caught a glimpse of the display he had ordered, should just this question arise.

"Your Majesty, what price would you consider fair for the display of power you can see by gazing from this window into the night sky?"

"What?" the king exclaimed. "What deviltry have you conjured, old friend?" The youth sprang to the window and surveyed the lands and the river below. "I see no display of power, wizard," he grumbled.

"Look to the horizon in the sky."

The king's head snapped back as he gazed into the far sky. Then his mouth dropped open in shock before his eyes glazed over a kind of ecstasy. "Oh! Oh, by the gods! Look at this Culdus! Look!"

The soldier came to stand by his king and his tired eyes peered toward the far horizon. What he saw froze him with fear. Winging toward the palace-fortress, in numbers sufficient to blot out a good eighth of the sky, were the hideous flying lizards known as wyverns. The ugly beasts were twenty feet long—though half of that was tail—and they could kill a man with a nasty bite from their jaws, with swipes from their deadly claws, or with the poisonous sting of their serpentine tails. Mounted on each wyvern was either a wizard of the League of the Black Wing or an armored man-at-arms, complete with lance and great helm. Onward toward the palace the armada of airborne warriors flew, until they passed within a few feet of the king's window.

"Wyvern riders, Your Majesty," Valdaimon said. "Power from the skies to aid your conquering armies on the ground. At their mere appearance many foes will break and flee, for their appearance almost reminds one of the dragons of old legends—does it not?"

"Indeed, Valdaimon, indeed!" the king enthused. "How fitting, given our choice of heraldic crest—the black dragon . . ."

"I am glad Your Majesty is pleased." Valdaimon smiled again, this time turning his full gaze on Culdus. "The riders are wizard members of the league and a few troops we have trained on our own. Their leaders will meet with you tomorrow to coordinate cooperative efforts on the field of battle. Agreed?"

Culdus was feeling trapped. How could he disagree? How could any commander turn down a force like this that would guarantee victory in the opening battles of the campaign? As for the long run, Culdus didn't see how these things could overcome elven magic or the hordes of Parona, but . . . But what about the eggs?

"Agreed, friend Valdaimon." Culdus returned the wizard's smile. "But tell me, what have these wyvern riders to do with the Golden Eggs of Parona?"

"It is a magical link—a technical matter for wizards. Do not concern yourself too deeply. Only those trained for decades in the magic arts could appreciate the nature of the connection."

"I see," Culdus replied. And he did see. Valdaimon was up to something, and neither Culdus nor the king was to be allowed to know what it was. And, Culdus thought, the question of price had been neatly sidestepped altogether.

Far below the great hall from which Ruprecht watched the display of power he imagined to be his, a solitary elf hung crucified against the cold, slime-covered walls of a tiny dungeon cell. The elf's hair shone in the darkness with a kind of silvery light of its own—a unique feature even among elves. Not that Ruprecht had noticed; this was the only elf the Black Prince had ever seen, and under Valdaimon's tutelage Ruprecht believed that all mature elves appeared this way. But this was no ordinary elf. Only elves who attained to legendary age were gifted with the glowing silver hair, and only one such elf remained. He was commonly called Elrond. This Elrond Ruprecht had made prisoner at Valdaimon's insistance and against the Covenant, but then this Covenant was not a matter that Ruprecht took seriously.

Elrond hung on the dungeon wall, his wrists and feet manacled to iron spikes driven deep into the stones. His near-naked body, withered with age, was a mass of bloody streaks and festering welts, the souvenirs of his periodic torture for the amusement of the Black Prince. Despite his wounds, Elrond at this moment felt no pain, for his mind, trained over five millennia in the arts of elven magic and elven mental discipline, was far from the dungeon.

He began his mental journey while the Black Prince still dined. First, his senses reached out to the creeping green slime that grew upon the wet stones of his cell, for slime, however disgusting to humans, is green and living, and wherever there are green and living plants, the mind and soul of an elf can dwell. Slowly, the consciousness that was Elrond made its way through the trail of the slime, inching over the cold stones, slipping between tiny niches and cracks the eye could never see, working its way upward and outward until, somewhere in the soil beyond the dungeon wall, it made contact with a tiny tendril of root sunk deep by an evergreen tree. From there, his mind flowed, faster now, with greater ease, upward, upward, upward with the running sap, until it broke above the surface of the earth and, in a thousand, thousand green needles felt the warmth of the last rays of the day's pale spring sun.

Onward and outward the consciousness that was now Elrond and slime and root and tree and then forest raced and expanded like a great, empty balloon expanding and discovering the nature of the air inside itself. His mind touched creepers that led up the wall to the great hall, and he heard all that was said between Culdus, Valdaimon, and Ruprecht. At the same time his mind counted the numbers of blue jay nests in the forest conifers and discerned that the spring, though still cold, was far advanced. His mind felt the coldness of death of the branches of trees that would not be renewed and sensed the joy of spring birth in the tendrils of tiny plants that would soon be saplings reaching for the sun.

Onward and outward raced the mind of Elrond, now at an astonishing clip, until the ancient elf, with his five millennia of memories and knowledge and love was part of all the living green things in the southern part of the world, reaching almost to the boundaries of the Elven Preserve, seeking for ... what? Whom?

Elrond searched his vast memory. He did not seek food, for his vast array of roots brought him food from the depths of the earth. Water, too, was provided in abundance. Warmth would be welcome, but Elrond knew that in time, just a little time, the warmth of the sky light would come again, as it always did. But there was something, someone. . . .

Shulana! It required all the discipline of his millennia of training to snatch the name of a single, discrete being from the vast consciousness of half a world of living things. But when Elrond's mind cried out the name of Shulana, the cry was so great that every tree, every budding flower, every blade of grass over a range of six hundred miles echoed that cry in the vibrations of their flowing sap. The cry, silent to human ears, leapt from the plants into the very air and was carried on the breeze until a little gust touched the fresh flowers in a vase on a table near a certain bedstead.

"Shulana!" The call of the most ancient of all elves roared in the mind of his stripling kinswoman. Shulana, who the instant before had felt the glow of triumph as she knew that Bagsby's own greed and pride had won him to her cause, trembled in her innermost being. True, in elven communion she had before encountered the minds of other elves, melded with little patches of green nature. But never before had so powerful another consciousness, so vast in its scope and extent, ripped into her own mind without warning and so focused on her own identity that she felt naked and completely alone. The young elf's hands trembled. Her eyes grew wide with terror and she gazed at the vase of flowers just in time to see it tumble to the floor and shatter.

"What was that?" Bagsby said, annoyed, glancing about. He saw the sheer terror in the elf's eyes and leapt to his feet, grabbing his dagger. "What is it?" he called.

Shulana neither replied nor moved. She stood stone still while her mind became a receptacle into which was poured all Elrond's knowledge of Ruprecht's plans and the single command, "Hurry!" For as both elves knew, once the Eggs of Parona were in Valdaimon's hands, the vile wizard would be unstoppable.

"Curse you, elf!" Bagsby complained, slinking around his own room in a crouch with the dagger held ready to strike at any shadow that moved. "I should have known you'd bring me danger!"

In a single instant, the mind of Elrond flowed back into the body of the frail elf in the dungeon of Ruprecht's castle. Elrond groaned in pain. He was no longer part of the of the Earth. He was merely a very tired, very old, very tortured elf. Indeed, he was the oldest elf in the world and the one in the greatest physical pain.

"Be still, Bagsby," Shulana replied. "You do not yet know what real danger is." Shulana shuddered, and goose flesh rose along her arms and legs. The thought of the eggs in the hands of Valdaimon chilled her. So did the thought of the power of mind that Elrond must possess to cry out to her over a distance of hundreds of miles. . . . "But you will learn, Bagsby. You will learn."

* * *

Ruprecht clapped his hands and rubbed his palms together in gleeful anticipation. So far, the evening had gone better than he had expected. The anticipation of victory was thrilling. The display of wyvern power that Valdaimon had showed him was elating. But now would come the best part of all. "Come, smelly old tutor of mine," he said eagerly. "Show me, show me in your ball of crystal the victories that will be mine."

Valdaimon smiled, his usual scraggly toothed, obsequious smile. His Majesty was in a fine form tonight, pleased and easily controlled. Even Culdus dared not cross the wizard now; the display of wyvern power had silenced him. The old mage's long staff thudded on the stone floor of great hall as he made his way back to his seat at the main table. Slowly, he eased himself into the chair. He breathed deeply, then began to wave his arms in broad circles over the crystal globe.

He would show the king victories, Valdaimon decided. He would even show the king something good about Culdus. This conference would end with hopes for victory high and the king with no doubts that his expectations would be fulfilled.

Slowly, Valdaimon spoke the words, handed from the earliest human mages who had mastered the arts of scrying and futuresight, that infused the crystal with their power. A tiny spark of green light appeared in the center of the clear ball. Gradually it grew, changing color to yellow, then red, then orange, then blue, then purple, then a blinding white. A great flash came from the ball, and then an image formed.

"Behold, Majesty, the scenes of victories to come," the old wizard intoned.

Ruprecht stood and leaned forward eagerly, gazing into the depths of the ball. Culdus, too, stood and looked over the young king's shoulder.

In the crystal, they saw the legions of Heilesheim marching forward against a foe already fleeing in terror, while wyvern riders swooped from the sky, laughing, killing at will with thrusts of their spears. In the far distance, great stone towers crumbled, and the king saw himself, mounted on a great black steed with its hooves raised to the heavens, crying out "Victory! Victory! On to another victory!"

"Valdaimon!" the young king exclaimed at length. "It is all as I had planned!"

"Yes, Majesty, truly your wildest dreams shall be fulfilled," the wizard answered humbly.

"Yes, yes, I see . . ." The king's voice broke off. A troubled frown passed over the face of Culdus. The crystal went suddenly dark.

"What was that, Valdaimon," the old warrior asked.

"Yes, you saw that. What was that?" the pale youth demanded, grabbing the front of the old wizard's robes. "What was that?"

"Nothing, Majesty," Valdaimon replied. But the mage could not keep uncertainty from his voice. For he, too, had seen the momentary image—a short man with graying hair and a chubby square face, slinking about a great bedroom with a dagger in his hand. By itself, that could mean anything. But, as though in a dream, a second image shimmered behind the little man: the gem-studded, gleaming Golden Eggs of Parona. "It is nothing at all," Valdaimon continued. He laughed, a kind of obscene, cackling laugh, to make light of the momentary vision that had deeply troubled him. "Perhaps," he said, cackling louder as if sharing a great joke with friends, "we have scried the secret dreams of some little thief!"

Ruprecht joined Valdaimon's laughter, clapping the decrepit wizard on the back. Culdus waited until his own eyes met the wizard's across the table, then he smiled a small, dry smile.

3

First Blood

Bagsby sat down again on the edge of the bed and eyed the elf carefully.

"This deal stinks," he said at length. "I don't know you. I don't know that you can pay me. I expect that you won't. And you want me to take on five hundred men in the pay of the Black Prince to steal a treasure that can't be sold because everyone in the known world will recognize it and know that it's stolen. Forget about Nebuchar's assassins— they don't scare me. Tell me again why I'm going to do this for you."

Shulana's thoughts were already far from Bagsby. So much had been implanted in her mind by her brief contact with Elrond that she needed time to think, time to sort it out, time to modify her own plans, if need be.

"What?" she responded, a little dazed.

"What?" Bagsby replied, mocking her. "What? I'll tell you what. I think this deal stinks and I want to know why you think I'll even consider stealing the Golden Eggs of Parona, that's what."

"Oh. That again." Shulana's fingers made nimble gestures in the air, and she muttered words that Bagsby could hear but not understand. In the next instant, he could see only her disembodied face.

"What'd you do?" he demanded incredulously.

"I must go," Shulana said, turning to leave the room. Then she turned back, and for an instant the elven face reappeared in midair. "You'll do it, Bagsby," she said softly and seriously, "because you think you can do it."

Bagsby glared at her, then slowly his face broke into a grin. "Well," he admitted, "there is that."

53

The face disappeared. The door to Bagsby's chamber swung silently open, then silently shut. Bagsby was alone.

"Yes," he said aloud to no one. "There is that. It would be the greatest theft of all time and I, the greatest thief." Laughing, Bagsby bounced up from the bed and strode to the large shutters that guarded the great window of his room. He threw them open in time to see the first rays of dawn light the gray, overcast sky. Yes, he thought, the greatest of all time.

Bagsby took a deep breath of the chilly morning air, smiling with self-satisfaction. He gazed out on the neatly manicured gardens at the front of the viscount's mansion, where the ranks of shrubs and carefully pruned low trees struggled to maintain their dark green coloration on a cold, gray day. He noticed the arrow just in time to do a back flip, the arrow whizzing past just beneath his short salt-and-pepper hair. He landed on his hands and, with a second flip, bounced to his feet, running toward the door. The second arrow thudded into the wood of the door about a half inch above his head.

He's good, Bagsby thought, dropping to one knee while opening the door. He had to make that second shot on pure calculation; he could not have seen me this far inside the room. The short thief held his dagger at the ready in case a second foe was bold enough to rush in the open door. No—nothing happened. The second man could be waiting in the hallway for the easy shot when Bagsby came running out. Bagsby crouched behind the door, slammed it shut loudly to raise an alarm among the household, then sprang in one leap toward the bed. He landed short with a thud on the hard floor.

Cursing at the pain, Bagsby reached up with his left hand and grabbed at the bedclothes. He pulled down a wad of satin sheet—that would do. He crawled under the bed—no use leaving his back open just in case someone burst through the door. He tied one end of the satin sheet to a leg of the bed, and then made his way in a sideways crouch back toward the window. Chances were the archer in the garden was already in the house. Bagsby would risk the window.

The little thief tied a large double knot in the remaining end of the sheet. He stuck his dagger between his teeth. Grasping the sheet tightly just above the knot, he hurled his body through the open shutters into space. He plunged straight down six feet before the sheet's length was run out; and the snap as the sheet unfolded to its full length brought him up short. His own weight pulled hard at his elbows and shoulders, but his vicelike grip held. It took him only three seconds to gain a foothold against the nearby wall, and three seconds later he was swinging, back and forth like a pendulum along the front of the building. As his swing reached its highest point near a fig tree, he let go and somersaulted through the air, landing in the branches with only a slight bump on one shin.

"Curses!" Bagsby whispered to himself. "Getting clumsy in my old age."

It took him five more seconds to scramble up the tree, climb onto a balcony, and position himself, dagger ready in his right hand, beside the large glass doors that led to the second-story hall. By now, Bagsby calculated, the assailant in the hall—for he was sure there was one—would be carefully making his way to the door to Bagby's chamber. Bagsby reached out with his left hand and opened the latch on the glass doors. Then, with one seamless motion, he threw open the door, whirled inside, and tossed his dagger, tumbling as it flew, straight at the back of the crossbow-armed figure in black who was creeping down the hall, just as Bagsby had assumed.

The short blade caught the man squarely between the shoulders, and the force of the throw pitched him face forward onto the thickly carpeted floor. Bagsby was on him in an instant. His right foot stamped on the man's hand; his right hand grabbed the crossbow; his left hand retrieved his dagger. Then for an instant, Bagsby hesitated. An assassin taken alive would be worth a small fortune in ransom money from the Assassins of the Compact in Kala. They despised failure and would actually pay to get back one of their own who had failed, just so they could put the hapless would-be murderer to death themselves in their own inimitable style. Still, it would hardly do for the "elder son" of the honest and pure Count of Nordingham to know too much about the ways of assassins in a land so distant from his home.

"Too bad, oaf. At least you'll have an easier death than your friends would have given you." Without further thought Bagsby slit the squirming man's throat. As the dying man's blood gurgled and gushed onto the carpet, Bagsby whirled toward the glass doors he had just entered and discharged the crossbow. The bolt caught the second assassin, the one who had fired at him from the garden, squarely in the right knee.

Bagsby shook his head in disgust. He was clearly getting out of shape.

"Hurts, doesn't it?" he called cheerily to the second murderer who had dropped to the floor, writhing in pain. "Kneecaps always do," Bagsby continued as he strolled down the hall to stand over the man. He reached down and pulled the black mask from his assailant's face. Though contorted with rage and pain, the man's face looked vaguely familiar.

"Tomar?" Bagsby asked.

"Damn you black, Bagsby," the tortured Tomar responded. "Finish it."

"Ah, ah, not so fast. Who sent you?"

"You know I cannot say."

"No need; you've handled plenty of contracts for Nebuchar before. This was a pretty bungled attempt, you know. Especially the first shot from the garden—a frontal shot, head-on, against an experienced guy like me. The odds weren't with you."

"You've grown careless with success," Tomar spat back.

"True, true, I must admit you've hit a sore point, there, Tomar," Bagsby said, nodding a sad acknowledgment. "But not careless enough for your purposes," he added, swiftly kneeling and slitting Tomar's throat from ear to ear.

Tomar's legs were still kicking when the first of the household servants arrived in the hall, drawn by the crashes, thumps, and wails of pain.

"Assassins, sent by some unknown foe to slay the viscount in his sleep," Bagsby announced to the wide-eyed staff as they surveyed the bloody hall. "Go quickly and tell your master that his life has been spared. And alert the guards to search the grounds. There may be more of these vile fellows about."

Shulana saw the assassins as she left the grounds of the viscount's mansion. She considered staying to defend Bagsby, but decided that the thief would neither need nor want her help. She did not think he was in serious danger; there were only two of them. If he couldn't handle that, he would never succeed at stealing the Golden Eggs of Parona.

The streets of Clairton were filling with busy humans, rushing about their morning activities with that usual combination of intensity and narrowness of focus Shulana found so alien. She used the magic of her cloak to wend her way through the crowded streets unnoticed. Faint stirrings of hunger tempted her for a moment to stop in one of the many small market squares, where dozens of vendors loudly hawked the virtues of their edible offerings, but her desire to escape for a while from the all-too-human world drove her on toward the city gates. Her stomach could wait; her mind and spirit needed sustenance.

It took her a full hour to find a solitary copse more than a mile beyond the city gates. This refuge proved to be a small growth of conifers, hardwoods, and scraggly, prickly vines not large enough to be dubbed a wood. Still, in its center, an old oak reared its head high above the younger trees around it, and at its base Shulana could not see beyond the edge of the copse to the muddy fields beyond. Her vision thus insulated from the world, she felt secure, almost as though she were at home again in the Elven Preserve. She sat on the damp moss that grew at the oak's feet, leaned her back against its rough bark, and allowed her mind to meld into the being of the tree.

Shulana's mind possessed neither the power nor the discipline of Elrond's. Still, in this state, undifferentiated from the living plant life around her, she was able to find the freedom from anxiety needed for clear thought. She considered the questions and problems presented by Elrond's communication one at a time.

First, there was the almost overwhelming fact that Elrond, the greatest, oldest, and most revered of living elves, was a prisoner in a human dungeon! That single fact, should it become known to the other elves of the preserve, could start a new human-elven war that would unleash so much magic and so much hatred that the entire world would die in its flames. No elf had thought anything amiss when, some twenty years ago, the ancient Elrond had announced he had a task to perform and left the safety of the Elven Preserve. No elf had thought anything amiss when he did not return, for an elf might spend twenty years on a journey that would take a human a mere fortnight. But Elrond's imprisonment by humans was unthinkable! Under the Covenant no human could slay or imprison an elf, and no elf could slay or imprison a human. This was such a basic tenent of the Covenant that the infrequent violations to date had always led to prolonged and tense negotiations. Of course, there were always some violations that went undiscovered, and both sides endeavored to show understanding and goodwill when unfortunate incidents arose. But Elrond! For a human to imprison Elrond was the equivalent of elves systematically destroying human temples to the gods they professed to worship! War would be the only honorable elven response to such an outrage.

But war would be suicide. So depleted was the elven population that it would take every elven mind and every elven spell to balance the sheer numbers of the humans. Horrendous, raw, elemental forces of nature would be unleashed—the forces of earth and air, fire and water, turned loose to roll like primordial chaos over the face of the earth. Even if anyone or anything survived, there would be nothing left to live for.

Therefore, Shulana concluded, she would not communicate the news of Elrond's imprisonment to her fellow elves. It would remain a secret, buried in her own mind, shielded by long tradition from the prying of magic and even from the sharing of mental communion, when elven minds, linked to trees and grass and green life of all kinds, merged into a kind of oneness.

Second, there was the warning in Elrond's message. He had told her to hurry, to do quickly what she must do. Therefore, Elrond, the great one, who could commune even with barren soil as long as plants had once grown in it, was aware of her own scheme, even though she had first thought of the plan only ten years ago, long after Elrond had left the preserve. Not even the Elven Council understood her full intent. Of course, if any elf could know her mind, it would be Elrond. Not for nothing was he her great-great-great-great-great-uncle. Not for nothing had he personally instructed her in the basics of elven magic. And not for nothing had he told her the tales of the elven-dragon wars, fought far beyond the memory of all living elves save Elrond himself. To her, and her alone, had he imparted the secret of the fabulous Golden Eggs of Parona. What his purpose had been, Shulana could even now only vaguely guess.

But urgency was what Elrond demanded. Her plan must be fulfilled quickly, lest the treasure fall into the hands of the Black Prince. The thought of that particularly vile human brought Shulana to consider the brewing human war. Through her contact with Elrond's mind she had full knowledge of all the plans laid by the Black Prince, his arrogant desire to subjugate the world to the whims of his juvenile and malicious will. Normally, the subjugation of one group of humans by another would hardly concern an elf. Humans who called themselves kings or emperors and thought of themselves as immortals came and went by the score in the lifetime of an elf. But in this case, there was a difference. The Black Prince, unless stopped, would also possess the Golden Eggs of Parona.

But what matter that? Humans had possessed the eggs for three thousand years, ever since the dwarves found them in the bowels of a rich vein of gold far away in the northernmost mountains of the world. Why would Elrond urge her to hasten in her plan?

The answer, of course, was Valdaimon. For there were three who knew the secret of the treasure of Parona, and

Valdaimon was the third. And should Valdaimon come to control the potential power in the Golden Eggs, not even the sum total of all elven magic could stop him.

Thus, Shulana could only conclude that Elrond knew her plan, approved it, and urged her to hasten lest Valdaimon come to possess the treasure and control its power.

That left only one final matter to consider. Shulana had a duty as a kinsman to Elrond. As the closest living elf with direct lineage to Elrond's parents, Shulana owed her kinsman her special loyalty and protection. She would not only have to complete her plan for the Golden Eggs. She would also have to rescue Elrond from the dungeon of the Black Prince.

Shulana focused her mind with a great effort of will, and her consciousness flowed slowly back into the receptacle of her elven body. She rose and inhaled deeply, savoring the scents of the few trees. Then she strode to the edge of the copse and gazed through the spring haze at the walls of Clairton. It was time to return to the human world. She felt refreshed, renewed, and grateful to have her tasks more clearly understood. Sadly, they were not tasks she could perform herself. Under the terms of the Covenant, an elf dared not steal from, nor bear arms against any human. To accomplish her purposes, she needed the cooperation of a human. In short, she needed Bagsby. It was time to get her human moving. Once her tasks were accomplished, she would slay the human, in secret violation of the Covenant, and all would once again be well with the world.

Three savage kicks to his ribs from a mailed boot snapped George the miller's son out of his deep slumber. A final kick to the side of the face ripped a strip of skin off his cheek and brought him to full consciousness.

"I said get up, you whoreson! Get up and get to your place in the ranks. We're finally moving out."

George sprang to his feet, careful to keep his head bowed in respect. "Ready, sire! Forgive me, sire!" he cried.

But the angry knight had already whirled and stomped away, his mailed footsteps splashing in the inch or more of water that covered the soggy ground. He kicked and cursed at two more sleeping men as he made his way to the bush where his heavy war-horse, its finely worked bards covered with thick, dripping woolen blankets, was loosely tied.

"Kiss me, sire," George muttered, spitting a wad of phlegm, blood, spittle, and a chip of tooth into the pouring rain. The water burned as it splattered against the open wound on his cheek, and his side felt like a dagger was probing it every time he drew breath.

All around, scores of men cursed, laughed, spit, gathered their gear, and tromped and splashed around in the thick mud the heavy rain had created beneath their feet. All but one had ignored the brutal interaction between the knight and George; if they thought about it at all, they were simply grateful it was George who got the boot this time and not them.

"There's what you get, George, for ignorin' the wake up," his companion Frederick said, pounding him on the back. "Hey, you lost a bit of tooth that time!"

"That great bastard. I 'ope he gets captured and the ransom breaks his family," George sputtered. He wiped his filthy, muddy hand across his face in a vain attempt to keep the cold rain out of his eyes and away from his throbbing cheek.

"Lot of good that would do us," Frederick offered. "Our lord gets captured and his family goes broke. Who'd be paying then for our supplies? Besides, it could be a lot worse."

"How's that?" George grumbled, looking about in the predawn darkness for his helmet, sword, long spear, and boots.

"Why, we could be in that poor bastard Dunsford's army!" Frederick roared with laughter at his own joke.

George, despite his foul mood, also laughed aloud. Rumor was that today they would attack Dunsford's army, and before nightfall, George believed, he would more than vent his anger on the hapless wretches who fought for the doomed count.

"You're right about that!" George allowed. "I wouldn't want to be one of them wretches. Wait'll we wade into 'em. I always likes to catch someone right in the eye with my spear, then step up with the sword. You know, like we've done in practice. They'll drop like wheat before the scythe."

"Come on, then. There's our company forming up, I think," Frederick said, pointing through the rain to a barely visible throng gathering near the muddy riverbank. "Can't see the standard, though."

"No matter," George replied, cheerful again at the thought of the action to come. "If we don't get in the right place, someone with 'sir' in front of his name'll kick us in the ass and set us right."

A mile away, Culdus sat on a powerful, white steed and watched as the last companies of the Fourth Legion's men-at-arms tramped across the badly swaying wooden bridge completed just the day before. The commander of the legion, also mounted on a war-horse, sat silently beside the king's appointed commander, thankful that his men showed no hesitation about using the bridge, which the swollen river threatened to wash away at any instant. The crossing of the Rigel at Shallowford had been carefully planned. As usual, Culdus thought, the careful plans were becoming worthless with their first confrontation with reality.

"My Lord General, that is the last of my legion." Count Otto, the legion commander, had to shout to make himself heard above the sound of the accursed rain.

"Only a full watch late," Culdus grumped. "May the gods curse the devil who sent this rain. It began while the bridge was still being built, and it hasn't slackened for over twelve hours. I doubt that bridge will last for the crossing of the Fifth." Culdus extended his mailed fist and pointed to the river, which now extended a good twelve feet beyond the bridge. The tops of shrubs could be seen poking above the surface of the swirling brown water. "Look how badly the river is already over its banks."

"Aye, Lord General," Count Otto replied. "I'd best cross myself unless I want to swim. What orders? If the bridge collapses, our first four legions will be isolated on the far side."

Water poured off Culdus's mustache as he pondered his reply. "Continue your march according to plan," he answered at length. "If you encounter Dunsford, the First Legion alone with its six thousand should be enough to crush any force he's raised. Tell Count Pomeran the honor of first blood shall be his should that occasion arise. The other three legions are to continue their march and try to make up the time lost here."

"As you order, Lord General," Otto responded.

Culdus leaned forward in his saddle, bringing his face close to Otto's ear so he could be heard in a normal voice. "It's that damnable Valdaimon. He's responsible for this delay. I wouldn't doubt that he conjured this rain to slow us down."

Otto raised an eyebrow, indicating both curiosity and agreement, but said nothing. He felt privileged to receive Culdus's confidence and afraid to speak lest he say the wrong thing and Culdus fail to say more.

"He tried yesterday afternoon, you know, to delay the attack," Culdus continued. "Something about not wanting the convoy carrying that damned treasure from Parona to be in Argolia when the war began. He's scried something in his spying ball that's scared him, though he dare not let the king know it."

"What could scare the greatest wizard in all the earth?" Otto queried, shaking his head vigorously to clear the water from the crest of his helmet, from where it poured into his face. "If the things he conjures don't scare him . . ."

"I don't know," Culdus said honestly. "But I know this. The king would brook no delay. Valdaimon earned some disfavor by counseling him to wait." Culdus stared into Otto's eyes. The man is a warrior, Culdus thought. His loyalty will be to his fellow warriors. And whatever has scared Valdaimon won't scare him. "That works only to our advantage," the lord general continued. "Ultimate power in this kingdom belongs to the sword, not some disgusting thing that may not even be human anymore. The more he hurts his position with the king, the better for the nobles and the army."

"Aye. I wager there's nothing the old wizard has seen that can't be killed with a sword of some sort," Otto said in a matter-of-fact tone. "Don't worry, Lord General. Your legions will fight, whatever it is they meet. I'll see to that." Otto dug his spurs into the sides of his mount. The great war-horse leapt forward into the still nearly blinding downpour.

Culdus watched Count Otto ride away with a combination of concern and amusement. True, if the enemy had strong forces across the river, he could catch four legions piecemeal. But Culdus trusted his experience and his instincts. Both told him that Dunsford could not possibly have gathered a force of more than four thousand of all social ranks. The four legions already across the river numbered almost six times that many men.

"Good man, Count Otto," Culdus answered, nodding his head. "Good man." Culdus turned his own horse and rode downstream to the head of the waiting columns of the Fifth Legion. There he spotted a man-at-arms with a large, red horsehair plume rising from the crest of his helmet. This identified him as a nonnoble leader, a "leader of a score" in the new military system Culdus had created for Ruprecht's army. The nobles had long resisted this innovation; they furnished the foot soldiers, armed them, and paid them from their own purses. In any traditional army the foot soldiers would have marched along behind their mounted lords, providing service on the march and protection in battle. But Culdus had changed all that. Now the foot soldiers were formed into "battles," "hundreds," and "scores" of their own, with nonnobles appointed as leaders of these groups. The men-at-arms responded well to the innovation; the nobles had cursed, protested, and resisted. But Culdus had the king's confidence—and the king's power—to enforce his will on the clamorous barons.

"Leader of a score!" Culdus shouted at the man.

The leader looked up, spat, smiled, and hefted high his great eighteen-foot spear with an eager war cry in response. Culdus was pleased to see that the rain had not dampened the spirit of this man. A high level of performance and discipline from these men was a critical element in Culdus's revolutionary military system.

"Tell your leader of a hundred to take his hundred, strip them of weapons, and get them into the river. The bridge must be reinforced against the flood!" Culdus roared.

"Aye, Lord Culdus! It shall be done!"

Valdaimon stared through the door of the thatched hut at the downpour outside. He could hear the roaring of the flooding river less than a hundred yards away. His yellow, skin wrinkled even more as his face drew up in a kind of malicious grin. He had conjured well, he thought. This should delay Culdus for a least a day, maybe two.

He turned from the doorway of the hut, which he had taken as his temporary quarters for the start of the army's march, and slowly made his way back to the crude table in the middle of the hut's single room. A fire roared in the hearth against the back wall, and a large black kettle hung over the fire, its contents bubbling. Thick, almost greasy steam rose from the kettle, filling the hut with a slightly nauseating odor. But Valdaimon paid no heed to his kettle; his small green eyes and his mind were focused on the large crystal ball set at the center of the small wooden table. Three times he slowly walked around the table, staring at the ball, muttering curses containing names known to less than a score of the world's elves and to even fewer humans. A fat, shabby, dusty black crow perched on the back on the room's only chair; it stood motionless, watching the old wizard's progress around the table. At length the old man stopped, leaned forward on his great staff, and stared silently into the ball.

"Curse him!" The shout leapt from between Valdaimon's thin dry lips, and the old mage raised both arms, shaking clenched fists toward the heavens. "Curse him!" he repeated, and then a third time, "Curse him!"

The crow gave a loud, angry cry, spread its wings, and

took to the air, flying through the open doorway into the rain-filled air. Valdaimon could hear its angry cawing for more than a full minute until the bird was several miles away.

The old wizard slowly stooped over, one hand placed on his pain-filled back, and retrieved the great staff he had dropped. Then he collapsed in the chair, hung his head, sighed, and mused.

It was Bagsby—there could be no doubt. He had scried him first during the meeting with the king and Culdus. He had watched the little man off and on now for two days. There was no question it was Bagsby. Who else could kill two of Nebuchar's hired assassins after letting them have the first shots? Who else could have gulled the nobility of Argolia into treating him like a visiting minor god? Who else could pose a threat to the most secret and most important element in Valdaimon's plan, a plan that had been brewing in his mind for centuries, a plan whose fulfillment was finally at hand, a plan that was now endangered by the existence of a petty thief!

Valdaimon's body quivered with rage. It was intolerable that this upstart, this rootless being with no ancestry, no heritage, no greatness of mind or spirit, this ... mortal should threaten the undoing of all that Valdaimon had worked toward.

At first, the wizard had not been certain. He dared to hope his scrying had merely wandered into a random room to show him a random human, who happened to look something like the pudgy little thief. Valdaimon remembered his jest to the king about a thief's dream; at the time it had been merely a jest. But even in that offhand humorous remark the deep recesses of Valdaimon's mind had found the truth and spit it up. Conscious memory came a few hours later, as he continued to scry through the night to determine the meaning of that first seemingly random vision.

Valdaimon closed his eyes and summoned again the hated face of Bagsby to his mind. What a mistake he had made, letting that whelp live some quarter of a century ago. "I should have killed you then," he muttered, focusing his mind more sharply on the hated face and on his memory of an event from years gone by.

It had been in Laga, a small city near the eastern border of Heilesheim, where the sand sea of the Great Eastern Desert begins and the reaches of civilization end. In Laga, barbarian desert tribesmen mingled in the streets with stout Heilesheimers who derived their living by trading grain, fine cloth, and baubles to the desert men in exchange for meat on the hoof, captured weapons, information about the relations of desert tribes and the contacts of merchants of other regions with them, and gold, silver, and gems from lands unknown. Merchants from all over Heilesheim sent traders to Laga to barter with the swarthy desert men with in their black, flowing robes. The streets of Laga were narrow, winding, crowded alleys lined with the cloth-covered booths of Heilesheim merchants, traders, and farmers. They were also filled with thieves, sons of the poverty of a great trading city who prey on Heilesheimers and desert men alike.

The day had been a torment, Valdaimon remembered. The sun, always bright over Laga, had beat down on the streets that day with unbearable vigor. The heat was so great that even the barefoot urchins of the city had congregated at the city's fountains and pools to soak their feet in the tepid water, for the paving stones were so hot the skin would burn from walking on them. If the heat had not been bad enough, the wind had joined it to contribute to the city's misery. It had been the hot, dry easterly wind off the desert, howling through the tunnels the folk of Laga called avenues, bearing on its back a load of swirling, stinging sand that crept into every nook, cranny, and crevice of every building and made its way inside the folds of every robe.

Valdaimon had gone to Laga to find a certain desert shaman and sage, reputed to know by memory verses and incantations learned by his people a millennium ago in the Unknown Lands, the lands beyond the mountains, where no civilized man had ever ventured, no wizard ever scried, no bird ever flown. Perhaps, Valdaimon had thought, those verses and incantations contained final confirmation of what he had long suspected. Perhaps they would verify the secret Valdaimon believed in the depths of his being lay in the great treasure of Parona.

Whether they did or not, Valdaimon never learned. He had been lying in his litter, the curtains drawn against the sun, heat, sand, noise, and the stench of the city, struggling to breathe the sandy air while four servants bore him down one of the city's endless snaking streets. The air was hot and dry, his old lungs paper-thin, and his throat so dry and scratched from inhaling the ubiquitous sand that he was forced to swallow small globules of his own blood. In desperation the mage had extended his scrawny arm and hand and yanked back the shielding curtains.

Just off to his right his eyes had seen a narrow, crowded, open square with one of the fountains in which the youngsters of Laga romped half nude. The old mage had kicked, thumped, and grunted, until the lackeys bearing his litter understood he wished to be carried to the fountain. Carefully, slowly, the bearers had picked their way through the crowd. Inside the litter, Valdaimon's impatience had grown; his entire being was focused on his need for water to relieve his pain.

At last the litter had come to a halt. The old wizard had parted the curtains with his great staff. The fountain was still several feet away, its base mobbed by playing children. In frustration, the mage had lashed out with his staff, striking the nearest adult to get the man's attention.

The man was stocky, naked to the waist against the heat of the day, his skin brown and his torso well muscled. His hair was long and coal black, tied into a tail that fell far below his neck. A gold earring dangled from his left lobe, and a tiny diamond flashed from one of his gleaming white upper teeth. The man's brown eyes had bored into Valdaimon's face.

"Water," the old mage had managed to croak. "I need water."

"See," the man had replied, kneeling and putting his arm around a young child, maybe five years old. "This old buzzard needs water. What say you, son? Shall we help him, or shall we make him croak a bit longer in order to teach him manners?"

The young boy had folded his arms, cocked his head, and stared straight into Valdaimon's eyes. A look of serious study had come over his face, and his fat lips had pouted outward as he concentrated.

"He looks rich," the boy had said at length. "The rich should have better manners. He should not have struck you, Father."

"Right on all three points!" the man had answered, a broad smile lighting up his face. "You see, old man, the boy has cunning. But, Bagsby," he had added, turning back to the boy, "a kindness that costs us nothing and could be richly repaid should not go undone."

The boy had continued to stare skeptically at the withered old figure. His father had laughed again, then had risen and started toward the fountain. Valdaimon, angered at the impudence of the pair but relieved that his request was being fulfilled, had flopped back down among the pillows of his litter, letting the curtains swing shut.

"Father," he had heard the child's voice cry, "he bears the mark of the dragon!" The little urchin had noticed the pattern on the curtains of the litter: a large black dragon, its wings extended fully to both sides. An instant later, the curtains had parted, and the father was once again gazing at Valdaimon. This time, though, he was drawn up to his full height of five feet three inches, and his barrel chest was puffed out to the full.

"Dragon wizard—Valdaimon! You are Valdaimon!" the man had shouted, pointing a finger as though the mere mention of the name was an accusation.

Valdaimon, too tired to argue, his throat burning and bleeding, had merely nodded his head in his pillows to acknowledge the recognition.

"You vile bastard—your wizardry has corrupted half of Heilesheim," the man had cried, "and you rob the better half by your influence with the king. You can fetch your own accursed water. And may Kirie, god of thieves, cause you to choke on it."

Valdaimon's rage had flashed. Despite the dryness of his

throat and feebleness of his bones, he had managed to sit bolt upright in his litter, jam the end of his huge staff into the man's chest, and shout a word of magical command. The man had exploded, and when the black, oily smoke had finally cleared, there was nothing left of him on the sun-soaked pavement save a pile of burning flesh and bones.

"Now, you," Valdaimon had commanded, pointing a bony, thin finger at the quavering child who stared dumbly at his father's smoldering remains. "You, fetch me water!"

The child had met Valdaimon's eyes, his own wide with fear—was it loathing? At any rate, he had quickly obeyed, leaping toward the fountain, swiping a cup from a beggar who sat near the edge of the crowd of children, dipping it in the lukewarm water, and hastening with it to Valdaimon's side without spilling a drop.

"Now you know how to serve your betters and the cost of defying the royal wizard," Valdaimon had snapped, grabbing the cup from the boy's outstretched hands.

As he had raised the cup to his lips, Valdaimon had felt a strange, sudden pressure in his groin that his brain instantly translated into nauseating pain.

"Oooomph!" the old wizard had croaked, spitting and dropping the cup. He had sat upright and doubled over, bumping his head against an elbow of the agile child, who had leapt into the litter and stamped on his groin. Valdaimon had raised his eyes to see the hate-filled face of the child snarling at him. A dagger had flashed, and the tiny boy had held aloft Valdaimon's coin purse. Finally, before the old mage could react, the child had kicked him, hard, right in the face, dislodging another of his already precious yellow teeth. An instant later, the child had vanished, melting into the gathering throng that clamored insults against the royal wizard.

It was then, Valdaimon now realized, that he had made two mistakes. Overcome with pain and rage, he had ordered his bearers to take him away to the shelter of the governor's mansion. There, in a matter of hours, he had left himself be overtaken by affairs of the moment. He had missed the chance to find the desert shaman, and he had let go his intention to have the child Bagsby sought out and killed.

Critical mistakes, Valdaimon thought as he sat in the cheap chair in the thatched hut, listening again to the pouring rain. When one is among mortals as a mortal, one must keep track of who one kills, who their relations may be. Mortals are essentially powerless beings, Valdaimon mused, but they can be a deadly nuisance when one grows careless.

This particular human whelp had become a great nuisance. Valdaimon had heard his name from time to time in his contacts with the thieves and cutthroats of a dozen baronies. It was Bagsby who had stolen the gems of the Countess Pomeran, whose husband now commanded the First Legion. It was Bagsby who had kidnapped the daughter of the leading merchant of Grullheim, whisked her off all the way to the lands of the Rhanguilds, then, when he ransomed her, stolen a ship and sold it to her father for their return journey! He had even dared touch the league; it was that fool mage Grundelson who had let Bagsby steal one of his books of incantations and then sell it back to him before he realized it was missing.

Now this Bagsby was in league with some elf—could there be any connection to Elrond? Would he know, would he dare go after the treasure of Parona? Could he know what it truly was? Valdaimon could only wonder. Once more he cursed the name of Bagsby. Then he opened his eyes, rose, and leaned over the table, turning his attention once again to his scrying ball. Bagsby must die. Until that could be arranged, Valdaimon would keep a watchful, secret eye on the activities of this thief. And he would worry until the treasure of Parona was safely through Argolia, where Bagsby now resided, on its route to his own anxiously waiting hands.

❧4❧

Battle Joined

THOMAS ARBRIGHT, COUNT of Dunsford, single-handedly hefted aloft a full keg of Heilesheim-brewed ale, a feat of strength few living men could have equaled. Roaring with frustration and rage, he hurled the keg down the rocky hillside, heaving for breath and watching with satisfaction as the copper hoops snapped, the wood splintered, and the brew imported from his new and hated enemy spilled out onto the rocky ground.

"So shall we do to Heilesheim's army, which dares to invade our land!" the count cried out to the assembled knights and minor lords who lined the hillcrest behind him.

A lusty, throaty cheer arose from the throng of warriors. Swords were raised in salute to the prowess of their leader. War hammers were banged against the backs of great shields. A stiff, cool, morning breeze conveniently snapped the count's large standard out to its full, colorful glory. The count's gasps formed steam that rose toward the pale blue spring sky, and the bulky war leader smiled. His men were ready for battle. It would go well.

"Barons, meet me for my council of war," the count shouted. "All others, attend to your men-at-arms. The enemy is not far distant. We will attack today!"

A second round of cheering, grunting, and weapon rattling rang out as the count tramped up to the top of the hill and off toward his large tent that served as sleeping quarters, mess, and military headquarters when he was in the field. A flock of barons fell in behind him. The remaining nobility—baronets and knights—shared back slaps and mock clouts and gradually drifted toward their waiting foot soldiers, who had neither seen Count Dunsford's display nor understood the reason for the battle they were about to fight.

Dunsford, always a careful warrior, believed he had done all he could to enhance his chances of winning the coming engagement. He had arisen early, bathed in the cold stream nearby to shock his system to full alertness, then knelt naked for half an hour in early morning air, humbly beseeching the numerous gods recognized in his barony for their aid in the coming fray. Then he had repaired to his tent for a light breakfast of eggs, poultry, venison, and hot mulled wine. He had dressed carefully, beginning with a clean woolen undersuit, followed by a plain gray tunic, his thick quilted underarmor, his chain mail, and his great white outer tunic, emblazoned with blue crossed swords and a boar's head between the blades, the emblem of his family. He had donned his great helm and strapped on his two-handed bastard sword with the jewel-encrusted pommel. Lastly, he had stared into the reflecting metal held by his valet and practiced the scowling, withering glance that was his trademark as a leader of fighting men. His valets had assured him that he cut an imposing figure. At five-foot eleven, he was one of the tallest men in the realm, and the strength of his thick arms and bandy legs was legendary. His hair, beard, and mustache were still thick and black despite his thirty-eight years, and his blue eyes could bore into the soul of either a friendly coward or a determined foe.

Heilesheim was famous for its ales, which were imported into Dunsford's lands in huge quantities. He had chosen the smashing of the keg as a demonstration both of his prowess and of the fate that awaited the Black Prince and his armies for daring to invade the Dunsford lands. As he energetically hurled himself into the large wooden chair at the head of the meeting table in his tent, he congratulated himself for choosing that particular demonstration. The troops had been fired up. They were ready for blood. All that remained was to state to the more important lords the causes of the conflict, so they would know that justice and the gods would fight with them, and then to give the final orders for the battle to come.

"My lords and friends," Dunsford began as more than thirty of the highest ranking nobles milled about in his tent, clanking in their armor, "hear me."

Dunsford did not yet invite the nobles to sit. First he would state the justness of his cause. That would take only minutes. Then, he would invite the nobles to sit and hammer out their positions in the line of battle. If all went well, that would take only one or two hours.

"We fight today to repel an invading foe who fights with neither gods nor justice behind him," the count cried.

Calls of "Yes, yes" and "Hear our liege, hear, hear!" arose from the assembled nobles.

"We have given no offense to Ruprecht of Heilesheim," Dunsford declared, "who is justly called the Black Prince. We did not raid his territories—yet he raided ours and destroyed our village of Shallowford."

Nods and murmurs of agreement arose.

"Now hear more!" Dunsford shouted. "The sack of Shallowford you know of. But hear now of what affront he has done to the honor of every one of us! When we sent our envoy to protest the sack of our village and to demand to know Ruprecht's intentions, the Black Prince saw fit to return to us our own protected ambassador's head in a cloth bag!" On cue, a servant appeared bearing a great platter on which rested a bloody, lumpy cloth sack. Dunsford opened it and held aloft its grisly contents. "Behold, how he treats the honored servants of your liege, the Count of Dunsford! Behold, how Ruprecht regards your own honor!"

"Vengeance!" cried one dull-faced lord, hefting his sword aloft and sadly thrusting it through the roof of the tent. His faux pas went unnoticed; the cry of "Vengeance" was taken up by all, mingled with shouts of "Reparations!"

Dunsford leapt up on the table, ducking his head to avoid the roof of the tent, and gestured for silence.

"That is not all, my lords," he continued. "This same Ruprecht has sent his own envoys with the following demands." A hush came over the lords; the demands of the enemy were always important to know. They gave clues to what advantages might be gained in negotiations after a battle when ransoms for prisoners were determined and reparations for acts of injustice were meted out.

"Ruprecht demands full freedom of passage for the armies of Heilesheim through all the territory of this barony," the count said calmly. The nobles fell stone silent; the first demand was unthinkable. "He further demands," Dunsford went on, "that collectors of revenue for Heilesheim be installed in each shire of this barony, to collect such taxes, tithes, fees, and entitlements to which he, as the true king of this realm, may declare himself entitled."

"Never!" shouted one baron. "Invasion and tyranny!" called out a second. In an instant the tent was a seething mass of angry men, mindlessly shouting, banging their weapons, and pounding upon one another with mailed fists. Dunsford allowed this demonstration to continue a bit before raising his arms, as best he could in the cramped space, and calling again for silence.

"My lords, silence! Silence I say! You have not yet heard all!"

"All?" one baron queried. "What more could that impudent usurper, who probably murdered his own brother, ask?"

"Hear me, and I will tell you. Ruprecht, who styles himself King of Heilesheim," Dunsford said, deliberately pausing for effect, "demands that all lands not belonging to the temples and the lords of the temples but held in fief and liege from the Count of Dunsford, along with their rights, privileges, fees, duties, and titles, be surrendered to the crown of Heilesheim as royal lands in perpetuity."

Pandemonium erupted in the tent.

From the low hilltop Culdus gazed on the level meadow that stretched for more than a thousand yards before him. In the far distance the crest of a second hill rose; there, he could make out unmistakable signs of the enemy force. Smoke rose in the air from countless cooking fires; little blobs of white against the mottled green and brown of the hillcrest were the tents of enemy lords. The meadow would be a battlefield within a few hours.

The position could not be better, Culdus thought, for his purposes. The little roadway from Shallowford to Dunsford's main city, Avon, wound through the middle of the meadow. The entire field was only about fifteen hundred yards wide; on the left the marshy banks of a stream that made its way south to the Rigel prevented the movement of troops, and on the right a large uncleared wood blocked any flanking movement.

"A good field for our tactics, Lord General," commented Viscount Karl of Sudlund, commander of the Fifth Legion that would bear the brunt of the fighting. He stamped his mailed boot on the cold, hard earth. "The ground is solid, making maneuver easy. Our flanks are protected," he added, pointing to the woods and then the marsh. "The enemy will be in a narrow zone, where we can easily slay them."

Culdus nodded, pleased. Sudland was one of the few who truly understood the new military system, which would now, after several days' delay, receive its first real test in battle. It was a good thing that this first test would come under the command of a man who understood and appreciated the system.

Only a few thin wisps of white cloud marked the sunny, pale blue sky. A light breeze stirred, but there was no sign of the accursed rain that had dogged the invasion of Dunsford for the first three days. Even though the schedule of march of the legions had been badly thrown off by the weather, this was a perfect day for battle, Culdus thought.

"Tell me, Karl, how you will proceed," Culdus said, clapping an arm around the younger noble's shoulders.

Karl surveyed the field one more time, shading his eyes to study the details of small rises and dips in the ground. He gazed at the enemy encampment on the opposite hill. He removed his mailed gloves, dropped them on the ground, stroked his chin, and then fiddled with the large ebony brooch that formed the clasp of his heavy, dark blue cloak. At length, he drew his longsword, and using it as a pointer, outlined his plan.

"I'll form the foot soldiers in line by battles," he began. "The first battle will take the center, with the second in standard formation behind it. The fifth I'll deploy to the right of the first, the sixth to the left."

Again, Culdus nodded. He could immediately visualize Karl's positioning on the field. The foot soldiers would form lines in their "battles" of one thousand men each. Each soldier was armed with an eighteen-foot spear and a shortsword. A full battle formed a line three ranks deep and about three hundred and fifty yards in length. Thus, three battles formed in line, side by side, with about one hundred yards between them for maneuvering room, would just about cover the frontage of the field. An additional battle, the second in Culdus's numbering system, would be formed up just behind the center of the line. So far, so good.

"What else?" Culdus prompted.

"The third battle in standard blocks behind the second," Karl responded. Thus, his center would be even deeper. Behind the second battle, a third would be divided in half, with each half formed in a kind of square. One square would be placed behind each flank of the second battle. "The archers will be distributed by hundreds behind the flanking battles to arch fire as the whole advances."

"And the cavalry?"

Karl laughed. "Yes, my tumultuous lords. They will be held in reserve and can advance at a distance of three hundred yards behind the rest of the legion."

"And if the enemy charges?"

"We will halt and form the block," Karl answered immediately.

Culdus was very pleased. This would be a good day for Heilesheim. "The Sixth Legion will be formed in the block behind this hill as a reserve. I doubt you will need it," Culdus said. "Form your legion and advance at will."

"Lord General, it shall be done. But what of the king and Valdaimon?"

"Let us pray to our gods that the king and Valdaimon

find other amusements today. This is work for soldiers. And Karl," Culdus cautioned, "mind you mark well the behavior of your mounted lords. The order of the day is, No prisoners."

Karl nodded his obedience.

Dunsford sighed. Goblets of wine were being hurled across the table in his tent. Four of the assembled lords had already left for the open field outside, there to hack away at one another over injuries to their honor. Shouts, curses, insults, and claims of precedence created a din around the table. It was always this way when it was time to form line of battle. The theory was simple; he would form with his troops in the center. The next lords in ranks would take station to his right and left. The next lower ranks would form to the right and left beyond, and so on.

Sadly, determining order of rank was always a complicated matter. It involved ancestry, conferred titles as opposed to inherited titles, reputation for prowess, performance in battles past, and social rank acquired by marriage. Councils of war always degenerated into name-calling matches, and not infrequently one or two lords would be killed in private duels before the line of battle was ever formed.

"My lords, I beseech you. This bickering over precedence is needless," Dunsford literally screamed at the assemblage. "It is not important how close you stand to me, but how well you close with the enemy!"

Murmurs of assent momentarily interrupted the shouting matches. Before they could resume, a young page, wearing a rapier and dagger but no armor, dashed into the count's tent.

"My Lord Count," he cried, "the scouts report that the enemy advances!"

"What strength does he show?" Dunsford asked.

"The scouts report more than six thousand, but only a few hundred mounted knights, and those held in reserve," the page responded.

For an instant Dunsford's brow wrinkled and his mouth formed a small *o*. What devilment was this? Only a few hundred knights? Foot soldiers advancing? But there was not time to ponder. Dunsford banged his fist on the table and bellowed his orders.

"Duncan, you will take position on my right. Sir Richard Grier, on my left. The rest of you, where you will. Go to your troops and form line of battle at the crest of this hill, now!"

The nobles, still bickering and casting angry glances at one another, clattered their way out of the tent.

"God of my homeland, grant me victory today," Dunsford said, his eyes raised to the sunlight that shone through the roof of his tent. The count rose and walked outside. Two servants awaited with his war-horse, and helped him mount.

Behind him, the camp was gradually transformed as his barons formed their troops. Each baron had with him between one hundred to one hundred and fifty men. Of these, ten to twenty were mounted knights; the remainder were men-at-arms, foot soldiers. The knights were armored as best they could afford, and most were armed with heavy lances, supplemented by longswords, or, in some cases, some other preferred weapon, such as a mace, morning star, war hammer, or axe. The men-at-arms were a haphazardly armored and armed lot. Most carried a standard twelve-foot-long spear along with some other weapon, though these varied from fine longswords for the more fortunate to daggers, mallets, or even clubs for the less privileged.

"Form up! Form up!" the count cried, riding along the crest of the hill, waving his great two-handed sword in the air above his head. "The enemy comes!"

As he rode along the hillcrest he could see them advancing across the meadow. Already they were only about eight hundred yards distant and coming on at a slow but steady pace. Never before had Dunsford seen an army advance in such a fashion. These were foot soldiers, but with peculiarly long spears. They were arranged in thin blocks, about three ranks deep, keeping nearly perfect order as they advanced. There were more troops in the center than elsewhere. Behind the main lines were little groups of men that didn't seem to carry the long spears. Probably archers or slingers, Dunsford guessed. But most peculiar of all was the behavior of the enemy knights. These formed a solid block, three ranks deep, nearly three hundred yards long, that advanced at a very slow walk, hanging far behind the infantry. What kind of knights were these, Dunsford wondered, who allowed infantry the honor of the first attack?

His own army took shape at the crest of the hill. His longtime friend and loyal vassal, Sir Duncan Wright, rode up on his right-hand side. Sir Richard Grier, a younger man of proven prowess in many a minor border dispute, thundered up on a magnificent charger to take his position on Dunsford's left. The remainder of the cavalry, some six hundred in all, gradually formed a ragged line that was at times one rank and at times two ranks deep. Behind the cavalry the foot soldiers formed up in irregular masses of spearmen, trying to get into positions somewhere behind and near their respective noble leaders. Pennants snapped in the breeze, revealing a colorful panoply of coats of arms.

"By the gods, what is this insult?" Sir Richard shouted to the count. "They attack with infantry—why? Do they think to tire us and thus avoid capture and ransom payments? Come, let us show these brigands false!" Sir Richard shot out his right arm and his young squire, who would not fight, handed him his great battle lance, a heavy, tapered, pointed twelve-foot shaft of wood coated with metal. Sir Richard raised his lance high in the air.

"No," Dunsford shouted. "Not yet. We need to think about—"

"For the gods, for the right, and for Dunsford!" Sir Richard screamed at the top of his lungs. His spurs bit into the flanks of his mount, and he was off, charing at the trot toward the slowly approaching enemy mass.

A tremendous shout erupted from Dunsford's lines. Rider after rider put spur to flank, and in less than half a minute the entire cavalry force was in a ragged charge. Pennants and banners snapped bravely against the pale blue of the cold, clear sky. The foot soldiers scrambled after the horsemen with no order to their ranks. Some waved their spears and shouted; others carried them lowered toward the enemy. A few paused after a hundred yards to catch their breath and let their comrades run on ahead.

Oh well, the count thought as his own steed charged forward, it's no worse than usual. "For the gods, for justice, and for me!" he called, lowering his own great battle lance. He spurred his mount to a full gallop. He had to overtake Sir Richard; it would never due for a vassal to be the first to make contact with the enemy.

The Viscount Karl of Sudland reined his horse to a halt and craned his neck forward. He held up his right arm, and immediately the drumming, which marked time for the marching ranks of his legion, ended with three heavy beats. As one man, the disciplined men-at-arms halted, their eighteen-foot spears held erect.

By all the gods, Karl thought, old Culdus was right. Everything he taught us was right! The fools are charging! Karl waved his upraised right arm in a broad, circular motion. The drumming began again, this time at a much faster tempo. The two huge battles on either flank of the center turned inward, forming three long lines. The heads of these lines then began a turn toward the rear. In less than a minute, during which time the oncoming enemy cavalry closed to within one hundred yards, the two flanking battles had moved to the very rear of the formation.

The archers, too, had changed position; they were now in the very center of the huge block of spearmen. The two squares in the middle, on the outside of the archers, did a smart change of face so they were facing outward, as did the flanking lines of the front and rear battles. The mass formation now looked like a giant block, with spears pointing outward in all directions except the very rear.

Karl wheeled his horse and galloped to a position at the rear right corner of the block.

"Lower spears!" he shouted. "Fourth battle, arcing fire, by hundreds!"

The long spears were lowered, allowed a clear flight path for the volley of one hundred short arrows that arced from the center of the block into the line of onrushing cavalry. The first flight was followed by another, then another, then another, all within a few seconds.

Dunsford, who rode in the very center of the charge, was only sixty yards from the enemy when the hail of arrows struck the line of charging horses. Two arrows bounced off the barding on his horse, but a third penetrated its right eye, and a fourth plunged into its left flank. The injured animal whinnied wildly and reared. As it did, four more shafts struck it dead-on in the chest. The mighty animal crashed over on its side.

"Aaaahhhhwwww!" The count howled with pain as the full weight of his dying mount crushed his right leg and the hard ground knocked the breath from his lungs. His great lance thudded to the ground beside him and rolled uselessly away. The count cursed his horse and kicked at its back with the mailed boot of his free leg. The painful blows only caused the panicked animal to thrash more wildly in its losing bout with death, and with each thrash of its legs, it pressed its weight more against the count's trapped, crushed limb.

Loyal Duncan, heedless of the menace of the volleys of arrows that sang through the air all around him, reined in his own mount and trotted to the count's side. Quickly seeing the hopelessness of horse's struggle, he raised his great lance like a spear and plunged it deep into the horse's head. The animal's struggles ceased.

"Onward, Duncan," Dunsford shouted through clenched teeth. "The men-at-arms can free me. Go! Fight them!"

"Ay, my lord," Duncan replied, raising his shield as another flight of arrows plunged to earth around him. One shaft buried itself in his shield; another bit into the dead flesh of the count's horse. Duncan handed his shield to the pinned count. "At least protect yourself, my liege."

"I shall, I shall," the grateful war leader replied. "Now go, lead the attack!"

But the attack was already faltering. No sooner had the tenth flight of arrows been loosed than Viscount Karl shouted another simple command. "Prepare to receive!" he bellowed.

At the front of the great block, the first battle, three ranks deep, knelt and planted the ends of their great spears on the hard earth. Their hands gripped the ends of the spear shafts and their strong arms kept the points, which included an extra metal hook for ripping armor, angled upward at about thirty degree.

Behind the first battle, the second hoisted their spear shafts waist high and aimed them forward. The third battle raised their spears high in both hands and, resting the ends atop their shoulders, likewise pointed the business ends dead ahead.

The result of this simple maneuver was a wall of spearpoints, now three rows high, extending outward some fifteen feet from near the earth to the height of a man's head. Similar maneuvers by the men facing the sides caused a similar bristling defense to be presented on either flank.

Sir Richard was the first in Dunsford's army to learn a basic lesson concerning animal behavior. A horse, even a trained, charging war-horse, will not willingly impale itself. Sir Richard was less than twenty yards from the enemy when his own mount veered off, slowing its pace, finally coming to a winded halt with its flanks presented to the enemy only a few feet away. Sir Richard shouted and howled and cursed. He gestured threateningly with his great lance, but could only touch the spear points and hooks, not the men behind them.

All along the front of the block the same scene was repeated: dozens of horses and riders were felled by the initial volleys of arrows. The remainder of the horses veered off just before the moment of contact with the wall of spearpoints, leaving their riders to dig their spurs into flanks and curse with helpless rage. It was the same on the flanks as the charging line wrapped itself around the block, only to find that spears pointed at them from all sides. In less than a minute more than a hundred of Dunsford's mounted knights were dead. The count himself was still pinned under his dead horse, beating the earth and writhing in pain. The remainder of his knights milled about helplessly in front of the spearpoints, unable to bring any weapon to bear on the enemy.

Even the Viscount Karl was stunned by the magnitude of the legion's success. Footmen had withstood a charge by mounted knights—not only stood it, but stopped it dead. And now these same knights were wandering about in rage and confusion, leaderless, virtually helpless. There were not even the usual sounds of battle to be heard—no clash of steel on steel, no resounding impacts as lance met shield or breastplate. Instead, there were only the curses and howls of the frustrated knights and the screams of the wounded and dying. So overwhelmed was Karl by the magnitude of this success that it took him longer than it should to issue the next, logical command.

"First battle," he shouted. "Attack!"

Drummers translated his order into beats. The front three ranks of the great block stood up, raised their huge spears to their shoulders, gave a mighty shout, and charged forward at a run. They had both superior weaponry and number on their side. Untouched by casualties, their battle numbered a full thousand. Only slightly more than a third of the enemy force had actually charged the front of the block, and of those more than a third had been felled by arrows. Now, the men-at-arms charged with a five-to-one superiority and a weapon that could outreach their foes' by a good twelve feet.

It was George the miller's son, in the second rank of the first battle, who happened to drive his great spearpoint through Sir Richard's leg just above the knee, pinning the limb to the horse that the hook of the spear then half disemboweled. "Hah, c'mon, Frederick, the fun's a' now!" George shouted with glee. He released his grip on the great spear—it was deeply embedded in man and horse, and, drawing his shortsword, wove forward at a crouch, avoiding the spear shafts of his friends as he made his way toward the enraged knight still atop the dying horse.

Sir Richard screamed with pain, but his agony did not completely numb his brain. Tossing aside his lance he drew his longsword and vainly twisted atop his mount, trying to bring the blade to bear on George.

"Begging your pardon, my lord," George taunted as he worked his way to the horse's rear. "Your mount seems to be hamstrung!" George let fly a mighty slashing blow at the back of the horse's rear left leg. The beast squealed from the pain of the blow, and the leg collapsed. Sir Richard's body snapped and rolled as the horse suddenly fell like a rag doll, but the knight could not free his leg from the impaling spear.

"Damn you, you peasant murderer!" Sir Richard bellowed. "May all the gods damn you!"

"Ask 'em about it when you see 'em," George called back, leaping onto the back of the dying steed and, with both hands, plunging his shortsword into Sir Richard's back. The blade bit through the chainmail. George felt the satisfying resistance of bone as the cold steel sliced through vertebrae and ribs. Blood spurted from Sir Richard's mouth as he tried to form a final curse, and his right arm vainly flailed up and down, beating his longsword against the unyielding ground.

"C'mon, Frederick, there's more for the taking," George called, looking about the melee for his friend. He finally spotted Frederick about ten yards away, hacking the head off a man who was pinned to the earth by a huge eighteen-foot spear shaft extending toward the heavens from the middle of his torso.

All along the front line of battle the scene was similar. The futile fighting of Dunsford's knights lasted only about ten minutes. In that time the more valiant tried in vain to charge again and again, but always with the same result. Duncan, veteran of many battles, saw the problem and tried to tackle it by approaching dismounted. A well-trained man-at-arms simply laid his spear on the ground, waited for Duncan to approach, then quickly pulled the spear backward, using the hook to grab Duncan's ankle and pull him to the ground. The knight was quickly impaled and cut to bits by three other men-at-arms.

Eventually the remaining knights saw the futility of fighting and turned to flee. As they increased their distance from the impregnable block of spearmen, more volleys of arrows were unleashed, and more and more of the knights found themselves fleeing on foot in full armor.

Dunsford's men-at-arms were useless at initiating battle.

Their function was to follow after their knights and finish off the wounded, occasionally taking a prisoner who could be ransomed. With the failure of the knights they had not the slightest notion what to do. They simply stopped and stupidly watched the debacle. And when the knights at length retreated, the foot soldiers turned and ran.

Only when the enemy was retreating with his infantry in panic and the knights in, at the very best, confusion and disorder, did Karl take a large green pennant from his saddlebag, tie it to the tip of his own lance, and raise it high. From three hundred yards in the rear, the fresh, untouched heavy cavalry of his legion began thundering forward in perfect formation at a controlled trot. The formation split in two as it approached the rear of the block of spearmen, swirled around them, and re-formed into a line at their front. Then the commanders gave the signal for a canter, and after sixty yards more, for the full gallop.

The results were decisive. The savage horsemen thundered into the scattered, fleeing men, sowing death and devastation with lance and sword, mace and morning star. A few of Dunsford's braver knights turned, swords in hand, and tried to stand against the charging horsemen; but such gestures were hopeless acts of courage. A few managed to get in a symbolic sword stroke at an enemy as he galloped past, then dropped their swords and offered cries of "I yield!" to the next passing knight.

Such as tried this time-honored course were stabbed and trampled as the knights of the Fifth Legion reminded themselves of their training with shouts of "No prisoners! No prisoners!" The mounted knights hacked, slashed, stabbed, and clubbed their way through the mass of fleeing men until at last they gained the crest of the opposite hill, where they dismounted and began systematically looting the enemy camp.

On the field below, the foot soldiers were doing the same, stripping the dead of Dunsford's force of anything of value, leaving the corpses to lie naked in the cold spring sun. George, having single-handedly killed a knight—and a rich one at that—did very well for himself.

"Lookie 'ere, Frederick!" he called across the field as

the soldiers of the first battle, having reaped the fruits of victory, lolled about on the field, resting, making fires, and hacking steaks of horsemeat from the mounts of their slain foes. "Lookie 'ere!"

"What did you get, George?" Frederick asked, his eyes wide as George approached with his arms laden with a pile of glinting loot. "Show me!"

"First, there's this here cloak. A fine one, see, thick and heavy, made of wool, with gold and silver thread worked into the seams at the edges and a fine coat of arms," George said, tossing aside his pile and spreading the cloak on the hard ground. "Look, 'ere's where my sword went through—a big slash, but I'll wager some fat Dunsford cow can fix it." George turned his head, staring for a moment at the source of a continuous wailing moan. "What's he on about? Why don't you kill him?" he asked, pointing.

Frederick followed George's finger to where a large man, stripped naked to the waist, lay trapped under a dead horse. The man sweated and moaned and cried out, but all ignored him.

"Oh, that's old Dunsford. Nobody dares kill 'im; the higher-ups'll want him, I wager."

"Yeah, yeah, I see," George replied. He grabbed another item from his pile. "And this clasp for that cloak—it's gold, Frederick!"

Frederick seized the clasp in his rough, blood- and dirt-covered hands. He raised it to his mouth and bit at the thinnest part. "By the gods, it is gold, George; it is!"

"Aye, and that's not all. Look at this." George retrieved the late Sir Richard's sword from the treasure heap. It was a finely made longsword crafted in the Rhanguild lands, with a blade honed to razor sharpness. The pommel was ebony, ending in a large ball with a ring of tiny, gleaming stones that fractured the sunlight into a rainbow.

"Diamonds!" Frederick exclaimed. "Them's diamonds."

"Aye. And there's this armor, which might be mended, a good tunic I could wear to any temple, and a fine suit of woolen unders."

A loud scream of agony from Dunsford interrupted George.

"Shut up, you bloody damned cripple!" George shouted. "You'll be dead soon enough." He turned his attention back to his loot. "Now these mailed boots," George said, rummaging through his pile, "don't fit me—too little. See if you can use 'em. If you can, you can have 'em."

Awed, Frederick scrambled after the boots and, with a mighty shove, forced one foot into one. "They fits good, George," he said hopefully. "Say, 'ere, 'ave a bit of this horse steak with me," he added, pointing toward the hunk of meat hanging from a stick over the fire he had built.

"Thanks, Frederick. I'm a bit hungry after this morning's work."

George pulled out his dagger and roughly cut a hunk of the rare, juicy meat. He popped it in his mouth and chewed vigorously. The hot red juices streamed from the sides of his mouth down his stubbly chin. "Hmm, not bad," he commented.

A fanfare of trumpets interrupted the feasting and looting of the Fifth Legion. The drummers were the first to their feet, running for the large kettledrums on which they beat the march and command cadences. A second trumpet blast sounded, and drummers formed a rough line and began beating the signal for "stand to." All over the field the happy, if tired, warriors of the Fifth obediently, but with a bit of grumbling, dropped meals and piles of loot. They grabbed their weapons and began falling in. In less than two minutes the entire legion was back in block formation, and Karl of Sudland, mounted on his charger, stood at its head, looking to the rear and watching the approaching riders.

He recognized Culdus first; then he made out the smaller figure, magnificently clad in gleaming, full plate armor with a tunic of snow-white satin overlaid with the arms of the House of Heilesheim in threads of scarlet, blue, black, silver, and gold.

"Men of the Fifth, prepare to salute!" Karl shouted. "The lord general comes! The king comes!"

A great shout arose from the Fifth. Their huge spears were lifted high in the sky, and a celebratory volley of arrows was loosed. Culdus and Ruprecht galloped up to

Karl, their right arms raised in acknowledgment of the legion's clamorous salute.

While the shouting continued, Culdus extended his right arm to Karl, who grasped it at the elbow.

"Well done! Well done, indeed!" Culdus said with enthusiasm. "Your triumph on this field was witnessed from yon hill not only by myself but by His Majesty."

"Yes. We are most pleased," Ruprecht said with a cold nod. The king turned is mount to face the center of the legion's front line and lifted both arms high, a sign of celebration and also a call for silence.

"Men of the Fifth Legion," he shouted, "hear me!"

The tumult was quickly replaced by silence, broken only by the continued wailing of one wounded man who lay beneath a dead horse a short distance from the king.

"You have done well. Victory is yours. As your king, I award you the spoils of this field." This announcement was greeted with another clamorous shout.

Again the king called silence, and again the tumult died down.

"The armies of Dunsford are broken forever," the king declared. "This land is now a conquest of Heilesheim and shall be part of our realm. But as punishment for its resistance, it shall suffer. Hear me well, soldiers of the Fifth; for your role in this conquest, Dunsford shall be yours. You may take what you will of food, wine, ale, and women. And each may take as much loot from any house or any village as that one man can carry!"

Not even the king's repeated calls for silence could still the cry that arose from the foot soldiers upon hearing that announcement. It was a soldier's dream: an entire province laid open for their plunder.

But still the wails and moans of Dunsford himself threaded their way through the shouts to the king's ear. He leaned forward to Karl.

"Who is that moaning knight over there, and why is he alive? Did I not order that all were to be put to the sword?"

"Aye, Your Majesty," Karl replied. "That is the Count of Dunsford himself. I spared him only so that Your Majesty could have pleasure as desired before he is dispatched."

"Ah," Ruprecht answered. "Well done." The king guided his steed over to the fallen, wounded count and looked down at his agonized countenance. "You rejected my demands, and now you are beaten," the haughty youth said. "What last requests, old warrior, would you make?"

Blood and white foam already flecked the count's lips as he spat his reply. "A quick and honorable death."

"I grant you a quick death," Ruprecht said. "But . . ." He paused, thinking. "Honorable? I think not."

Suddenly inspired, the king rode back to his legion and point a finger at a random soldier. "You there! Yes, you!" the king called. "Go kill me that rebel!"

George the miller's son shrugged off his fear and broke from the ranks, running at the side of the king's horse over to the fallen count.

"See, Count Dunsford, you shall die at the hands of a commoner!" the king crowed. High-pitched, squealing laughter erupted from the pale youth's mouth. "Kill him," he shouted at George. "Stick him like a pig!"

George nodded. He gripped his huge spear high up, nearly five feet from the butt end of the shaft. He raised it so the back end rested on his shoulder and pointed the tip slightly down. Then, lunging forward, he rammed the business end straight into the count's skull. The point penetrated all the way into the cold ground, impaling the broken head upon the earth. Brains oozed out around the shaft of the spear that protruded from the hole in the man's head. George released his grip on the spear; it stood upright on its own, as if to direct the eyes of heaven toward the brutal scene upon the earth.

The king's shrieking laughter grew even louder, and a cheer went up from the Fifth Legion. George drew his breath in shallow pants. He had killed a count. Today, he had killed first a knight and now a count! A broad smile broke over George's face, and he raised his countenance to his laughing king.

"Lookie 'ere, Your Majesty," he shouted above the tumult. "These 'ere nobles bleeds and dies just as easy as any soldier!"

The king continued to laugh, ignoring the man's remark. But for an instant, Culdus felt icy tongs grab at his heart, and a thrill of terror ran through him. The feeling lasted only an instant, and he could not understand its origin. He shrugged it off, but later, he would ponder that moment deeply.

Sir John Wolfe, the son of the Count of Nordingham in the distant kingdom of Pantania, known to most of the world outside Clairton as Bagsby the thief, laughed heartily, slapped the giggling serving wench on her plump behind, and drained another mug of wine in three great gulps. A cheer went up from his dozen noble companions, a lusty cheer led by the Viscount Marco D'Alonzo, who believed he owed to this multitalented visiting gentleman nothing less than his very life.

The viscount's misguided belief had resulted in a great windfall for Bagsby. In gratitude, the viscount had opened his own credit in the best gambling clubs of the city to Sir John Wolfe's draw, and he had done the same with the finer merchants. Bagsby, in his role of Sir John, was meeting the highest nobility of the city, enjoying wine, women, clothes, gambling, and all the pleasures of the idle rich. He had only to stay alert enough to foil the next troop of assassins sent by Nebuchar.

For that reason he sat at a long table in a far corner, his back against the join of two walls, so that the natural direction of his gaze took in the main entrance to the establishment. He had, as a matter of routine, already planned three routes of exit for himself in the event of trouble. But the evening was merry, and thoughts of trouble were flying further and further from Bagsby's mind.

The viscount was not a bad sort, Bagsby thought. He was typical of the higher city nobles. His family had made a fortune about a century ago in the merchant banking business. Kings always needed money, and they were willing to exchange titles for it. Hence there had arisen, in Clairton and other wealthy cities throughout the Holy Alliance, a breed of idle, wealthy courtiers, living off inherited wealth and enjoying purchased titles. These men provided a few services to their kingdoms; as far as Bagsby was concerned, they were worth having simply for decorative purposes at court. A few, like Marco D'Alonzo, were actually educated—they could read and work numbers, and they could tell stories about the great empires of the past gleaned from their youthful reading of ancient books.

But most of all, these men were fun. Bagsby glanced around the table and loved what he saw: laughing men, men of polish and wit, men clothed in brilliant silks and rich furs, men interchanging sly allusions to the classics with a touch of bawdy wit. By the gods, Bagsby thought, it is good to be alive!

And it's good to be a hero, he noted to himself.

"Another toast to this noble gentleman who combines wit with decisive action," D'Alonzo was saying, raising aloft his mug. "Sir John, I salute you with gratitude."

"No, no," Bagsby interjected, leaping to his feet and swiping the viscount's mug from his hand. "I forbid any more tributes to my humble self. I am but a grateful guest of your lordship, and did no more than any honorable man of any station would do in the same situation."

"Hah!" the viscount interrupted. "My servants told me you were swinging from window to tree to balcony on a rope improvised from the sheets of your bed. A dagger toss dropped one assassin, and the second you wounded with the first's bow—and all in the blinking of an eye. No false modesty, Sir John."

Bagsby raised his hands with palms forward and tilted his head to one side, averting his eyes from the approving stares of the assembled lords. "Gentlemen," he said, "I risk an accusation of ingratitude by daring to disagree with my gracious host. But I must insist that this salute go to the Viscount Marco D'Alonzo, a man of distinguished family, whose services to the crown of Argolia are such that some enemy, as yet unknown, thought it essential to slay him. A man whom the enemies of his country would slay should be honored by his countrymen." Bagsby raised the mug in the viscount's direction and smiled. "I give you that most valuable servant of His Majesty, the King of Argolia, the Viscount Marco D'Alonzo. Long life and noble service!"

"D'Alonzo!" came the joyous answer from the lords, and more draughts were drained.

"It may be, Sir John," wagged one of the looser tongues of the assembly, "that the unknown enemy you name has shown his hand and his identity already."

"Eh?" Bagsby responded. Concerned glances shot back forth and up and down the table. The idle rich did not welcome serious talk in the midst of their carouses. Still, Bagsby knew it was essential for him to know everything relevant to his cover story. "What enemy is that?"

"Have you not heard? The Black Prince of Heilesheim has marched an army against the Count of Dunsford. It is only a matter of time until Dunsford's envoys arrive at our court to ask for aid under the terms of the Holy Alliance," the drunken lord explained.

"I had not heard," Bagsby said, his eyebrows knitting together in concern.

The lords fell silent, each staring at his own cup.

"It is true." D'Alonzo broke the awkward stillness. "I had not wanted to trouble my guest with these rumors of war. But you should know now, Sir John, that two days hence I am commanded to appear at the king's court to give counsel after the reception of Dunsford's envoy. All those at this table have been so commanded to appear."

Noble heads bobbed silently up and down, acknowledging the truth of D'Alonzo's words.

"By the gods!" D'Alonzo said, a sudden inspiration bringing light to his face and fire to his eyes. He leapt to his feet, pointed at Bagsby, and said, "You, Sir John Wolfe, shall attend our council and provide your opinion to our king!"

Cries of "Aye!" and "Great idea!" rang out from the lords.

"My lords, my lords," Bagsby protested. "I am but a humble stranger in your land. You overvalue my poor opinion. I know nothing of war or politics."

"Nonsense," the viscount responded for the entire

group. "You are a man of action and discernment. Did you not just reveal to us that the attempt on my life was part of a plot by an enemy of the crown? Who else among us could have arrived at that conclusion from the meager evidence on hand? You shall attend, and we shall have your counsel."

"My lords," Bagsby said humbly, cocking his head again with feigned modesty, "I bow to your judgments, which are wiser than mine. I am but a robbed, beaten stranger in a strange land. Here I have received wonderful hospitality. If I can repay but a portion of it by offering my valueless opinion on your matters of state, how can I refuse?"

A round of applause rose from the lords, and six voices rang out for the serving wench. It was time for more wine.

The evening's revels lasted into the dark hours of the night. Bagsby's head was reeling as he tumbled through the doors of the club and, with guidance from two charming ladies, fell face-down upon the soft orange and blue pillows of the litter provided for him by the viscount. "Home," he muttered, waving a drunken hand randomly at the bearers. He felt the first motions of the litter as it rose and started forward, and began to drift toward drunken sleep.

An instant later, pain shot through his scalp as his hair was grabbed and his head pulled backward and upward. He felt the cold, needle-sharp point of a dagger pressed just behind his left ear.

"Make no sound. The tip of this blade is envenomed, and you will die instantly from the slightest scratch," a vaguely familiar voice whispered in his ear.

"You don't want to kill me or you would have already," Bagsby said. "I may be drunk, but I'm not stupid."

"Hmmph," the voice answered, but the pressure of the dagger point was removed. "We must talk, and then we must act."

Recognition finally filtered through Bagsby's drunken brain. "It's you," he groaned, "the crazed elf."

"Elf, yes, crazed, no," Shulana replied.

"That's a matter of opinion. Why don't we tell everyone

what you want me to do and take a vote?" Bagsby
snapped. "And let go of my hair. It hurts."

Shulana made the slightest gesture with her right hand,
and Bagsby's head flopped down into the pillows.

"Oohh," he moaned. Then, suddenly concerned, he
rolled over and sat up. "Hey, how did you manage to grip
my hair? It's too short for anyone to grab."

Shulana stared into Bagsby's eyes and raised both eyebrows, her face crinkling into an expression of disdain.

"Oh yeah, magic," Bagsby muttered, falling back into
the pillows. "Go away, elf woman. You're crazy, and I'm
in the middle of a good thing right now."

"We have an agreement. I'm here to see that you get
started on our task. Immediately."

"Look . . ." Bagsby said, trying to be patient. Why he
didn't just draw his dagger and . . . the Covenant, he remembered. Can't kill an elf because of the Covenant. Big
trouble, even for a professional. *Especially* for a professional. "Look, I don't want any trouble with you. I don't
know you. I don't know anything about you. All I know
is you want me to steal the treasure of Parona, which is the
single most stupid idea I've heard in my life. I'm not going to do it."

"You agreed," Shulana persisted.

"Yeah, I agreed," Bagsby said. "Big deal. You've
learned a valuable lesson. Never trust the word of a thief,
especially when given under duress. Leave your address
and I'll send you a bill for my professional advice."

"You want to do it," Shulana said.

"I want to do lots of things. I can't do all of them. I
want to fly, but I'm not going to hurl myself off a cliff and
hope for the best. It's called being realistic. Maybe you
elves have heard of that."

"I could just kill you right now if you don't agree to
what I demand," Shulana said. She was truly puzzled now.
Just a few days ago, he'd been willing enough. Now she
was resorting to ridiculous threats to get him to do what
she knew in his heart of hearts he wanted to do. Humans!
How frustrating to deal with!

"Yes, but you won't," Bagsby said tiredly. "I'm only of

value to you as a thief. I'm worthless to you if I won't do what you want—which I won't—and I'm worthless to you dead. It's the same either way. So there's no reason to kill me."

"Spite. Revenge," Shulana shot back.

"Human traits, not elven. You'd be more likely to kill me if I did steal that accursed treasure for you. That way, you wouldn't have to pay me. Now go away and leave me alone."

Shulana sat silent for a long time, thinking. The litter bobbed up and down a bit as the servants bore it through the dark streets. The occasional shouts of drunks and laughing cries of lovers penetrated the curtains, but not Shulana's thoughts. How could she persuade this creature? She concluded that she could not.

"Very well. Let Valdaimon gain the treasure. Let the world be destroyed by war. Or let you rot. I'll find another thief," she said in frustration.

Bagsby sat bolt upright, his brain suddenly clear. His arm shot out and his hand grasped the elf's thin arm so tightly she flinched.

"Valdaimon? What has Valdaimon to do with this?"

"He is the royal wizard of Heilesheim, the principal advisor to the Black Prince," Shulana responded, surprised at having to state what was common knowledge.

Bagsby shook his head vigorously. He grabbed the elf by the shoulders and shook her harshly. "I know that! Everybody knows that. What has Valdaimon to do with the treasure of Parona?"

"Unhand me, human!" the elf barked, her thin arms snaking between his and her right fist smashing into his sternum. Bagsby fell back, clutching his chest. The pain was immense.

The litter stopped suddenly and the curtains parted. One of the servants looked inside to see Bagsby lying on the pillows, clutching his chest, and a red-faced, angry looking creature the likes of which he had never seen before staring at the little man.

"Sir John, is everything all right?" the servant stammered.

"Perfectly." Bagsby coughed. He waved his right hand in an impatient gesture. The servant eyed him questioningly, then closed the curtains. Bagsby could hear the man muttering to his fellows, but in a moment the litter was raised and was moving again.

"Elf," Bagsby said at length, "I beg you, tell me what connection there is between Valdaimon and the treasure of Parona."

Shulana tilted her head and smiled wryly. She lifted one eyebrow and gave Bagsby a look that, had she been human, he would have taken as coy. "Steal it for me," she said in a whisper, lowering her face to only inches from Bagsby's, "and I'll tell you."

Bagsby looked into her dark elven eyes and felt a strange, drunken desire stirring. "Will it . . ." he whispered back, placing a hand gently on the back of the elf's head, feeling the fine texture of her dark hair with his sensitive fingertips, "will it hurt Valdaimon if I do this?"

"It will." Shulana said. She raised a single, white, thin finger to her full lips, then gently touched it to the aching spot on Bagsby's sternum. Bagsby's pain evaporated. "It will hurt him very much. And my name," she added, her lips brushing Bagsby's ear as her whisper grew even softer, "is Shulana."

The rotund little man's plain gray robe hung down to his sandaled feet. The top of his head, no higher than Bagsby's, was clean shaven, with a ring of soft brown hair around the rim. He whistled a cheerful air as he maneuvered a ladder against the bookshelves that formed the back wall of the crowded room, and scrambled up it to retrieve a heavy, leather-bound tome.

Bagsby glanced around at the remainder of the tiny hole in the wall that served as the sage's place of business. The room was no more than ten feet square, and so filled was it with wooden shelves laden with books, table tops piled as high as seven or more feet with parchments, ancient scrolls, recent leaflets, with still more piles of books, papers, and parchments stacked on the floor that Bagsby hardly dared to move for fear of toppling something.

The little man scampered down the ladder, carefully picked his way over and between the seemingly unarranged stacks and piles, and made his way to a stool behind a small reading stand. He removed the three open books and, glancing about for a convenient vacant spot and finding none, handed them to Bagsby.

"Hold these for a moment, will you? Won't take long now," the little man said.

"Hmmph!" Bagsby snorted. "You don't look much like a sage, and you certainly don't act like one."

"Hey," the little man snapped, his head popping up from scanning the large opened tome, "I'm the best in Clairton. Twelve years in holy orders before I quit the religion business and went into this. Twelve years of deep study, and I'm a fast study at that. I know a lot, and I know where to find out a lot more. What were you expecting, anyway?"

"Well," Bagsby said, "I'm not sure. Someone a bit more, more . . ."

"You expected a soft-spoken wise old man, tall, skinny, with white hair and soft white beard, right?" the little man challenged, his eyes twinkling.

"Something like that."

"Well, forget it. Never met a sage who looked like that. Now, I get ten crowns an hour, whatever we talk about. Do you want to know about me, or do you want to know about the treasure of Parona? Makes no difference to me— I've seen your gold."

"Keep your voice down!" Bagsby commanded, irritated. He turned his head this way and that, looking for a clear place to set down his burden of books. "I told you, this is a strictly confidential inquiry. No telling who's listening around here."

"Nobody's listening around here," the sage said off-handedly. "Elven magic—paid for it years ago. Cost me a small fortune—part of the reason I get ten crowns an hour. Nothing said inside this room can be heard by anyone outside this room. This room is proof against scrying, clairvoyance, clairaudience—all the usual magical means of spying. And we're alone." The sage reached into the reading stand and pulled a bare-bladed dagger from a small shelf. The blade glowed with a greenish-gold hue. "Magic. Protects me when I'm alone in here with folks I don't trust, just in case you were getting any funny ideas."

"Nothing of the sort." Bagsby tried to sound reassuring. But the truth was, this man was so irritating that Bagsby at this moment would enjoy slitting his throat.

"Well, a man in my kind of business can't be too careful. You understand, don't you, Sir John Wolfe?" the impudent, fat stranger asked.

"Of course. I'm not paying for the last two minutes," Bagsby added.

The sage chuckled. "Well enough, you are a sharp one. Now, what is it you want to know, Sir John Wolfe, from the county of Nordingham which doesn't exist, in the kingdom of Pantania, which doesn't exist? Do you exist, or am I talking to thin air?"

Bagsby grew alarmed. This man could be dangerous. He pitched the books to the floor and drew his own dagger.

"Now, now, sir," the sage said, wagging a finger at him. "It would never do to lose your temper. Your little secret is safe with me."

"I'm not paying for the time that exchange took, either," Bagsby said flatly, his dagger visible in his hand.

"All right then, all right," the sage replied, chuckling. "Let's see—the treasure of . . . here we go." The little man lowered his head close to the page and read, muttering softly to himself as he did so.

Bagsby waited impatiently. In the back of his mind he pondered whether or not the sage should be killed at the conclusion of this interview. Clearly, the man wasn't buying his Sir John Wolfe routine. He knew too much geography. Would he talk? Probably not, unless he were paid to or found something "fascinating" about the situation. Sages were usually driven by a combination of curiosity and greed. Greed was predictable; curiosity was not. Unpredictable people were dangerous.

"Well, now, this bears out what I already knew from several dwarven, elven, and ancient imperial sources," the sage said at last. "Here, sit down, and I'll try to put this

all together for you." The fat little man came out from behind the reading stand and began rearranging the hopeless
piles until he had cleared a spot on the floor big enough
for a chair. Then he popped through the one door that did
not lead to the street and returned with a three-legged
stool. "Here, sit, sit," he said, his excitement growing.
"This is a grand story."

Bagsby sat.

"The treasure of Parona," the sage began, clearly excited by the prospect of delivering a long and enlightening
lecture, "also sometimes called the Golden Eggs of
Parona, was first discovered some four thousand years ago
by the Odenite tribe of dwarves. You know about
dwarves?"

Bagsby nodded. "A bit. Short people, shorter than you
and me."

"That is a most rudimentary definition. Actually, they
are not people at all, in the sense of 'human beings.' They
are as different from us as the elves. Their race has a long
and rich history—"

"Which probably is not relevant to my query," Bagsby
cut in. "At ten crowns an hour, I expect relevant information, thank you."

"Very well," the sage said, irritated that his erudition
was not respected. "The Odenite dwarves were a tribe that
lived in the extreme northern mountains, those mountains
that form the northern boundary of the present kingdom of
Parona. Now, these dwarves were great miners of precious
stones and metals, and they had mined the northern mountains for centuries, perhaps millennia. The dwarven tales
indicate millennia, but the most authoritative human
sources question the dwarven tales, pointing out that legends often involve exaggerations of fact—"

"Get on with it," Bagsby interrupted again. "These
dwarves found exactly what?"

"They found nodules of gold," the sage snapped. "They
were working deep in the mountains—far north of the
foothills that form the border of Parona. They were in the
high mountains, where they winter cold stays all through

the year, and the snow never melts. That is, on the tops of the mountains. There are valleys where, it is said, the seasons turn not unlike they do here in the temperate regions."

Bagsby began grinding his teeth.

"All right, all right. They were mining a particularly rich vein of gold when they discovered two large gold nodules."

"What exactly do you mean by the word 'nodules'?" Bagsby asked, leaning forward, furrowing his brow.

"The ancient dwarven texts indicate that the find consisted of two large lumps of gold, which the dwarves termed 'nodules.' Later, when humans saw them, they called them 'eggs' because of their shape. Now, these nodules were entirely smooth and appeared to be made of gold."

"Appeared to be?" Bagsby asked.

"Oh, yes. Even the dwarves very early determined that the nodules were, in fact, not solid gold. There is something else within them."

"What?"

"No one knows."

"They were entirely smooth?"

"According to the ancient texts, yes."

"Then they were made by some intelligence," Bagsby concluded.

"Not necessarily. The dwarves did not dwell much on that point; they were not much given to speculation, you know. But, several human authors who examined the nodules shortly after they came into human hands were divided in their opinion as to the origin of these strange objects. One school held that the gold had been formed into its peculiar shape by the same forces that shape certain solid rocks into perfect spheres. You have no doubt seen these for sale by some of our local merchants."

"Yes. They are found near streambeds most often, and inside they contain crystals of great beauty but little real value."

"Precisely!" the sage said, his enthusiasm returning as

his listener showed some knowledge. "Now, some say the nodules were formed in the same way as these rocks."

"And others?" Bagsby asked.

"Others put forth a multitude of theories. Some humans maintain these are part of a long-lost treasure fashioned originally by the elves, but elven authors have always denied this. Other than that, elven records that are available to us contain no mention of the nodules."

"Very well," Bagsby said. "The origin of the eggs is unknown. The dwarves found them a long time ago and didn't know what they were even then. Do the dwarves today have any ideas on the subject?"

"Alas, the Odenite dwarves have passed into history. Their tribe is unknown today."

"All right. What happened next?"

"We humans being what we are, the nodules soon found their way into human hands. I'm afraid the exact process involved both duplicity and violence that do no credit to our race."

"Why am I not surprised? Skip the moralizing and give the facts," Bagsby said.

"Parona, even in the days of the three ancient empires, was a well-consolidated territory with a hereditary ruling house. The nodules became the property of the kings of Parona, and the treasure has remained in their hands from that day until quite recently. Two thousand years ago some modifications were made. Skilled jewelers were hired by a particularly rich Paronan king, to engrave the surface of both eggs with a wide variety of designs. There are numerous drawings of these designs available, even in the most common sources."

"I have seen them," Bagsby acknowledged.

"Then you also know that these same jewelers enhanced their designs by inlaying the surface of each of the eggs with a mixture of precious stones—emeralds, diamonds, rubies, sapphires, opals, and the like. Each stone actually has a history—"

"Not important to me," Bagsby said, "unless they bear on the magical significance of the treasure."

The sage looked nonplussed. "Magical significance?" he asked.

"Yes," Bagsby said casually. "What value would this treasure have to a practitioner of magic—especially to one highly skilled in the blackest secrets of magic?"

"I—I don't know," the sage said simply.

"Well, surely," Bagsby pressed, "there must be something in the ancient tales that grew up around these eggs— perhaps in some of the various theories of their origin—that suggest a magical purpose."

The sage walked back to the reading stand, perused the volume more deeply, closed it, and placed his fist against his bald brow. After a while, he said, "I know of only one reference to any magical powers the treasure may possess, and that reference tells us nothing of their significance."

"Well, what is it?" Bagsby demanded.

"It is said that there are certain barbarians in the Great Eastern Desert who believe the Golden Eggs confer the power to call down fire from heaven—devastating, devouring fire that could consume the world. But whether this is true or not, no one knows or admits to knowing."

Bagsby sat silently on the stool for a long while, pondering the sage's words. The sage during this time stared intently at Bagsby. The protective dagger continued to glow and pulsate atop the reading stand.

"Now, sage," Bagsby said quietly, breaking the long silence, "what do you know of me?"

"You are a thief," the sage replied, just as quickly. "You desire to steal the Golden Eggs of Parona as they pass through Argolia on their way to the Kingdom of Heilesheim in the south. Why you desire to do this, I do not know."

"What else?"

"You have enemies. The assassins you are credited about town with killing were sent for you, not for the Viscount D'Alonzo."

"What else?" Bagsby demanded.

"You do not know whether to kill me, buy my silence, or leave it to the gods and fate to determine what happens to me."

Bagsby smiled and nodded. He stood, took out his coin purse, and counted out ten gold crowns. These he pressed into the sage's palm.

"I will leave it to fate," he said.

➣5➢

Bad Eggs

"AND THUS, YOUR Majesty," the Viscount Marco D'Alonzo declaimed, "my own life was saved by this man, whose courage and noble character were proven to be above reproach. It is with great pleasure that I present to Your Majesty my guest, our guest in this our Kingdom of Argolia, Sir John Wolfe, son of the noble Count of Nordingham in the distant land of Pantania."

Bagsby stepped forward, and with a flourish of his large, black, feather-bedecked hat, bowed deeply. He looked, he hoped, resplendent in his new red velvet doublet, trimmed with gold piping, that fit snugly and comfortably over his silver silk-over-linen tunic. His breeches, yellow with green stripes, extended down and tucked neatly into his high, shining black boots. He wore a stiff, white, full ruffled collar, and at his side hung a slim rapier. He was, he believed, the perfect court dandy in this new attire, one of several rewards extended him by the grateful, if somewhat mislead, viscount.

"We are not familiar with Pantania, Sir John," King Harold of Argolia said in his deep and gracious voice. "If you are a fair example of the nobles bred there, we must establish relations with this kingdom."

"Your Majesty is too kind," Bagsby said, his head kept lowered. "I am grateful to receive such a welcome, for as a stranger far from home, deprived of my sustenance by thieves, I had no right to hope for such graciousness as Your Majesty and his loyal servant, the Viscount D'Alonzo, have shown me."

"Thieves and assassins are not welcome in our kingdom," the king replied. "We are grateful to you for ridding

105

us of two such and for saving the life of a servant dear to our heart."

"Sadly, Your Majesty, it was necessary to kill the brigands before they could be properly interrogated."

"Yes," the king agreed. "That is sad. And where, did you say, exactly is the Kingdom of Pantania?"

The old boy is no fool, Bagsby thought, though at first glance, it would be easy enough to mistake him for one. The great audience hall was packed with personages of importance in the minor kingdom. Bagsby had already classified them into three groups. There were the courtiers, such as the viscount and his friends, who had money, influence, beautiful clothes, and fine houses. There were the military, the knights and lords tied to their rural lands, who still wore armor into the king's audience chamber. From what Bagsby could tell, most of these were barely articulate, although he did not doubt their personal courage or brutality. Then there were the women, lots of women, young, beautiful, amoral, and scheming—the kind of women created by a society such as Argolia's and kind of women Bagsby loved. Yes, Bagsby thought, this king is surrounded by sycophants and dandies on the one hand, and armored louts on the other, but he's no fool himself. Better be careful. . . .

"I did not say, Your Majesty. I fear Pantania lies so far distant from Your Majesty's fair land that there is little cause for intercourse between our two kingdoms. However, be assured that the nobles of my land share Your Majesty's values, and that any future relations between us, limited though they may be, will be of the most cordial and courteous nature."

"I perceive," the king said, "you are a man of action, of wit, and of courtesy. We are pleased to have you join us in council this day, for a matter has come to our attention that will require action and wit, coated with the sweetness of courtesy."

The king rose from the hard, uncomfortable cherry wood chair that served as a throne in his audience chamber. The court bowed as one. Brightly dressed pages scrambled to open the side doors, which led to the king's

council room, and the huge, tall doors at the far end of the
audience hall, through which most of the court were expected to exit.

Bagsby could feel scores of pairs of eyes burrowing into
him. The dandies, he knew, would be impressed by his
costume and not a little afraid of his now-reputed prowess.
Of course, he was already well regarded by the Viscount
D'Alonzo's party. The rural lords, on the other hand,
would no doubt disdain him as a dandy but grudgingly respect the fact that he had, at least, killed two villains in
personal combat. Now it was time to capitalize on his position. With a nod to the viscount, he strode boldly behind
the king toward the council chamber.

King Harold graciously indicated a seat for Bagsby near
the end of the table farthest from the throne. In all, there
were only a dozen besides Bagsby invited to join the king.
Five were town dandies, six were rural lords. One was a
fashionably but conservatively dressed older man who
wore around his neck a large chain of office; an appointed
chief councillor or administrator, Bagsby guessed.

No sooner were the doors closed and the council invited
to sit than the king began.

"The situation, to put it plainly, is this. Heilesheim has
invaded Dunsford, putting to the sword all who opposed
their large armies," the king said flatly. "The Count of
Dunsford had appealed to us for aid under the terms of the
Holy Alliance, aid which we are honor bound to provide.
However, since the time of his appeal a battle has occurred. Dunsford is dead, and his lands seized by Ruprecht
of Heilesheim."

A few murmurs broke out among the rural lords, which
were quickly stifled as the king raised his arm for silence.

"There is more." The monarch paused a moment, raised
his hand to his brow, and wiped off the light sweat that
had broken out. "Unseasonably hot in here," he commented. "The window," he added, gesturing toward the
large, double windows of colored glass that opened out on
a large garden. One of the courtiers sprang to his feet and
threw the windows open. In the garden, flights of birds
twittered and flew and hopped about in the branches of

large yew trees. A single, large, scraggly crow joined the throng of finches, sparrows, robins, and cardinals, but its presence went unnoticed by the humans in the council chamber.

"Thank you, Lord Gilford," the king acknowledged as the courtier scrambled back to his seat. The monarch leaned forward, his gaze intense. "We have received information from our scrying," he announced.

The murmurs rose again, louder this time from the rural lords, and the court dandies twisted uncomfortably in their seats.

"Do not disdain the use of magic to protect your own purses and your own lands, my lords," the king said, his voice suddenly edged with anger. "Wizards may be vile creatures, but I would use the vilest things on the earth to protect this realm. If you are loyal subjects, you will do the same when I bid it."

The room fell silent. Bagsby noticed that the very mention of magic made the lords jumpy, and he saw a chance to enhance his own position.

"Your Majesty," he said, standing and bowing his head. "If I may intrude with a sudden thought . . . ?"

The king nodded his permission.

"I know nothing of magic, save that it often works. If it works to protect your realm, I applaud it. However, I have one worry: if Your Majesty's wizards can scry the enemy through their great crystal globes, cannot the enemy scry Your Majesty? Indeed, might we not be under magical observations, even as we speak?"

The courtiers exchanged nervous glances as the implications of Bagsby's words sank in. The rural lords said nothing; each stared dead ahead, their faces grim and growing pale.

"Well spoken, Sir John," the king replied, "and an intelligent observation. Be assured that our court wizard has given his word that this room cannot be scryed, for he has placed invisible magical wards and protections upon it that no form of magical seeing or hearing can penetrate."

"I should have known," Bagsby said quickly, "that Your Majesty would have so provided for the security of his deliberations." He bowed his head again, and sat quietly. He noticed with some pleasure the king's admiration for his intelligence and the continued discomfiture of the lords, who seemed no happier with the thought that there were invisible "protections" around them than with the thought of enemy scrying.

"Now, thanks to the magic you nobles so much despise," King Harold said, "I know that the Heilesheim forces are divided into three groups. One group marches west from Dunsford. As we speak it stands on the border of Alban. This force consists of more than twenty and four thousands."

"Twenty and four thousands!" a rural lord exclaimed, leaping to his feet. "Could there be that many knights in all of Heilesheim?"

"Their number is mostly footmen," the king said simply. "A force of similar size has already marched eastward out of Dunsford and crossed the border into the County of Kala, where it clearly makes for the Tower of Asbel."

"Forty-eight thousands," a courtier muttered.

"But footmen," one of the rural lords sneered.

"Your Majesty, have Alban and Kala also appealed for aid under the terms of the Holy Alliance?" Viscount D'Alonzo asked politely.

"Their envoys have already crossed our borders. We expect to receive them by the morrow," the king replied. "But these attacks on our neighbors are not the greatest threat. A third force, some twelve thousand strong and"—the king turned to glance at the lord who had sneered at the notion of foot soldiers—"the same force of footmen that vanquished an army of four thousand under Dunsford, has struck deep into the County of the Wyche, and even now is approaching its border with Argolia."

"For the gods, for the right, and for King Harold!" shouted the lord who had suffered the king's mild rebuke, standing and drawing his great bastard sword. "And death to the usurper Ruprecht of Heilesheim!"

The rural lords cheered aloud, thumped their fists on the table, and cried out, "War! War!" The city nobles also rose, and with restrained bows of their heads, acknowledged the sentiment of their rural peers. But it was clear from their silent, grim faces that if there was to be war, the city nobles had little enthusiasm for it.

King Harold rose and again called for silence with upraised arms. "My lords," the monarch said with a nod to the armored, rural contingent, "I appreciate your enthusiasm. But, officially, it is my duty to point out that Heilesheim, too, appeals for our aid, claiming that the smaller counties are to blame for the current conflict for their refusal to certain just and reasonable demands made upon them by the Heileshiem crown."

The rural lords glowered with anger. The king nodded; they were no more impressed by Ruprecht's excuses for aggression than he was.

"As for you, my lords," the king added, turning to stare down the row of city nobles, "I think you should understand what fate awaits your cities and your fortunes should Heilesheim gain a victory in the field." The king lifted his head toward the far door of the council room. "Guards," he shouted, "send in the poor wretch."

Two royal men-at-arms thrust open the door. Through it walked with forced dignity an obese, lower-class townswoman, dressed in a plain white gown that tied behind the neck. She awkwardly made her curtsy to the king as the door slammed behind her.

"I believe," King Harold said gently, "your name is Marta."

Fat Marta, her head down and eyes averted as she had been instructed, nodded.

"This woman was the only survivor of Heilesheim's first act in this campaign of aggression, the seizure of the town of Shallowford on the Rigel in Dunsford," the king explained. "Marta, kindly tell my lords here what happened to your village and what is now happening throughout Dunsford."

The fat woman drew a deep breath. She had never spoken in the presence of a king before. But when she raised her head to speak, every man in the room could see the determined hatred burning in her brown eyes.

"They came to Shallowford before dawn," she began.

"Knights, lords, and foot soldiers. Our men had no chance to resist. Most of the villagers were still asleep when the murdering scum fired their houses. When the people ran out into the street, archers shot them down. Except for the three better houses in town. I lived in one of them. These the knights came to. They butchered everyone—men, women, babies. They took everything they could carry. Then they left."

An embarrassed silence hung in the air as Marta paused to collect her thoughts. That knights should attack commoners was unthinkable to the lords of Argolia; knights should fight only knights. A knight who attacked a peasant would lose his honor. Worse, to despoil a prosperous village was stupidity; who would till the fields, gather the crops, pay the taxes? Only men who had lost all sense of control over their vilest instincts would conduct war in such a way.

"They were about to kill me, too," Marta continued, "when one of the knights said, 'Let's save this one for the Black Prince's amusement.' They beat me, then dragged me by the hair through the burning village to the place where he sat, mounted on his big war-horse, watching it all."

"Where who sat, Marta?" the king interjected softly.

"Ruprecht, the Black Prince. I'll be damned to all the torments of all the gods before I call that murdering swine a king," Marta snapped.

Shouts of "Well said!" erupted from the rural lords.

"Then he said he wanted me to take a message to my lord the Count Dunsford," Marta went on as stillness settled over the room again. "He said he wanted Dunsford to know what would happen if all his demands weren't met." Marta paused and raised her chubby arms. Her fat fingers pulled at the ties of her gown behind her neck. "Then," she said, turning her back to her audience and letting the top of the gown drop, "he did this to me."

The eyes of the nobles grew wide with horror as they gazed upon the sign of the dragon branded into the flesh of Marta's broad back. Bagsby dropped involuntarily back into his chair, his eyes shut tight, his fists clenched, and his taut muscles trembling as a wave of uncontrollable rage swept over him. The sign of the dragon, with its outstretched wings, had been branded on him as well, only his brand was deep within the recesses of his mind in a place where he seldom let his consciousness wander.

Marta stood erect, tied her gown, and turned to face her audience once again. "Now," she went on in a calm, cold voice, "Dunsford is a wasteland. What happened at Shallowford the Black Prince lets his men do everywhere, to every village. There is nothing but rape, murder, pillage, and waste. Dunsford is made a desert." Marta paused, thinking. From the looks of the assembled lords, she had made her point. These men were not lazy and were not cowards, she thought. They would do the right thing. It was time to be still, she decided. "With Your Majesty's leave, that is all I have to say," Marta concluded.

"You may go," the king said softly.

Marta plodded her way to the door and slowly opened it. She was pleased to hear the shouts of "War! War! War!" that erupted as soon as the door was closed.

"Your Majesty! Your Majesty!" Viscount D'Alonzo shouted above the din. "I pledge you my wealth, my honor, and all the men at my disposal. Honor and prudence now combine to demand that we assemble at once a great army to meet this unholy foe. Let us summon the aid of the remainder of the Holy Alliance, and let the priests call upon all our gods to aid us!"

The city lords cheered their support and loudly indicated that each of them, too, would throw the total of his financial and manpower support into a war with Heilesheim.

The most senior of the rural lords banged his fist on the table, demanding the floor. At length, he was able to blurt out, "Your Majesty, let an army be assembled at once, and I will lead it to the borders of the County of the Wyche, where we will deal with this threat from Heilesheim in such a way as to reflect glory and honor upon Your Majesty."

"We are agreed, then," the king said. "It shall be war. Lord Keeper of the Seal, you shall summon the royal troops to assemble at Clairton with all haste." The tall, silent man wearing the chain of office acknowledged the order with a bow of his head. "My lords, I shall expect your contributions of money, supplies, and troops here in Clairton within the week. May your men march swiftly! My Lord Comminger," the king said, indicating the rural knight who had offered to lead the armies, "you are appointed Lord General of the Realm and shall lead our forces. We ourselves," the king added, "shall accompany the army."

The king basked in the applause of his nobles and in the success of his plan to achieve quick unanimity in favor of the defense of the realm. Only one detail caught the royal eye as somehow out of place, and he addressed it immediately.

"Sir John," the king said, "you have not spoken to the issue of this council."

Bagsby remained frozen and shaking in his chair, his eyes tightly shut. At the king's address, he strained to regain control of his violent emotions. Slowly, he opened his eyes, unclenched his fists, and stood to address the monarch. Now was his time to strike.

"Your Majesty, I applaud any and all actions against the forces of Heilesheim and against that imposter of a king, who, dethroning his own brother, now lays waste to a great land."

"Then it is settled. Even a foreign lord can see the justice of our cause," the king crowed.

"But I would point out to Your Majesty," Bagsby suddenly continued, "that you need not wait until a great army is assembled to strike a devastating blow against Ruprecht."

"What?" clamored a dozen voices. "Where? How?"

"Speak plainly, Sir John," the king demanded. "What blow could be struck at once?"

"Your Majesty, and these assembled lords, know full well that wars cost money," Bagsby said. "An army without money is almost as poorly off as an army without swords."

"True enough," the king agreed. "But our treasury is not poor. These last several years—"

"I do not refer to Argolia but to Heilesheim," Bagsby said, daring to interrupt the king with his enthusiasm for his idea. "At this very moment, the greatest treasure owned by Heilesheim is on Your Majesty's soil, and within two days will pass through the very streets of Clairton."

The king's eyebrows rose. "You mean the convoy carrying the treasure of Parona, recently purchased by Heilesheim?"

"The same," Bagsby said. "Why should the greatest treasure in the world be delivered into the hands of your enemy?"

The king hesitated. "We have given our word to Heilesheim that this trade convoy may pass unmolested through our land. And, while war is imminent, honor cannot ignore the fact that Heilesheim has not yet attacked us," he said.

"Quite true, Your Majesty," Bagsby agreed. "Nor will Heilesheim attack until that treasure is safely across your borders and in the hands of Ruprecht's army in Kala."

King Harold at once saw the thrust of Bagsby's thought. "But," he countered, "our word was given. On what grounds could that word be broken? This dishonorable action would taint our person."

"Not, Your Majesty," Bagsby continued, "if the treasure was taken into your royal custody because it was found to be in the possession of spies against this land. Can any lord here doubt now that the 'escort' of five hundred troops that guards the treasure as it passes through Argolia is anything other than a military spy mission? What better means could the Black Prince have to ascertain the lie of the land, the locations of roads, castles, fortifications, lakes, streams, and every source of communications and supplies than by marching five hundred trained soldiers through this land?"

"By the gods!" Viscount D'Alonzo exclaimed. "Sir John, you are a man of discernment. We entertain within our own borders the very scouts for Heilesheim's invasion forces!"

"Do not forget," King Harold snapped, "that the honor

of your king and the value of his word is here at stake. Now, if it could be proved that these escorts to the convoy were spies, we would have grounds to take action and would do so gladly."

"Then proof you shall have, Your Majesty," Bagsby declared. "I volunteer my services to Argolia to furnish that proof, and, with that proof in hand, to seize the treasure of Parona for Your Majesty's safekeeping until such time as peace negotiations decide who shall be the rightful owner." Bagsby puffed out his chest and stood to his full height. He drew his slender rapier and held it high. "This I swear," he declaimed. "The spies who operate against the safety of Argolia shall be brought to the king's justice, and the treasure of Parona shall not be allowed to fall into the hands of Argolia's enemies!"

"Sir John Wolfe," the king responded, "your intelligence, courage, and honor shall not go unused or unrewarded. We name you lord commander of the Second Company of our Royal Guard, one hundred mounted knights of proven courage, and we charge you with the task of gathering evidence against the spies in our midst. Further, we charge you that, should you discover conclusive proof of Heilesheim's spying against us, you shall confiscate all wealth belonging to our enemy and return it safe to our person."

Loud cheers greeted the king's pronouncement. Bagsby beamed. Not only would he have a chance to get vengeance at last on Valdaimon but also he would have a small army to help him do it. The king ordered food and drink for the lords of his council, who continued to cheer their cause and curse their enemy through the day. With all the boisterous racket of their preparations for war, they never noticed the screeching of the large crow that took flight from the king's garden, circling in broader and broader circles over first the palace and then the city of Clairton before winging to the south, where a certain ancient wizard eagerly awaited its return.

"By all the gods of Argolia!" Bagsby cursed. A light breeze swept through the open entrance to the large tent, rifling the piles of parchment charts and maps spread out on the big table in the center. "I was a fool to take this army with me to do a thief's job," he ranted, disgustedly tossing his measuring string onto the table atop the map he had been studying. "How do those overmuscled dolts in armor ever manage to do this?"

"They are bred for war," Shulana said flatly. "They think of nothing else from childhood. It is their nature to solve these kinds of problems."

"Well, I don't even know where to begin," Bagsby confessed. "Only a hundred men—I thought it would be easy. I never dreamed I'd have to coordinate such a mob." Bagsby walked to the open entrance and looked out on the green, grassy plain that extended for more than a mile from the low rise on which his tent was pitched. The forces of the lord commander of the Second Company of the Royal Guard of Argolia consisted of one hundred mounted knights, large, crude men whose sole goal in life was to bash some other knight in the chest or head with lance or sword or mace. At the moment they were milling about their own tents, about twenty tiny, tall, white structures pitched at random across the plain. But mingled in with the knights were more than five hundred other people: squires, cooks, bakers, valets, wagon drivers, grooms, blacksmiths, armorers, cartwrights, carpenters, shoemakers, tailors, tent makers, pages, lackeys, flunkies, whores, wives, children, and thieves—all the usual troop who followed an army. Then there were the wagons—huge wagons hauled by teams of mules or oxen, carrying food, beer, wine, tools, and other raw materials.

Bagsby's first plan had been to wait in Clairton, sit at the head of his company of knights, and simply surround the Black Prince's convoy as it passed through the streets. But King Harold would have none of that: the presence of a Heilesheim force in the city streets while rumors of the coming war spread like wildfire among the population could trigger a riot or worse. Instead, Bagsby was instructed to march north and intercept the Heilesheim convoy as it came south along the great highway that ran from Clairton all the way to far Parona.

The first day of the march had been a disaster. Bagsby had been totally ignorant of the entourage he would have to command until "Sir John" was asked, slightly before dawn, what orders he had for something his knights called the "order of march." He had told his knights to arrange their "order of march" however they preferred; at the time that seemed like a good idea to win their favor and cooperation. Of course the opposite had occurred, as each knight chose to have his own retainers march with him, where he could keep a watchful eye on them, and the knights then spent hours squabbling among themselves over who would follow whom out of the city. The chaos was so great that the force of one hundred fighting men, mounted on some of the finest horses available in Argolia, had covered less than six miles before nightfall.

The disordered mob he surveyed on the broad plain was the result of Bagsby's second, and final order, for the first day. "It's dark. Let's camp here," he'd said.

The sun was already high toward the center of sky and no progress had been made toward sorting out the mess. Bagsby's tent, a huge affair with broad red and gold stripes, was the scene of endless comings and goings all morning. Knights would stride in, complaining that they did not know where the wine was. They couldn't find the boot maker. They didn't know where to find the blacksmith to shoe a horse, the armorer to fit a new cuirass, or the tailor to mend a ripped tunic. Throughout the throng on the plain, the feeling was spreading that the man in the great tent, above which the huge, square banner with a silver lion imposed over red and gold stripes snapped in the gentle breeze, did not have the slightest idea what he was doing.

Bagsby was forced to agree with that spreading opinion. He had to do something, and do it soon, or troop would lose the entire day's march. But how to begin? He didn't dare set them on the road until he had somehow brought order out of this chaos.

"What would you do?" Bagsby asked casually, continuing to survey the disorder. "I mean, if you were in my position."

Shulana was startled. It was the first time Bagsby had even hinted to anyone, to her knowledge, that he needed advice. True, he had been treating her kindly, in his own way, since the night she had accosted him in his litter. And, in a strange way, Shulana realized, she had been treating him more kindly in return. A kind of gentleness had settled over their relationship that was strange to her. And now this.

"I don't know," she replied honestly. "I'm not in your situation."

"Hmmmph," Bagsby snorted. "No help from you, eh? Just use me to get the treasure, that's all you want. Never mind how much trouble I get into doing it. And I am doing this for you, you know.'

Shulana laughed, and a quiet thrill ran through Bagsby. The sound of elven laughter was light and tinkling, like tiny, silver cymbals hung on a string and colliding gently in a breeze. It was almost as thrilling as the fall of her breath upon his ear, or the . . .

Bagsby stopped himself. What was he thinking?

"You're doing this because you want to," Shulana was saying. "I've given up trying to get you to do anything for anyone except yourself," she added.

Despite himself, Bagsby laughed too. What a woman, he thought. Elf! He quickly corrected his thinking. And what a caper! Here he was, a royal general. What would a real general do? He'd kick some order into things, that's what he'd do. And he wouldn't worry about currying favor with the troops.

"Page!" Bagsby bellowed. A thin young lad came at the run from somewhere nearby. "Tell the knights to assemble here, in front of my tent. In full armor, ready for battle. Now!" The youth ran off, wide-eyed with fear at the anger in the eyes of the lord general.

"What are you going to do?" Shulana asked.

"Something these louts will understand," Bagsby said, grinning widely. "I'm going to bully them into submission and then into doing what they know how to do."

Bagsby knew that his knights were low on respect for him and probably resentful as well. He had managed to learn, by means of a few discreet questions before leaving court, that the knights of the Royal Guard were socially the low men in the knightly hierarchy of Argolia. Knights sold themselves into the royal service as a last resort. Most were second or third sons of poor nobles who could not hope to inherit lands or money and needed some means of support other than honest work or thieving. War, which was essentially honest thieving, and which they were trained for from birth, was their best opportunity. Naturally they would resent a higher ranking commander, especially a foreigner whom they didn't know, who had displaced their usual leader. It was time to turn things around, Bagsby decided.

As the first few knights began straggling slowly up the small hill, Bagsby disappeared inside his tent, taking Shulana with him and pulling the entrance flap shut. Inside, he began the tedious process of choosing which of the pieces of armor he should wear from the full suit provided him by the king. If he were going strictly for show, he would wear the whole suit—it was most impressive, full steel plate with fine fluting and designs inscribed on the arms, legs, and cuirass. But he might have to fight in a few minutes, and the full suit would weigh him down. He couldn't hope to beat a real knight at his own game. Bagsby thought for a moment, then pulled on the great helm he'd been given, strapped on his cuirass, and thrust his hands into the pair of mailed gloves. He belted on a longsword, stuck a dagger inside his high boots, and picked up a mace. Then he turned to Shulana and gave her a look that was at once a scowl, a frown, and a promise of violence in the immediate future.

"What is suddenly troubling you?" the elf asked. "A moment ago you were laughing—now you look as if you want to kill me."

"Good," Bagsby said, breaking into a muffled laugh. "That's just the impression I want to create." He carefully placed the scowl back on his face and stepped outside to confront his disgruntled troops.

He was greeted by a wall of silent, staring, sullen, armored men, any one of whom, he knew, could happily kill him with a single blow. It was a pleasant advantage, he thought, that they didn't know that—not with certainty. Bagsby deepened his scowl.

"I called you here to find out whether you are cowards or merely fools," Bagsby shouted at the assembled host. "I know you are one or the other. I hope you are fools, for fools can still be taught something. If you are cowards— and I hope you are not—I have no use for you."

The startled, angry reaction was exactly what Bagsby had expected. Murmuring broke out among the men, and one of the larger ones stepped forward quickly, his hand on his sword hilt, an enraged gleam in his eye.

"Are you calling me a coward?" Sir John of Elamshire demanded.

"No," Bagsby replied calmly. "If you'd a brain to go with your brawn, you'd understand that I'm asking you a question. Are you a coward or a fool?"

"I'm no fool!" Sir John thundered.

"Then, I conclude you are a coward. There. Happy? Now I'm calling you a coward," Bagsby said with a sneer.

The air rang with the sound of Sir John's cold steel blade being pulled swiftly from its scabbard. With a roar the knight sprang forward, the blade raised in both hands high over his head, ready to cleave in twain the little man who had insulted his honor. Bagsby stood his ground, quickly shedding both cuirass and helm, until the large man was only one step away, his blow already slicing downward. Then the little thief collapsed into a ball and hurled himself forward in a somersault between the charging knight's legs. Sir John's blade was buried in the earth. Bagsby sprang to his feet behind Sir John and whirled with his right arm extended upward, mace in hand. The short, heavy metal bludgeon caught Sir John squarely in the back of his helmet, knocking the knight forward onto his face. Bagsby leapt onto the man's back and once again struck with the mace, crushing the back and top of the knight's helmet. Blood began to puddle beneath Sir John's face.

Bagsby stood up and faced the wall of knights again. "He was wrong," Bagsby said flatly. "He was a fool, not a coward." Bagsby strutted up and down in front of the confused mass of fighting men, who were struggling to comprehend what was happening. "What are the rest of you?" Bagsby suddenly roared. "You!" he screamed, pointing out one of the knights at random. "What are you?"

The man looked at Bagsby, then at the motionless form of Sir John, then back at Bagsby.

"A fool?" he asked.

"By the gods, you are, sir. You are a fool. And so are the rest of you," Bagsby snarled. "I gave you leave to organize your march and your camp as you saw fit, in the manner to which you were most accustomed, for my way of doing things would be different from yours, and I wanted you to concentrate on our task, not on learning a new order of march. And look at this mess! Knights bickering among themselves, almost a full day's march lost, whores and children and thieves running hither and yon—who but a fool would organize a march or a camp this way?"

Bagsby paused and glared, making eye contact with as many of the men as he could.

"Answer me!" he demanded. *"You!"* he screamed, pointing at another randomly chosen knight. "Answer me!"

"Why, uh, why, uh, uh, I think, uh, only a fool would organize a march or a camp like this," the man managed to stammer.

"That's the first intelligent comment I've heard since taking this command," Bagsby said. "Now, here is your new order of march. You five," he said, pointing to the five knights standing nearest the left end of the assembled throng, "will ride ahead to scout for the enemy. Find him, but don't be seen and don't get into a fight."

The five knights stepped forward, flabbergasted to a man. One raised his voice in anguished protest. "Lord General," he began, "we are knights, nobles. We are not scouts. Scouting is not a fit task for a noble. We have never scouted," he said. The other four men slowly nodded their assent.

Bagsby whirled to face the man, his face contorted with faked anger. "I command here by order of the king. You're noble, are you? Well, now you're a noble scout. Now go!" he ordered. "Or join this knight whose blood waters the grass."

The five knights looked at one another, then at Sir John, then at Bagsby, who stood with his feet spread wide, thumping the business end of his mace against the palm of his mailed left hand. Slowly, the five began to stomp off toward the chaotic camp, looking for their horses.

"The rest of you will mount and form a column, four men wide," Bagsby ordered. "This column will proceed north on the road. I will ride at its head. Wagons and workers will follow in this order: first armorers; then the water, beer, and wine wagons; then the food wagons. Next will be the cartwrights and carpenters. After that, the rest of the fools and whores can come however they want—they'll soon be far behind us, because I intend to move fast and strike hard. Now go mount up. We leave in a quarter of an hour."

Bagsby turned his back on the stunned assemblage and started into his tent. He paused a moment, then turned back and stared at the knight he had clouted.

"He'll live," he told the others. "My elven servant will see to that." Then, with an arrogant shake of his head, Bagsby entered his tent, pulling the flap shut behind him. Inside, he stopped dead and caught his breath, listening.

After a prolonged silence, one voice said quietly, "We'd better get our horses." There were mutters of agreement, and soon the mass of knights was clinking and clanking back down the small hill. Orders were bellowed; the camp began to stir into purposeful activity.

Bagsby let out a long breath.

"Elven servant?" Shulana said, looking up from the large map on the table.

"Just see to it that that fool I had to clout doesn't die," Bagsby snapped. "Please," he quickly added, holding out both hands toward her, palms up. "Please?"

It was Shulana's turn to let her face grow dark. "You're suddenly a general," she said.

Bagsby wondered if he could detect a bit of begrudged admiration in her tone of voice.

"Well, I'm acting like one. Let's hope that's the same as being one."

"No, no, no!" Culdus shouted at the top of his lungs, stamping his feet on the hard-packed dirt floor of the King of Heilesheim's tent. "We must not delay, not for an instant!"

"Truly," King Ruprecht agreed. "I do not see why we should pause when our armies are enjoying a glorious victory march through these southern provinces of the Holy Alliance. Already, we are moving into position to besiege Alban. The city of Kala is being reduced tonight, as we speak, and we have force to spare to begin the encirclement of the Tower of Asbel. Two legions have overrun the County of the Wyche against minimal resistance. Why should we delay the invasion of Argolia for even a single day?"

The king waved off the servants who had trimmed the lamps in royal campaign tent. The flames, spaced at intervals around the walls of the tent and in rows through the main interior room, cast a golden light that made the richly decorated interior seem even more luxurious than it truly was.

Ruprecht reclined on a couch covered with thick pillows and rich furs. Next to the couch, on a small table, a plate of delicacies was placed for his sampling; he cleansed his fingers in a bowl of rosewater after tasting one of the stickier honied fruits. As in any commander's tent, there was a large table laden with maps and charts. Culdus stood behind it, staring gloomily at a large map that showed the current positions of Heilesheim's forces, and the last known positions of their now numerous enemies. Behind the king's couch a wall of curtains was drawn to construct a separate room altogether, the room where the king would sleep, attended by such prisoners as he chose from the day's taking.

Valdaimon stood with head lowered by the main entrance to the tent. He knew full well that to approach the king too closely would risk offending with his odor; his mission tonight was difficult enough without adding to the displeasure he must create.

"Your Majesty, please understand," the old mage wheedled. "It is essential that the treasure of Parona, the Golden Eggs, be safely delivered to our forces before we strike Argolia. King Harold must be given no pretext to seize the treasure before it is in ... Your Majesty's hands."

"Essential to whom?" Culdus thundered. "To you? When last this subject was discussed, you evaded the issues of both the cost of this purchase and its necessity. We have had no need for your wyvern troops, and no need for your armies of the dead. What is it that makes you crave that treasure so?"

"That is not important," the wizard replied. "What is important is to protect His Majesty's investment. Would you prefer to see that treasure in the hands of Harold of Argolia?"

"We'd take it back soon enough," Culdus declared.

"Culdus's point seems well taken," the king concurred. "So what if Harold gazes upon our golden treasure a few days before his head is lopped off? Our victory is certain. Our legions are invincible." The young monarch tossed his head arrogantly. His long black hair flipped about in greasy strings. He ran his thin, white fingers through it, then dabbled them in rosewater. "Really, Valdaimon, you tire me. It is past time for my bath. And shortly thereafter, I must retire." He gave Culdus a lecherous wink. "After reviewing the prisoners taken today, of course," he added, breaking into his high-pitched laughter.

Valdaimon suppressed his loathing for merely mortal beings. How easy it would be to cast a quick enchantment, seize their minds, and run things himself! But all such spells had their limits. The king could be easily controlled, but Culdus, Culdus was strong of will. The spells would not hold his mind. And he would rally other humans to his cause, perhaps even cause dissension within the league, where the other mages jealously observed Valdaimon's closeness to the throne. No, it was best to be cautious, patient, and safe, even when the goal was so close at hand.

"I apologize, Your Majesty," the old mage said, flicking his dark tongue between his few yellowed teeth to wet his thin, white, dry lips. "I had hoped not to disturb Your Majesty with troubling news. But I see now," the wizard said, casting a withering glance at Culdus, "that I must tell you that your treasure is in danger not from the King of Argolia, though indeed he intends to seize it. Rather, the real danger comes from a certain thief who even now is seeking out the Golden Eggs as they pass through Argolia."

"A thief!" Culdus exploded. "One thief? Your magic and my armies combined cannot destroy one thief? What fools do you take us for?" the warrior demanded.

The king sat up on his couch, his eyes suddenly alert. "No, no, Culdus," he said. "I'm intrigued. Tell us of this thief, Valdaimon."

"His name is Bagsby. He is even now in Argolia, plotting to steal the treasure and using the King of Argolia as a pawn. This man is as filled with cunning and tricks as Your Majesty is with grace," the wizard said in his oiliest, most soothing voice.

Ruprecht searched among the delicacies on the table with his fingers, scrunched up his nose at the lot, and sighed. "Come to the point," he said wearily. "Why couldn't our armies handle one thief. Or your magic, for that matter. Cast a spell, old man, and turn this Bagsby into a frog or a fly, and squash him for your amusement."

Valdaimon tottered forward, leaning on his great staff. Culdus eased himself along the edge of the table, carefully keeping out of smelling distance from the vile mage.

"It is not so easy, Your Majesty. One does not use a siege engine to fire at a common fly; neither will our armies be able to find or capture this thief. And as for my poor, weak magic—he is, at the moment, protected against it," the wizard said with a sad shrug.

"Protected by whom?" the king asked immediately. Culdus nodded his approval of the question. This impudent young pup of a king was learning a few things.

"He has struck up an alliance with an elf," Valdaimon said simply. "Not even I dare strike an elf."

"And this elf uses magic to protect him from your magic?" the king asked.

"Yes, Your Majesty."

"How fascinating," the king declared, rising and striding about the room. "I never knew there was anything that could protect against your magic, dear Valdaimon." A broad smile spread on the king's thin, young face. His eyes twinkled with merriment. "Perhaps I should look more carefully into this matter of elven magic."

"Your Majesty's point is well taken," Culdus snarled. "The army, too, might well want to investigate this point. Now, Valdaimon, what has this to do with delaying our campaign?"

"As a precaution, Your Majesty," the wizard began, turning and walking back toward the tent entrance, "the treasure being conveyed by our guards through Argolia is a fake."

"What?" the king exclaimed. "Where is my real treasure?"

"Being safely escorted through that same land, cleverly disguised by numerous spells, carried in a plain peasant's cart that no one would suspect contained anything of value," Valdaimon explained. "But, if we attack before that simple cart with its meager escort is safely across the border in Kala, Argolia will seal its borders. This Bagsby will soon enough discover the fraud we have perpetrated and begin a quest for the real treasure. I would rather it were safely in our hands before he does so."

"*My* hands, wizard," the king snapped. "My hands."

"This is nonsense, Your Majesty," Culdus insisted. "To delay the march of thousands of men to easy victory, just to wait for a peasant cart to cross a border—"

"Consider His Majesty's investment," Valdaimon interrupted.

"I would," Culdus replied, suddenly smiling, "if I knew how much that investment was. That particular question," he said, extending his arm and pointing a finger at the wizard, "you have never answered."

"Yes, wizard!" the king agreed. He ran toward Valdaimon, only to stop short several feet from the mage and raise an arm before his face, a futile gesture against the foul stench the wizard exuded. "*Aaagh,* by the gods, you stink more with each passing day! Now, tell me plainly. How much did I pay for this famous treasure?"

"A small price compared to its true value," Valdaimon said, purposely moving closer to the king. Offense would be given, but it would lead to a swift conclusion to this interview, which was not going well at all. "Only one million gold crowns."

"A million gold crowns," Culdus sputtered. "A million? In gold? All at once? With funds like that our armies could be three times, no, four times their current size, maybe more. How did you get a million crowns in gold? How did you transport it to Parona?"

"How dare you spend such a sum without my knowledge?" the king said coldly. "We are much displeased."

"The sum is large," Valdaimon agreed, continuing to walk toward the king, driving the youth back toward his couch. "All the more reason to delay our attack to protect Your Majesty's investment."

"Go! Both of you," Ruprecht commanded. "This subject much vexes us. We will talk of it in the morning."

"'As you command, Your Majesty," Valdaimon replied, beating a hasty retreat to the tent's entrance. "Enjoy the fruits of your victories, Your Majesty."

Culdus bowed curtly and followed the wizard out into the cool, clear spring night. He intended to confront Valdaimon, but the wizard was nowhere to be seen. Culdus snorted and stomped past the ring of guards. He watched with disgust as the day's catch of females was paraded into the tent. The old warrior stalked off to a nearby deserted hilltop and gazed out over the fields and forests of Kala, soon to be part of Heilesheim. He sighed deeply, sat down on the cool earth, already damp with dew, and raised his eyes to the star-filled sky.

"What," he asked his gods, "is that wizard plotting?"

* * *

Bagsby rode at the head of his column of knights with Shulana on his right and a page bearing the great square standard of his company on his left. The sun was already well up in the morning sky; Bagsby judged that it was near mid-morning, about halfway to noon. Bagsby whistled a light air as he rode. Things were going well again, and he anticipated a great event today.

The previous day's march had gone without problems. His instinctive decision to group his fighting men together as a formed force and leave the camp followers behind, except for those bearing essential supplies, had proved wise. The company was making good time; the camp last night had been orderly, with the supplies grouped in the center of a ring of tents and watches posted. His scouts sent one rider back every three hours to report. That man was relieved and another sent up in his place. In this way, the ignominy of being forced to serve as a scout was reduced, since the apparent "dishonor" was shared throughout the company in rotation.

Now his command was good score of miles or more north of Clairton. Morale had improved with the establishment of order. Even Sir John, who rode without his helmet with his bloody head bandaged, would occasionally banter with his fellows. Bagsby expected that today his scouts would encounter the Heilesheim convoy; by late afternoon, or tomorrow morning at the latest, he would attack. It should be a quick battle; by all accounts most of the Heilesheim guards were footmen. All that was needed was a nice level field where his knights could charge. The footmen would scatter; the convoy would be overrun, and Bagsby would grab the treasure—and some kind of papers showing that the Heilesheimers were spies, of course, to keep King Harold happy.

The only cloud on Bagsby's horizon, as he thought about it, was the changing nature of the terrain. The "great highway" had never been more than a wide, well-beaten track; now that they were well north of Clairton, it narrowed. Earlier in the morning Bagsby had ordered his column to switch to two abreast rather than four. As the highway wound its way north, it curved more and more, first to the right, then back to the left, meandering through the increasingly high and rocky hills that made up much of the north of the kingdom. Here there were few of the wide, flat meadows that characterized the southlands. Instead, fields were hacked out of the steep slopes of the hills, and furrows wound their way around outcroppings of rock too heavy to be removed. In many places, the land was untilled, and the highway wound through patches of light forest. The trees here were not the tall oaks, elms, maples, and yews of the southlands, but short, stout firs and pines, with an occasional scrub oak competing for the nutrients of the thin soil. Finding a level field for battle might not be easy. Whenever they passed an appropriate section of terrain, Bagsby made a mental note of it and of the distance to the next level ground.

Bagsby's mount crested a low rise in the valley between two steep hills. In the distance, Bagsby saw an approaching knight, riding hard, almost charging down the highway toward him. No doubt one of his scouts with a report, Bagsby thought. Shulana, who always rode bareback, whispered a word in her mount's ear, and the big horse trotted up close beside Bagsby's.

"The scout comes to report before the usual time," she said.

"Yes!" Bagsby answered, his eyes lighting up with the implications of the event. "They must have found something." The lord general of the Second Company of the Royal Guard of Argolia reined his steed to halt and raised his right arm, halting the column behind him. "Dismount!" he cried. "Five minutes for rest!"

Bagsby took a deep breath, drinking in the piney scent of the crisp spring air. The cloppity-clop of the galloping horse's hoofbeats came closer. Bagsby gazed at the sky; only a few, long, thin white clouds, scraggly and shifting, slowly drifted across that vast field of light blue. It would be a perfect day for battle, he thought.

"What is your plan upon encountering the enemy?" Shulana asked.

"We'll meet them on level ground, our knights will charge and scatter them, and we'll take all their stuff,"

Bagsby replied with a shrug of his shoulders. "These knight fellows do this kind of thing all the time. Shouldn't be too hard."

"You have only a hundred knights," Shulana objected. "The Heilesheim force consists of five hundred men."

"Foot soldiers, mostly," Bagsby said, unconcerned.

"Do you remember the full reports of the battle that Dunsford fought? He had four thousand men, some six hundred knights, against a Heilesheim force with many footmen and only a few knights. Yet he was defeated," Shulana cautioned.

"Huh?" Bagsby replied, his attention focused now on the approaching rider. "Oh, well, he probably did something stupid. These warrior types are not over bright. Perhaps you've noticed that characteristic," Bagsby said, chuckling.

"Perhaps he did do something stupid," Shulana agreed. "Like what?"

"What?"

"Like what?" Shulana persisted.

"Huh? What? Like what? Well, you know, probably one of the usual stupid things, like, uh, well, like, uh ..." Bagsby stammered and stopped in mid-sentence. His cheeks puffed out and his lips pursed; his forehead furrowed. Then his shoulders slumped. He leaned over in his saddle, bringing his face very close to Shulana's ear, and whispered, "I don't really know. But I don't want these knights to know that I don't know. So please don't keep on asking me questions I can't answer. It's embarrassing."

"My Lord General!" the galloping rider shouted ahead. "The enemy approaches!"

"Well, then," Shulana whispered back to Bagsby, "perhaps it would be well to give it some thought if you intend to lead an army into battle."

The galloping mount of the scout was reined to a halt not three feet from Bagsby's horse. The great steed snorted and shook its head, exhausted by the long ride at full tilt. The rider, too, was gasping, even as he gestured excitedly, pointing back the way he had come.

"We have found them, Lord General," he reported. "Not

more than three miles ahead. A convoy of ten huge wagons, drawn by oxen, very slow. They have with them a guard of footmen—we counted them at about four hundred—and a smaller body of knights, not more than sixty."

"Good, good," Bagsby said, putting on the scowling face he found so effective in dealing with these knights. "You have done well. How far ahead to the next valley, where there is level ground to deploy our force?"

"About a mile and a half, maybe two," the excited rider declared. "If your lordship rides promptly, the column can be in the clearing and deployed before they arrive there. They must top a hill before spotting the place; they will not see you. They have no scouts riding ahead."

"Hah! No scouts!" Bagsby crowed.

"Our own scouts are staying out of sight in front of them, working their way back here while continuing to watch them," the rider added.

"Good. Take your place in ranks. Rest your horse. We move out in three minutes," Bagsby declared.

"Very good, Lord General." The man dismounted and led his horse back toward the throng of knights who, taking full advantage of the rest time, sat or lay on the hard, rocky ground, sharing swigs of wine and swapping tales of battles and of women.

Bagsby turned his horse around and surveyed his men. Soon, he thought, I'll know their mettle.

"Royal Guardsmen of Argolia," he cried, "the enemy approaches. We ride to meet them." Bagsby drew his longsword and held it aloft, its tip straight up toward the pale blue sky. "Prepare for battle!"

A cheer went up from the knights, with shouts of "For the gods, for the right, and for King Harold!" The knights began to busy themselves checking armor, straps, weapons, and horses.

Shulana again drew up beside Bagsby. He felt a small chill of excitement as he felt her warm breath touch his ear.

"Better think fast," she whispered.

* * *

Bagsby sat alone on his war-horse, wearing his full armor. Behind him, arrayed in lines deep over a short front of about fifty yards, sat his knights, deployed and eager for battle, but silent at his command. The great banner of the company, with its silver lion emblazoned over red and gold stripes, was held in the center of the front line, the honor having gone to Sir John, a gesture by Bagsby that guaranteed good morale among his men. Shulana and the camp followers Bagsby had placed out of sight, behind the hill to his rear.

Now he sat, patiently waiting for the approach of the enemy. He would call out, demanding their surrender as spies. His demand, of course, would be refused. Then he'd give the order to charge. Naturally, Bagsby thought, it would only make sense if his own mount dropped back during the charge, giving the honor of the first impact to the front rank of his knights.

From the distant north, Bagsby heard the sound of hoof-beats. He strained his eyes to the hillcrest, over which the enemy must pass to enter the flat, narrow valley where his force was deployed. There they were!

A column of knights, their leader carrying a huge square banner featuring the form of a black dragon with its wings extended, thundered over the crest of the hill. Immediately the knights fanned out, and without the slightest pause, formed a single, long, thin line, facing Bagsby's lines. This line continued forward, then suddenly halted, about four hundred yards in front of Bagsby. Farther away to the north, Bagsby could hear drumbeats in a rhythmic pattern, but the line of knights blocked his view of the hillcrest. The leader of this force continued forward at the gallop, his banner snapping, his black armor gleaming in the near noonday sun.

The rider suddenly halted about midway between the two opposing lines.

Something's wrong, Bagsby thought. Something's wrong, and I don't know what it is. Worse, I don't have time to figure it out.

Not daring to show hesitation, Bagsby spurred his own mount forward, slowly riding forward to meet the enemy commander. He approached to within ten yards of the man. He was a large man, with swarthy skin and a thin black mustache and beard. Even at a distance of ten yards his eyes conveyed hardness, cruelty, and arrogance.

"Who dares block the path of the forces of King Ruprecht, the Black Prince of Heilesheim?" the knight demanded. His horse pranced skittishly from side to side as the man cried out his challenge.

"Sir John Wolfe, commanding forces of the Royal Guard of Argolia," Bagsby answered. "Who marches an armed force through the lands of King Harold?"

"Sir Otto von Berne, commanding forces of the Black Prince, Ruprecht of Heilesheim. I have the word of King Harold of Argolia granting safe passage through these lands. Stand aside!"

"In the name of that same King Harold," Bagsby answered bravely, "I order you and your men to disarm and submit to inspection of your persons and your chattels. If no evidence of crimes against this land is found, you may pass in peace."

"We shall submit to no such search," the knight snarled. "If you attempt it, you shall die."

"To what gods do you pray, Sir Otto?" Bagsby asked.

Sir Otto tilted his head, puzzled. What kind of question was this? "To the war god of Heilesheim, to Wojan who wields the Hammer of Might and the Sword of the Gods," Sir Otto bellowed back.

"Good," Bagsby answered. "Then pray to him, and tell him to go to his own hell, where he can try to retrieve your own black soul within the hour!"

Having hurled this taunt, Bagsby reined his horse around tightly, turning his back on the foe, and rode at a trot back to his position in front of his lines. Sir Otto's curses followed him a short distance across the field, then that knight, too, turned and spurred back to his own lines.

That seemed to go well, Bagsby thought as he approached his own men. Now, let's see what these Argolian louts can do. He spurred his mount again and rode across the front of his lines, calling to his men.

"These enemies of your king dare raise swords against

his name, his orders, and his Royal Guard. Guardsmen, give them your answer!" Bagsby brought his trotting mount back to a position in front of the center of his line. He raised his sword, pointed at the enemy, and screamed, "Charge!"

With one mighty shout the lines of knights surged forward, lances lowered. Those who had no lances waved huge one-handed bastard swords high in the air. Bagsby fell in beside Sir John, who bore no weapon save the great banner of the company.

"Lead on to glory, Sir John!" Bagsby howled above the din of the charge.

Sir John nodded, his face aglow with battle lust. He spurred his mount to even greater speed, and tilted the great banner slightly forward. Bagsby slowly reined back his own mount, letting the three waves of knights overtake and pass him. It's their show now, he thought. But, by the gods! He wished he knew the meaning of that continued, damnable drumming.

From the rear of his own lines, where he finally brought his mount to a halt, Bagsby could see little of the battle that quickly developed. As his charging lines approached to within two hundred yards of the enemy, he heard a second great shout rise from his own men. From the rear, he saw his own lines surge forward with even greater speed, as the knights pressed their horses for the last measure of speed. Abruptly, the sound of drumming from the enemy's side of the field ceased. His knights continued to surge forward, and Bagsby held his breath, awaiting the sound of the great clash that must come momentarily.

Instead, he heard screams, shouts, and curses. From the rear of his own lines, he saw his knights charge forward, then suddenly slow and begin to mill about in a confused mass. Some steeds reared on their hind legs, throwing riders to the ground. Knights disgustedly tossed their lances to the ground, drew their swords, and disappeared into the mass of horses and men, only to emerge again, cursing, raging, and furiously spurring the flanks of their horses, but with no response. Something, Bagsby realized, was very wrong. Then that drumming began again, slower this time, and the mass of Bagsby's men—a confused swirl of horses, men, and weapons—began slowly backing toward Bagsby.

Bagsby considered his options. He could rise forward, see what was the matter, and try to correct the situation. He could flee; neither the war nor Shulana was likely to follow to him if he made it as far north as Parona, where he could continue his life very much as he'd lived it so far. He could order a retreat, fall back a few miles to the next open field, and try again. What to do?

Without even making a conscious decision, Bagsby dug his spurs into the flanks of his horse and rode forward, angling toward the left of the melee. As he trotted around the line of his own men, he saw at a glance the entire problem.

"A thousand demon's tricks!" he exclaimed. His horsemen were not in melee with knights: the enemy knights had retreated, and waited now in a single line, far behind the line of battle. As Bagsby's men had charged, the enemy mounted force had turned and run, revealing the impregnable force of footmen that had formed behind them. The footmen, who now surged forward as a solid mass against his helpless knights, were formed in a great block that bristled with the points of spears extending fourteen feet or more beyond the men in the front ranks. Bagsby's knights would approach that bristling wall and attempt to strike, but they had no weapons that could reach the foe, and their horses refused to advance against the spearpoints.

"Withdraw!" Bagsby bellowed. "Withdraw! Retreat!"

Again without thinking, he guided his steed into the mass of his knights, waving his sword in the air, crying his order for the retreat. One knight looked at him, incredulous, not believing that a retreat order could even be issued.

"Retreat, you fool! We'll re-form and hit them again! Retreat!" Bagsby screamed. Tears of frustration began to flow down the little man's cheeks.

Bagsby saw the light of understanding flash in the man's eyes. For an instant, the lord general felt a sense of relief. Then the pointed, hooked blade of huge spear split through the man's cuirass and lifted him from his horse. Blood gushed from the knights' mouth, and his legs kicked helplessly as he dangled on the ear of the broad spear before crashing dead to the ground.

"Get back! By all the gods, get back!" Bagsby cried in even greater rage. He spotted at length the great banner of the company, still held aloft by Sir John, whose armor was stained with flowing blood. Bagsby galloped up, grabbed the banner, and cried, "Follow your flag! Follow your flag!"

That seemed to gain some attention from the bulk of his surviving men. Slowly at first, then more hastily, Bagsby began riding toward the rear, holding aloft the emblem of the company. In scattered clusters, his knights began to follow, until within a minute the Second Company of the Royal Guard of Argolia was a scattered mass of knights, strung out across the battlefield, riding at the best speed their winded horses could manage toward the rear.

Now was Sir Otto's moment. With the enemy in ragged retreat, they would be helpless against a formed charge. With a shout and a wave of his sword, Otto ordered his knights forward. They came first at a slow trot, the line splitting to weave its way around the block of footmen, which now halted its advance. Re-formed in front of the foot force, the cavalry dressed their line on the move, then, knee to knee, tightly disciplined, advanced their mounts' gait to the canter.

Bagsby reached the crest of the hill on his own side of the field as the line of enemy horse began its canter. He stopped, looked back, and saw that the enemy force would overtake a good third of his own men, whose winded horses could not possibly outrun the fresh force. Tears began to flow freely down Bagsby's face; his men would be slaughtered, and there was nothing to blame for it but his own folly and arrogance.

It was then that a flashing line of flame shot forth from among the fir trees off to the east side of the highway at the top of the hill. Longer and longer the streaking line of fire grew, arcing out across the plain, flowing through a seam in the ragged, scattered mass of retreating men, flying with increasing speed toward the line of charging horsemen.

Bagsby watched in silent awe and wonder as the line of flame went on and on until suddenly, it disappeared in a great, blinding flash, replaced by ball of fire some thirty yards across that exploded in the middle of the charging enemy line.

The concussion from the blast knocked down horses for a distance of sixty yards, friend and enemy alike. Those who retained their mounts saw flaming pieces of men and horse raining from the sky, and some quickly began attempting to beat out the flames the heat had ignited in their own blankets and tunics. The enemy charge dissolved; the survivors of that blast quickly reined their mounts and milled about in stunned, frightened confusion.

"I've bought you time," said a voice simply.

Bagsby turned his stunned gaze back from the field of battle to the woods from whence the line of flames had shot. Shulana emerged from between the trees, a look of deep sorrow and even fear on her pale elven face.

"What was that?" Bagsby gasped.

"Magic," Shulana answered. "Protect me. I have broken the Covenant."

"Protect you? Lady, I will protect you to the day I die," Bagsby replied, carried away with admiration and some other emotion he could not quite identify.

The retreating mass of Bagsby's force began to crest the hill now, turning in toward the highway. The mounted men looked stupefied; their eyes turned to Bagsby for answers as their winded mounts trotted by.

"Fall back to the next clearing and re-form," Bagsby shouted confidently. "Fall back to the next clearing and re-form." Then, in a flash of insight, Bagsby added, "I'll join you there. I'll join you there."

As Sir John, raging and shocked, trotted past, Bagsby extended to him the great banner. "Fall back to the next clearing and re-form the men. Do not attack. I will join you there. Victory will yet be ours," Bagsby said.

Sir John nodded, too tired and bewildered to answer. He

took the standard and stood in the center of the spot where the highway crested the hill, waving on the remainder of the retreating force.

"Sir John," Bagsby called as he began to ride back down the hill, "protect the elf on pain of your life!" Then Bagsby galloped away, back toward the field of battle, shedding his armor as he went.

"Give me water," the panting soldier called as he approached the halted line of large, wooden wagons. "You there," he said, pointing a weary arm vaguely toward a wench who lounged on the ground, leaning her back against the front wheel of the lead wagon, "get me some water."

"What's going on up there?" the wagon driver called down from his seat, where he half reclined, puffing on a pipe. "Is the way clear yet?"

The soldier shook his head. "No. Still fighting going on. Shouldn't take much longer though. Those Argolians are a stupid lot—charged right into us, just like Sir Otto said they would."

The driver chuckled, then leaned back again, reassured that his rest could continue and that no danger lurked in his future.

"Aren't you the lucky one, sent back here—for what?" the wench asked. "Why ain't you up there if there's still fightin' goin' on?" She cocked her head and stared at the man with her hard blue eyes.

"Orders," the soldier replied. "Them lords left some papers in with Sir Otto's stuff—maps, I'd reckon. The enemy is retreating off the main road—I'm to fetch Sir Otto's charts. And you, wench, had better fetch me some water or feel my boot on your backside."

"Ain't we proud?" the woman said with a sneer, but the soldier noted with satisfaction that she sauntered off to fetch the water.

"Say, driver," the soldier called again, "where here is Sir Otto's gear stored?"

"What, didn't he tell you?" the driver replied. "Just like them lords; expect us common men to know everything, do everything, and then kick us when we don't do it right 'cause we don't know any better."

"No soldier can talk like that," the armed man replied. "Which wagon?"

"Third one back, of course, where it always is. Wagon just before the treasure wagon," the driver said, as if instructing a doltish child.

The woman returned with a cup of water and handed it to the soldier. "So," she said, "in a hurry to get back to your battle?"

"No time for you, wench. Not now. But," he added, removing his helmet and pouring the water over his short salt-and-pepper hair and his bloodied, dirt-smeared face, "maybe later, when the fightin's done."

"I'll be 'ere," the woman answered with an attempt at a seductive smile.

No doubt you will, Bagsby thought—for it was he—but there'll be a few other things missing.

Bagsby sauntered down the line of wagons, smiling, nodding, occasionally rubbing a pretended aching muscle in his arm, thigh, or back, looking for all the world like a Heilesheim man-at-arms fresh from the battlefield. The armor had been easy to come by. He had ridden onto the battlefield, shedding his own armor, then slipped down on the side of his horse as he approached the scene of carnage where Heilesheim knights had been blown to bits by Shulana's magical ball of fire. There he had simply dropped on the field, letting his horse go free. In a short time he had managed to crawl farther back on the field where some Heilesheim men-at-arms were stripping the dead Argolian knights slain in that first, fatal charge. As Bagsby had worn no armor and no identifying symbols, the Heilesheim soldiers took him for a camp follower who had wandered out onto the field.

"Here, you!" one of the soldiers had called gruffly. "Help me gather up this loot." The man had tossed a pile of armor toward Bagsby, then begun stripping the tunic off a dead Argolian knight. It had been a simple matter for Bagsby to locate a dagger, isolate the plundering soldier, and quietly slit his throat. Piece by piece, posing as a plunderer, he had dressed in the man's armor, until he could pass for a Heilesheim man-at-arms. Then he had alternately crawled and played dead across the battlefield until he reached the rear of the Heilesheim lines. A hike down the highway had brought him to the wagons.

The sides of the highway were crowded with the camp followers, all the usual sorts that had so impeded his own progress just two days earlier. None paid him much attention. Soon he came to the third wagon and saw further down the road the fourth. These two were guarded. Five men-at-arms stood slackly around the third wagon, exchanging jokes, gossip, and small talk with the throngs that milled about beside the road. A ring of twenty men-at-arms, Bagsby estimated, stood all around the fourth wagon, where the fabled Golden Eggs of Parona were stored.

The wagons were large—nearly twenty feet long with flat beds that sat a good three feet off the ground. They had wooden sides that extended up about another three feet. Large wooden hoops then arced over the top to form supports for the thick linen and canvas that covered the contents and, presumably, kept them dry. The wagons were made of ash, rather soft and easy to work, and economical. The wheels were solid, not spoked, with rings of copper around the rims to prevent their wearing out too quickly. At the front of each wagon was a driver's seat, and a large tongue extended, suitable for hitching a team of oxen or mules.

Bagsby's mind raced over the multitude of problems: how to get in, how to handle the treasure, and above all, how to get it out. Instinctively he positioned himself out of sight of the guards, wandering off the side of the road and losing himself in the crowd of camp followers, until his plan was formed. He paced about, thinking hard, until his stride became more purposeful. A smile spread on his face, and he worked his way through the crowd back toward the front of the column of wagons.

He got back to a point about even with the second wagon in the line and, when no one was particularly paying him any mind, began running as fast as he could, up to the highway, then down the line to the fourth wagon. As he ran, he put on his scowl that had proved so effective on his knights. He hoped it would work as well on lower class men-at-arms.

"You there, guard!" he called to the first of the guards he spotted as he trotted up to the treasure wagon. "What in the name of all the gods of Heilesheim have you and these other fools done?" he demanded.

The guard lowered his spear as best he could. "Who are you?" he demanded, confused. His fellows in line also became alert, readying their weapons.

"I'm sent from Sir Otto himself to ask you louts how you managed to lose the treasure, that's who I am!" Bagsby announced at the top of his lungs. Murmuring began immediately among the throng of camp followers. Bagsby was confident that before this conversation was over, the entire crowd would know that the treasure was missing, the guards were in deep trouble, and there was danger in store for all.

"I'm to send you to the front, now! Start marching! The lot of you—go on now! Sir Otto's orders!" Bagsby bellowed.

"Wait a minute, wait a minute!" the first guard rejoined. "That treasure ain't gone nowhere, see? It's right 'ere in this wagon." The guard's firm declaration elicited a chorus of affirmations from his fellow guards, who had now approached Bagsby in a cautious ring, their long spears pointed skyward as they relaxed their guard to see the outcomes of this conversation.

"Then maybe you can explain why the enemy is riding off the field of battle with them golden eggs, plain as day, throwing taunts back at us," Bagsby said sarcastically. "Maybe you'd like to explain that to Sir Otto yourself."

"Well, maybe I would," the guard shouted back. "I'm telling you, that there treasure is 'ere in this wagon, right where it belongs, where we been guardin' it, and it ain't gone nowhere."

Bigsby threw his hands in the air as if exasperated by dealing with a complete fool. "All right, all right, have it your way. You say the treasure is safe inside that there wagon?"

"That's right. It's right 'ere, inside this 'ere wagon."

"All right, all right. I'm a reasonable man; I don't want to see you boys 'anged for no good reason—although them is me orders, you understand, to bring the lot of you to the front for an 'angin'," Bagsby said. "Show us the treasure, then," he demanded.

"An 'angin'?" the chorus of guards echoed. Exhortations broke out among the suddenly white-faced men.

"Go on then, show 'im, Alfred," pleaded one man. "Right, show 'im, Alfred. That treasure is in that wagon." Similar cries were echoed by all the guards, until Alfred, both frightened and angry, held up his arms for silence.

"Right then, right!" he said. "I'll show 'im the treasure, all right. C'mon back 'ere, you, and just you take a look inside this wagon." The guard stomped back to the rear of the wagon, loosened the iron chain that held the back gate shut, lowered the gate, climbed up on it, and threw back the flap of the canvas top. "C'mon, it's right in 'ere," he called to Bagsby.

Bagsby hopped up onto the gate and peered into the wagon. The interior was loaded with wooden barrels, reinforced with iron hoops.

"I don't see no treasure," Bagsby said, folding his arms and looking the guard coldly in the eye.

"Of course not," the guard said, with a look that indicated Bagsby must be the stupidest man in Sir Otto's service. "You don't think we'd leave it lyin' about out in the open, now, do you? It's in them two barrels in the middle. 'Arder to get at, that way."

"Well, then, let's go open 'em," Bagsby said, stepping into the wagon bed.

"*Aaaggghhh,*" the guard grunted. He tossed his great spear down to another guard, raised his hands, and rolled his eyes, as if to say to the large crowd that had gathered around the sight, What does it take to convince this fool? Then he turned and followed Bagsby into the wagon.

Bagsby already had his dagger out, digging at the lid of the first barrel. The guard joined in the effort, prying at the iron hoop that held the lid tight, until at last the slab of wood rattled loose. Then the two dagger blades slid between the lid and the side of the barrel, and the top lifted off.

"There!" the guard said, triumph on his face. "There's one of them golden eggs."

Bagsby stared at the contents of the barrel. The sides and bottom were lined with loosely packed cotton to cradle the contents. And poking up from the packing was the gleaming gold top of what appeared to be a large, golden nodule in the shape of an egg, fully three feet tall when stood on its end. A ring of gemstones was set near the top of the egg, and fine lines of some design were etched in the gold. Bagsby caught his breath. This was it! Then he noticed the play of the faint light from the rear of the wagon in one of the diamonds.

"Bring that out on the gate where I can see it in the light," Bagsby ordered. He turned and walked back out to the gate, leaving the exasperated guard to obey.

"All right, you bloody bastard, I'll lug it out there. Don't think to give me an 'and; I'll manage all right by me self," the guard groused. Tugging and straining, the guard worked the large barrel through the narrow wagon bed to the lowered gate.

As soon as the open barrel was in the clear daylight Bagsby knew the mission was for nothing. He glared at the top of the egg and the gems embedded in it, thinking quickly. Was it better to accept the guard's "proof" that the treasure was here, or was it better to create chaos? His own recent experiences in command led Bagsby to opt for chaos.

"See, the treasure!" the guard was proclaiming to the crowd and his very concerned fellows.

"That ain't the treasure," Bagsby said indignantly.

"What!" the guard screamed. "You can see it! What in all the bloody 'ells of an 'undred gods do you mean?"

"I mean, that ain't the treasure," Bagsby said, drawing his dagger again and gripping it around the pommel with the blade pointed upward. "See them diamonds there?" he asked the guard.

"Yeah, I sees 'em," the guard replied.

"Watch," Bagsby said. He lowered the dagger in a savage blow, using the pommel like a hammer to strike one of the large gems. The alleged diamond shattered into a hundred fragments. "You ever see a diamond break from a man's blow?" Bagsby asked. "That's glass. These gems is fake, and so is this egg. That ain't even real gold, not more than a tiny bit thick," he added, scratching the surface of the egg with the dagger blade. The gold plate, thinner than a hair, peeled off, revealing dull iron. "No wonder that barrel was so 'eavy, mate. That there egg is iron, not gold."

"By all the gods," the stunned man said, "it's true." He looked up, casting helpless eyes on his fellow guards. "This 'ere egg is a fake," he said simply.

Bagsby struck his dagger pommel again against the side of the egg, which emitted a metallic ring.

" 'Ollow, too," he said. "Now, you lot ready to come with me?"

Howls of protest emerged from the guards, who expressed their dismay, their disbelief, and their protestations of innocence. Bagsby let the din continue while the crowd listened with growing horror. At length, he held up his hand for silence.

"All right, then, I know what you're startin' to think. But killin' me won't make that iron egg into a gold one, will it? An' if I ain't back to the front soon with some kind of report, there'll be 'ell to pay, there will. Them lords'll come back 'ere soon, lookin' for their golden eggs, and when they sees 'em gone, they'll think somebody 'ere swiped 'em. They'll blame the lot o' you," Bagsby declared. He gestured broadly out over the crowd of camp followers. "Not just these guards, mind you, but the lot of you!"

As Bagsby had hoped, the result was pandemonium. The crowd of camp followers turned into a frightened mob, screaming, running, looting the wagons, and scattering into the forest with whatever their arms could carry. The guards looked at one another, then at Alfred, then at Bagsby.

"Well," Bagsby said. "Go on then. It's better to disap-pear than to 'ang. I know you lot didn't do it, and I'm an okay sort, see? You take off, and I'll cover it some'ow."

The guards scattered. Within ten minutes the wagons were stripped of the bulk of their goods and Bagsby sat alone on the tailgate of the treasure wagon, with not another human soul to be seen or heard.

The instant he was certain he was alone, Bagsby ran to the already ransacked third wagon. As he had expected, the personal papers of Sir Otto—his maps and a large book of loose sheets covered with Sir Otto's scrawl—were untouched. Bagsby picked up this loot and began walking south. A glance at just a few pages of Sir Otto's notes were enough to prove to any sane man that the Heilesheim troops were also spies. Bagsby closed the book and picked up his pace. He had to make his way back through enemy lines, catch up to the remains of his own force, and get word to King Harold to close the borders.

Of course, he thought, he'd been a fool. It was too obvious for the treasure to be in a heavily guarded convoy. A snake like Valdaimon would never have done anything so risky and so simple. No, Bagsby thought, the treasure is right now somewhere where no one would think to look for it; probably near the southern border of Argolia on its way to Valdaimon's hands. The little thief shook his head in disbelief. He must be getting old, he thought. He'd been duped twice in one day, and lost both a battle and a trea-sure.

⇜6⇝

Surprising Outcomes

Bagsby's victory parade through Clairton was as great a surprise to him as it was to the four assassins, paid by Nebuchar, who had been scouring the city for him. The family Pendargon, too, privately voiced considerable shock when, as the triumphal procession of the Second Company of the Royal Guard marched through the square nearest their spacious home, young Reynaldo recognized the Guard commander as none other than the swindler who had conned him out of four hundred crowns not many days ago.

The victory had been even a greater surprise to Bagsby. It had taken Bagsby almost a day to circle the enemy forces and return safely to his own small command; by the time he arrived, Sir Otto von Berne had negotiated terms of surrender with Sir John! The Heilesheim force, having discovered themselves deep in what was clearly now enemy territory, with no supplies and with a major army gathering south of Clairton, was forced to seek terms. The only alternative would have been to try to survive in hostile territory without food or vital supplies, surrounded by a vastly superior foe. Sir John, valiant in battle but not overaggressive at the negotiating table, had agreed to accept the surrender of the Heilesheim force's arms. In exchange he extended a promise that the entire force could march unmolested out of Argolia. Further, each Heilesheim man-at-arms and knight was made to swear an oath before Wojan that he would not bear arms against Argolia for the duration of the current conflict. Bagsby had merely ratified the agreement upon his return to his own force, where he had been hailed as a hero, revered as something of a military genius, and suspected of being that rarest of rare things, a human wizard with prowess in physical combat.

Sir John of Elamshire, who had pondered as hard as his sore knightly brain would allow on the strangeness of his commander, found the courage to give voice to the new assessment the knights had of Bagsby. When he had returned to camp, Bagsby had set things in order to his satisfaction, dispatched a rider to the king with the captured documents and instructions to quickly close the southern border, and retired to his tent for the night. Sir John had begged permission to enter.

"Come," Bagsby had called in answer to Sir John's entreaties.

The knight, still in full battle gear, had stepped hesitatingly into the tent, where Bagsby sprawled, exhausted, on his bed, with Shulana seated cross-legged on the floor by his side. "My lord," Sir John had begun.

"Speak your speech, Sir John," Bagsby had said wearily. "I am tired and need to sleep."

"My lord, on behalf of the company, I have come to . . . say—to say that . . . well, we had thought, my lord, prior to the battle, that my lord was, well—"

"You had thought," Bagsby had interjected, "that I was a fool who knew not what he did. You also doubted my prowess at arms, given that my defeat of yourself in personal combat was, as you thought it, unconventional."

Sir John's face beamed. He nodded. "You understand perfectly, my lord."

"And now that I have single-handedly caused the destruction of the enemy's supply train and forced his surrender," Bagsby had droned on in a fatigued monotone, "your estimation of me is quite different."

"Just so!" Sir John had agreed. "By the gods, you are a man of understanding."

"A tired man of understanding," Bagsby had said, yawning.

"Your wizardry tires you," Sir John had suggested.

"Wizardry?" Bagsby had asked, forcing himself to sit

up in bed as the back of his brain felt the approach of danger in that remark.

"The magical fire," Sir John had explained.

"My lord does not discuss magic with those who do not practice it," Shulana had said quietly.

Bagsby had quickly nodded his agreement.

"Well, no harm intended," Sir John had said agreeably.

"None done. And may our future relationship be one not only of commander and his second in command," Bagsby had said, confirming Sir John's de facto role, "but also one of friendship. Now go, good Sir John, before I rudely fall asleep in your presence."

Sir John had bowed and hastily but happily exited. Bagsby had begun snoring almost immediately but not before he muttered, "Oh, Shulana, what a day this has been. . . ."

Shulana had sat quietly through the night, maintaining the same secret vigil she had maintained ever since her communion in the woods: a vigil against things magical, for there were powerful currents stirring in the sources of magical energy, currents that were slowly and subtly being shaped against Bagsby and against her. Shulana had also used this time to ponder her recent actions. She had broken the Covenant by attacking humans, and what was more, she had used magic to do it—not what one could call an inconspicuous outburst. Why had she done it? At the moment of action, she had not thought at all. She had seen the rout of Bagsby's force, she had seen danger thundering across the field, and she had acted without thinking. It was almost as though the fireball had surprised her as much as the enemy. She remembered hearing Elrond say that in battles against the humans, many elves found that they simply reacted without thinking. Perhaps that was what had happened to her. But Shulana was too honest with herself to believe that simple explanation. Somehow, her behavior had its roots in the strange new emotion she was feeling toward Bagsby, an emotion for which she had no name and which she little understood.

This emotion frightened her, for she knew that if and when Bagsby was successful, her duty would require his death; and she wondered now if, after protecting him, she could be the instrument of that death.

But neither Shulana nor Bagsby had thoughts of death two days later, as Bagsby's triumphal procession weaved through the streets of Clairton. The day was perfect for a public celebration: a warm, spring day with sunlight pouring down like pale melted gold to drench the broad avenues of the city, bouncing off the sparkling whitewashed walls of the better buildings and dancing among the brilliant colors of the citizenry's costumes. Hurrahs rose to the blue, cloudless heavens from the thousands who lined the streets. Some waved banners with the colors of Argolia; others waved bright red, white, or gold cloths of all descriptions and types—anything to contribute to the explosion of color, sound, and joy that greeted the victorious band as they paraded in tight formation with Bagsby at their head, the troops of Heilesheim walking without arms before them, their own banner held respectfully dipped downward in acknowledgment of their defeat.

The celebration, startling as it was to Bagsby, made a kind of sense to him as he mulled over the information he'd gathered from the scuttlebutt among his own troops and from the shouts of the crowd. Even though he had not consciously planned the defeat of the enemy force, Bagsby had, while pursuing his own ends, stumbled onto the one weakness of the Heilesheim military. Invincible as their troop might be on the field of battle, they still had to eat, drink, and maintain themselves. Without the resources to do that, they were harmless. Thus, he had inadvertently produced a victory. And, at a time when the forces of Heilesheim were reaping victory after victory with lightning speed—in Dunsford, in Kala, in the County of the Wyche—it was of immense political value to have demonstrated that the Heilesheim armies were not invincible, that they could be defeated, even by a smaller force.

And so, Bagsby reasoned, as he bowed to one side of the street and then to the other, grunting at the difficulty of moving in his gleaming full suit of armor, King Harold was no fool. He was using this fluke victory to arouse public enthusiasm for the war with Heilesheim. Smart, Bagsby thought. No doubt riders were already on the way to the other counties of the Holy Alliance, bearing word of the Argolian victory and holding out the promise of participation in the fruits of victory for those who responded to the call for assistance.

That there was full-scale war with Heilesheim was no longer questionable. Bagsby had learned at the gates of the city, where the Lord Mayor had presented him with an honorary gold-plated key, that the Heilesheim legions had crossed the southern frontier within the past day. Already they were on the march toward Clairton. And so, Bagsby concluded, the Golden Eggs of Parona were already far south, most likely in Kala, making their way each moment closer to Valdaimon's hands.

The procession turned a final corner, and Bagsby saw that he was riding into the gleaming white square in front of the great Temple to the Gods of Argolia. The square was immense, fully three hundred yards from side to side. The vast space was empty, calling even more attention to the enormous temple on the east side of the square. As the only approach was the broad avenue from the west, the Temple to the Gods of Argolia dominated one's vision as soon as the square was visible.

A set of one hundred marble steps led up to the entrance to the white marble temple, which was almost blinding in the spring sunlight. The front consisted of twelve fat, fluted columns that supported a huge, triangular frieze. Depicted on the brightly painted frieze were the great stories of the Argolian gods. Gia, the goddess of the earth, embraced her consort Lamdos, the night. From their union sprang great Argram, ruler of the gods, the god of the sky, who wielded the thunderbolt in fearsome fashion against Karmos, the bringer of evils. Golden Parmen raced across the sky, carrying aloft the great torch of the sun, while Aeris, who brings forth the fruits of the earth, gazed up at him in romantic admiration. Fierce Wogon, the Argolian version of Wojan, stood laughing on a heap of human and elven corpses as he held aloft his mighty spear, a dragon's head with gaping jaws impaled upon its point. The other minions of the Argolian pantheon walked, ran, leaped, and wrestled their way in blazing colors across the frieze, which was more than one hundred yards long. Bagsby was relieved and pleased to see, as he approached the holy temple, that even Shima, the universal patron goddess of thieves, was represented as a minor deity.

King Harold of Argolia, resplendent in a gold-trimmed robe of crimson whose train extended more than ten feet behind him, stood in the center of the steps, awaiting the returning hero. By his side, dressed in a pure white tunic with trim of green and gold, stood the old, revered high priest of the great temple, a man with a great mane of gray-white hair, which exploded around his head, and a wiry white beard that plunged to the middle of his chest. Bagsby rode halfway across the square, halted his column, and dismounted. The Heilesheim warriors, their flag still dipped, formed two lines through which Bagsby approached the steps of the temple. The people of Argolia flooded into the square behind the troops, the throng scurrying to gain positions from which to view and hear the royal reception of their newfound military idol.

Bagsby's brisk step belied the uneasiness he felt as he clanked up the marble steps toward the outstretched, welcoming arms of the king. Being in the presence of so much purity and holiness made him vaguely anxious; he had not even been faithful in offerings and prayers to Shima, and her most powerful friends, he thought, who in some sense resided here, might not welcome a thief, murderer, and imposter who had tried to use the wealth and power of a kingdom for personal gain and for a personal vendetta.

"Welcome, Sir John Wolfe, in the name of the kingdom and gods of Argolia!" King Harold boomed as Bagsby approached.

The little man stopped about two steps below the broadly smiling king, and knelt, bowing his head. "Your Majesty, I have the honor to return with news of a victory achieved by your forces."

The king descended a step, reached down, and raised Bagsby to his feet. "Hail to the victor!" the king shouted.

"So may all our armies return from encounters with Heilesheim!" The crowd roared. "We go now," the king shouted, continuing his prepared welcome, "to give thanks to the gods of our land, who have prospered our arms and sent to us this brave knight who has been the first to bring Heilesheim to heel!"

The din from the crowd, which now packed the vast square, made hearing impossible. The king gestured for Bagsby to follow him, and led the way up the steps to the temple entrance. The high priest followed. A small crowd of servants, attendants, and lesser priests followed at a respectful distance.

As Bagsby passed beneath the frieze between the two center columns of the temple front, he saw a maze of corridors, defined by more columns, leading to a number of different altars behind which stood gleaming statues of the various gods—some painted, other plated with gold and silver and encrusted with precious stones. The sight was a thief's dream.

King Harold walked with unfaltering step into the maze of columns and shadows. Bagsby had little choice but to follow, and soon was lost in the intricate interior of the temple. From time to time they encountered walls barely higher than a man's head that formed the back of altars on their opposite sides. Some areas of the temple, Bagsby noted, were roofed, and these areas increased as the king worked his way through the main sites of worship toward one side of the structure. Eventually he came to a corridor at the end of which was a set of plain, six-foot-tall wooden doors. These the king opened and motioned for Bagsby to step inside.

Bagsby entered a small, dark chamber with a simple altar at one end, with light provided by torches in wall brackets. The air was thick with incense from the large burners on each side of the altar. But there was no statue, no sign of the presence of the god. The high priest entered after the king, closing the doors behind him and leaving the three men alone in the small, strange chamber.

Bagsby watched with concerned curiosity as the king approached the altar, knelt on one knee, and bowed his head in silence. After a moment, his respects paid to whatever deity was worshipped in this room, King Harold stood and turned to face Bagsby.

"Well, Bagsby," the king said, "you've done well for yourself and for me."

"Your Majesty," Bagsby began—and then froze, as he realized what the king had said.

"I see for once you are speechless," the monarch said sternly. "I don't doubt why. Impersonating a noble is a capital crime. So is lying to the king, not to mention betraying his trust and taking command of a portion of his Guard under false pretenses!"

Instinctively, Bagsby's eyes darted about the room, seeking exits. Save for the double doors, against which the high priest leaned, grinning, there were none. Nor, aside from the torches and the incense burners, were there any items that might be useful as weapons in a brawl. Bagsby wondered if he dared draw sword against a king.

"There's no escape from this room, thief, if that's what you're wondering while your skin grows so pale," the high priest boomed. Bagsby noticed that his voice, though deep and somewhat somber, was edged with humor.

"He's right," the king said, approaching Bagsby with his hand outstretched. "Nonetheless, before we talk more, I'll have that sword and dagger, if you don't mind. It wouldn't do for a successful monarch to be murdered by his most successful general, would it?"

Bagsby kept his silence. He drew his sword and handed it, hilt first, to the king. He did the same with his dagger. Best not to say anything until he knew which way the wind was blowing, Bagsby decided.

"Thank you," the king said, handing the weapons to the priest, who hid them quickly in his white tunic. This surprised Bagsby, for the tunic seemed to have no folds and no openings.

"Priestly magic," the priest said, acknowledging Bagsby's wondering stare.

"Now," King Harold continued, "what are we to do with you, Bagsby? You have cost me a great deal already. In your absence we learned who you truly are—how does not matter—and of the frauds you have already perpetrated against our subjects. Young Pendargon will doubtless never forget how you parted him from four hundred crowns. No doubt his father will be in my law courts by the morrow, clamoring for justice."

"Ah, that matter," Bagsby replied. "There really is no reason to believe that Pendargon even knows who I am. However, I will gladly make restitution if Your Majesty desires," Bagsby began.

"Do you think old Pendargon blind?" the king demanded sternly. "The entire city witnessed your triumph. It will cost me a great deal more than four hundred crowns to ensure the silence of the Pendargons."

"Silence?" Bagsby asked, hope rising.

"Don't play the fool with me, thief," King Harold snarled. "You know as well as I that I can ill afford to publicly proclaim that my great general, the bringer of the first victory against Heilesheim, is a thief and a fraud."

"Oh, my," Bagsby replied. "Oh, my, indeed, that would be somewhat embarrassing. Well, then, perhaps it would be best if I simply disappeared from Your Majesty's realm."

"No doubt it would be best were it not for one thing," the king answered. "You are a war hero. Genuine war heroes are hard to come by. You are useful politically. Otherwise, I assure you Bagsby, you would have already disappeared from our realm. If not by my own hand, then by the hands of the assassins that our spies tell us roam the streets seeking you."

"Certainly, I may be of further service to Your Majesty," Bagsby began broadly, "I would only be too happy—"

"Silence!" the king commanded. "You have two options. Death and disappearance, which we could tolerate but which would not serve our greater end, or military service to us for the duration of this war in return for a pardon for your previous frauds against our person and our kingdom."

"I'll take the pardon," Bagsby said flatly.

"All in due time. First, you will kneel before this altar and place both hands upon it," the king commanded.

"What is this?" Bagsby said, allowing his natural disrespect for authority to show through. After all, he reasoned, he had little to lose at this point. "Some kind of religious initiation?"

"Not exactly," the priest interjected. The large man walked up to the altar and extended his hands, palms down, over the flat, plain stone.

"Gods of Argolia, seen and unseen, grant us now the use of this truth stone," the priest intoned. "Let the lips of him who touches this, thy sacred altar, speak only the truth. Let all ability to dissemble flee his soul. Make pure the words of his mouth." His incantation completed, the priest turned to Bagsby. "Kneel and place your hands on the altar," he said.

"Now, just a minute," Bagsby objected. "There really isn't any need for all this religious—"

The priest, who despite his age was a man of immense physical strength, grabbed Bagsby around the neck and clanged his helmeted head down upon the stone. Without thinking Bagsby placed his hands on the stone in order to push himself up. But no sooner had he touched the stone than a strange kind of dizziness overcame him, and a nausea made him sink to the floor. Vainly he ordered his arms to raise his hands from the slab of granite, but to no avail; the muscles of his arms would not obey.

"Now, Bagsby," said the king, "tell me this. If I spare your life, will you give me loyal service as befits a pure knight? Or will you betray me to the vile forces of Heilesheim?"

Bagsby's head swam. He understood the king's words. In normal circumstances, he would have eloquently sworn loyalty to the death to Argolia and the king, and not thought twice about breaking such an oath when the occasion demanded. But now he found he could not glibly lie—only the truth would come from his lips. And Bagsby found, as he searched inside his nauseated, dizzy soul, that he did not even know what that truth really was.

"I don't know," he replied, the words coming slowly, as though he might gag on each syllable.

"Explain yourself," the king demanded.

"I—I wish no harm to Argolia," Bagsby stammered slowly. "I wish harm to Valdaimon, the royal wizard of Heilesheim. If I could harm him by betraying you, I would. If betraying you was necessary to preserve my life so that I might harm him, I would."

"What enmity have you for Valdaimon?" the king asked.

"He killed my father!" Bagsby screamed. Hot tears poured down the little man's cheeks. "He killed the only person I ever truly loved. And I have never had a chance for revenge until now."

The king ignored the misery of the thief and pressed for more. "Tell me, Bagsby, what chance for revenge have you now?"

"I can steal the Golden Eggs of Parona," the thief wailed.

"How will that harm Valdaimon?" the king demanded.

"I don't truly know, but it will deprive him, somehow, of some great power he seeks. It will spoil his plan and bring his efforts to dominate the Land Between the Rivers to nothing," Bagsby screamed. "At least," he added, beginning to gasp for breath, "that is what I believe."

"And why do you believe this?" the king asked quietly.

"The elf told me," Bagsby whispered. He collapsed with a clatter on the floor, his hands above his head, still glued to the truth stone.

"What is the relationship between you and this elf," the king pressed.

"I don't know. I may be falling in love with her, even though she is an elf. How she feels about me, I do not know," Bagsby muttered, his voice barely audible.

The king stared long at Bagsby's body as it lay on the floor. His neither smiled nor frowned; he simply stared and pondered. At length, he raised his gaze to meet the questioning eyes of the high priest. The king cocked his head, as if asking a question of his own, and the priest, pursing his lips, slowly nodded his head. Then the big man extended his right arm and passed his hand, palm down, over the altar stone. Bagsby's hands slid off the chunk of rock onto the floor.

"Help him to his knees," the king ordered. The burly priest slipped his arms beneath Bagsby's shoulders and hefted the bulk of the little man up. Bagsby felt strength slowly returning to his body at the cleric's touch. Still, he burned with shame, as his deepest feelings had been revealed, not only to himself but also to these strangers. He raised angry eyes to the king, whose back was to him, and saw the monarch draw his great sword.

No matter, then, my embarrassment, Bagsby thought. I am to die.

The king turned and faced the kneeling thief. "The use of the truth stone is distasteful to us," King Harold said. "It engenders hatred, if the one it is used on is allowed to live. We ask your forgiveness for so prying into your very soul. It was necessary."

Bagsby stared back at the king silently.

"Bagsby, thief, you have served us well. Therefore," the king said, raising his great sword above his head and lowering it toward the thief, "we dub you a knight of realm of Argolia."

Bagsby was already cringing in anticipation of the death blow. The words of the king stunned his already numb mind. He felt the flat of the blade slam against first his right shoulder, then his left, as the king continued to speak. "We award you certain estates in the north of our kingdom," King Harold said, "which you may claim at the conclusion of the current war. We name you, henceforth, John Wolfe. Whereupon, rise, Sir John Wolfe, knight of Argolia."

The unbelieving Bagsby clawed the air, as though an invisible arm would be extended to help him to his feet. The priest came to his assistance, and the now-noble Bagsby stood before the King of Argolia.

"I know not what to say, Your Majesty," Bagsby humbly confessed.

"Then say nothing. You will command our entire Royal Guard in the forthcoming battle. And see to one thing: should your elf use magic again in our cause, be certain its use is imputed to you." The king winked at Bagsby and smiled, the smile of one thief to another.

"Your Majesty can make light of such an important matter?" Bagsby asked.

"I do not make light of it. Neither do I refuse aid against so powerful a foe as Ruprecht, even if that aid comes from the elves."

"I will keep it secret, be well assured," Bagsby said. "The elf fears the revelation as much as we do."

"No doubt. Well, Sir John, honor among thieves, eh?" the king said, jesting.

"Your Majesty is no thief," Bagsby said solemnly.

"All rulers are thieves," the king replied. "We simply legalize our thefts and call them taxes."

The sputtering flame of a single oil lamp threw occasional illumination on the yellowed, wrinkled face of Valdaimon as the old wizard stared into the dark, hard eyes of Nebuchar, the leader of all thieves and assassins in the land of Kala. This Nebuchar, Valdaimon decided, does not scare easily.

"You have not explained to my satisfaction why four professional assassins cannot accomplish the death of one insignificant man in the middle of a minor kingdom undergoing all the confusions of war," Valdaimon hissed.

Nebuchar leaned forward across the plain wooden table and stared back into Valdaimon's rheumy eyes. "I owe no explanations to you, wizard," he replied. "Take care. Your king may rule here now, but no king truly rules the streets of Kala. There I alone am king."

Valdaimon studied this man carefully. He was arrogant and stupid, like all humans, but with more reason than most. His power could not be disputed. Even in far-off Parona Nebuchar was famous as the one man who could cause anything to be done, regardless of law and custom, and the one man who could supply anything, regardless of its rarity. The only thing Nebuchar was said to care about was money. But, to maintain his ability to make money, Valdaimon reasoned, Nebuchar must also care about his reputation. It was clear enough he did not care about his appearance: he was fat, with short greasy black hair, flabby jowls, and a scar across his forehead which he made no effort to hide.

"That is why I engaged you in the first place," Valdaimon replied. "You are the king of assassinations. I paid my money. I want results. If you cannot deliver, no matter. I will not even ask for my money back. I will simply pass the word that you have become ... unreliable."

"I am reliable," Nebuchar snapped. "I want Bagsby dead as much as you do—whatever your reasons may be. He's the only man who ever crossed me and lived to talk of it. Taking your money only assured me of a profit for a job that was going to be done anyway."

"Yes, but when?" Valdaimon goaded.

"You could help, wizard," Nebuchar said. "You are supposed to be so powerful that no human can resist your spells. Do him in with your magic, and I will pay you." Nebuchar stabbed his dagger into the wood table top to emphasize his point.

"Those who do not practice magic can hardly appreciate its limitations," Valdaimon answered. "My powers are needed for the support of the war effort now."

"You lie," Nebuchar stated.

"I cannot get at him at long range. He has protections against magical attacks of certain types," Valdaimon admitted.

"Then use another type," Nebuchar said, shrugging.

"Then you use another type of assassin," Valdaimon snapped back.

Nebuchar grunted. "I don't want unhappy customers. Let's work together. I'll return your money, but let's work together to see that little monster dead."

"I could provide information about his whereabouts. Do you get along well with animals?" Valdaimon asked, grinning.

"What kind of animals?" Nebuchar asked. "I've got a lot of the human kind working for me now."

Valdaimon reached into the folds of his tattered robe and produced a vial of clear, blue fluid. He set it carefully on the table and smiled. "A crow will come calling on you. When he does, drink this," the wizard said.

"How do I know it's not poison?" Nebuchar asked, looking skeptically at the wizard.

"You don't. Welcome to the new regime in Kala. There will be other changes in your business operations in the future—but for now, we'll work together for our common good." Valdaimon wheezed. The wizard pushed back his chair and rose. "Our business is done. We will speak again when Bagsby is dead." Using his great staff for support, the old mage trudged toward the door of the small, dark room.

"Where will you be if I need to speak to you?" Nebuchar asked.

"I will be at Lundlow Keep—my new personal estate here. But you will not need to speak to me. I will know when the deed is done, and if it is not, you will not want to speak to me." The wizard made his exit.

"Valdaimon," Nebuchar called after him, "you stink. Don't come again yourself—send your damned crow instead!" The fat man broke into laughter at his own taunt.

Valdaimon merely shrugged and made an indistinct gesture with one hand. He didn't smile until he was making his way out through the dimly lit main room of the cheap dive that served the powerful, wealthy Nebuchar as his headquarters.

Though from the outside the place appeared to be like any of a score of other cheap taverns, none entered here without invitation. Here, swilling cheap wine and ale, debauching with some of the ugliest women of Kala, were the most ruthless cutthroats, the cleverest thieves, and the vilest assassins of the Land Between the Rivers. To enter here without invitation—and sometimes with—was to condemn oneself to the most ignoble death possible. Valdaimon realized it was a testament to his power that the room became silent as he entered and that not a single eye turned to gaze upon his person as he slowly dragged himself toward the only door. These, the worst of the worst, feared him. Only Nebuchar did not fear him—yet.

Valdaimon paused by the door. A scream came from the tiny back room, a blood-freezing scream that caused all the scum of Kala to exchange frightened, worried glances.

Yet not one of Nebuchar's followers dared move toward the tiny room, where the voice of their leader called again and again for aid in the high-pitched screams of a man totally overcome by terror. At the sound of those screams, Valdaimon chuckled. Now, Nebuchar, too, would fear him. The delayed fear spell he'd cast would wear off in less than an hour, but the memory of that fear would haunt Nebuchar for the rest of his mortal life.

Valdaimon's chuckle broke into a full laugh as he stepped through the door out onto the dark street. The rambling tenements and taverns of the Thieves' Quarter of Kala were illuminated by the flames that leapt skyward from the rest of the city. Shrieks, screams, and cries for help echoed through the dark streets as the troops of Heilesheim burned, pillaged, and raped their way through the once-great city that had dared to resist the will of Ruprecht. The sight gave Valdaimon a cold thrill; like Nebuchar's screams, it was a testament to his power— power that soon the entire Land Between the Rivers would acknowledge.

But first there was more work to do. The old mage shuffled down the narrow street—really no more than an alleyway—ignoring the drunks, the staring thieves who did not yet know him by sight, and the blandishments of hookers. The Thieves' Quarter, of course, had been spared the fate of the rest of the city on Valdaimon's orders. There was no point in destroying people who by their very existence would undermine any resistance to Heilesheim's rule—and thereby, his rule.

Malak, Orgon, and Barak, the three chief wizards of the League of the Black Wing, other than Valdaimon, stood at the end of the alleyway, their solemn, dark forms silhouetted by the orange flames from the square into which the street emptied. They watched as Valdaimon shuffled toward their planned meeting, a meeting that they, with some fear, had demanded. Anxiously they peered into the dark, trying to read the mood on Valdaimon's face as he approached. It was not an easy matter to force an issue with Valdaimon, especially an issue that might call forth his rage.

"I can't tell what his mood will be," Malak commented, straining to see. "He's coming from talking with Nebuchar, who is truly an evil fox; usually people like that amuse him."

"His mood doesn't matter," Barak responded in a whisper. "It can change as quickly as a cloud can cover the sun."

The threesome fell silent as Valdaimon came within earshot. The old wizard slowly trundled his way to the end of the street, and, ignoring his longtime followers, gazed about the square, a broad smile on his ancient face, which glowed more yellow than usual in the orange flames.

"A burning city is a fine sight," Valdaimon commented at length. "So, of course, are loyal friends. You requested a meeting, Malak. Speak. My time is short, and I have much to do." Malak removed his cap and shook his bushy white hair. He straightened his back from its usual stoop, brushed a bit of soot from his scarlet velvet cloak, and cleared his throat with a raspy grunt. Then the lean, thin-faced old man looked straight into Valdaimon's face and said simply, "There is trouble within the league."

"What kind of trouble?" Valdaimon asked calmly. "And do you speak for all three of my most trusted lieutenants or only for yourself?"

"He speaks for us all," fat Orgon interjected. The rotund, balding figure, overdressed in a gaudy silk print tunic and a shimmering cloak of yellow satin, rested his hand on his protruding belly and smiled benignly. "We have all heard the same things from the mages of our sections of the league. For each of us to report the same . . . concerns would be to waste time and breath," he said with his throaty, soothing voice.

"You waste both already," Valdaimon replied, smiling with fake sweetness. "And you, Barak, does Malak speak for you as well?"

Barak, youngest of the three senior mages, nodded once, sharply. Quickly removing his ostentatious green hat, adorned with blue and yellow feathers, he made a short bow and spoke briefly. "Malak speaks for us all," he said. "Our problems are the same."

"Well, Malak, tell me of these ... problems," Valdaimon responded. "Ah, but a moment ..." he added, looking suddenly playful. He quickly raised his huge staff and pointed one end toward a young man running from a burning building with two drunken soldiers in pursuit. Valdaimon breathed a single word, and a tiny yellow ball shot forth from the end of the staff, striking the man in the head. The man exploded in mid-stride. The astonished soldiers nearly fell over in their attempts to come to a halt, and gaped in astonishment at the foursome.

"Just helping you tame the locals," Valdaimon called. "Carry on with your work." Valdaimon flicked out his narrow tongue, wet his thin lips, and turned back to Malak. "You were saying?"

"This is a serious matter," Malak said, thrusting his defiant jaw forward, his old rheumy eyes suddenly aflame with anger. "It is not something to be settled by a few intimidating spells. The league now numbers more than two hundred, all trained in magic, all intelligent, ambitious, and eager for the fulfillment of those promises with which you bound us all together many years ago. Your threats and intimidation have kept discipline up until now, but not even your power is sufficient to contest the entire league!"

"Is this rebellion, then?" Valdaimon hissed.

"This is loyalty—we three come to warn you before there is rebellion," Malak rasped back. "The league grows restless. Our armies move forward relentlessly, carrying all before them. But the league does not participate in either the victories or the fruits of victory. The nobles gain glory and lands; the league is snubbed. Not once have the mages marched, as practiced, in the center of the formations of the legions. Not once have they been called upon to mount their wyverns and attack from the air, as we practiced and studied to do for many years. And while the nobles reap lands, we reap nothing."

"Is that all?" Valdaimon said disdainfully. "Are you children to come to me with these petty complaints? Discipline the offenders, if need be; kill one or two of them in some spectacular way, and the rest will fall back in line."

Malak's stomach tightened and his palms felt damp for the first time in years. "The rest—" he began, than fell into a coughing fit.

"The rest," Barak said flatly, taking up Malak's sentence, "will fall upon us with all the magic we have taught them if we don't give them some response other than violence and terror. They are no longer frightened, and they do not trust you, who alone have the ear of the king and of Culdus."

Valdaimon raised his thin, pale, sooty hand high into the air. Barak visibly flinched. Then Valdaimon, grinning, brought the hand down on the top of his head and scratched his yellowish scalp with his dirty, scraggly nails.

"Well, then," the old mage said, "I suppose we shall have to do something. Tell the league a great battle is brewing. It will take place within the next four days south of Clairton in Argolia. At that battle, the league will take its rightful place as the greatest force for war and magic the world has ever seen. It shall share fully in the spoils of victory. And more, the league shall soon thereafter share in the greatest treasure in the entire world. For I shall make available to the league the fabulous riches of the Golden Eggs of Parona."

The three wizards stared at one another in surprise, then at Valdaimon. "That is truly wondrous news," Malak croaked.

"Tell me," Barak said, a note of challenge in his voice now, "how the riches of the Golden Eggs of Parona can be shared with anyone. Do you propose to melt them down and dole out the gold and gems of which they are made? Such a course would be foolish."

"I will share the magical riches, young Barak, of which you know nothing," Valdaimon replied. "You three think you are powerful wizards, and as men judge such things, you are. But you do not yet know what power is. Soon, you shall. Now go. Assemble the entire league here, at Kala, with the wyverns. Be ready to march north at Culdus's order and to join the army in battle."

Without awaiting a reply Valdaimon began to shuffle his way through the burning square.

"Take care, Valdaimon," Orgon called after him. "The streets teem with the vermin of Kala eager for vengeance against us."

The three men heard Valdaimon's laugh; he did not turn his head to respond. They watched in silence until Valdaimon passed through the square and into the darkness of the street on the far side, where spurts of flame from the burning buildings occasionally allowed them a glimpse of his stooped, slowly moving form.

"That went well," Orgon suggested. "We got what we asked for."

"We received the promise of what we asked for," Barak said, correcting him.

"You grow too bold," Malak snapped, rebuking the younger man. "Valdaimon could have turned you to stone or, worse, to one some undead thing, with a mere flick of his fingers. I'm surprised he showed such restraint."

"Despite your fears and his boasts, Valdaimon knows he cannot fight the whole league," Barak retorted. "Let us see if Valdaimon delivers on his promise. If he does, all is well. If not, perhaps the league should consider new leadership."

Once out of sight and hearing of his rebellious underlings, Valdaimon cursed them aloud. Soon, soon, he reminded himself, there would be no need for the league, no need for Ruprecht, no need for Culdus, no need for the army, no need for anything that he did not want. And soon, soon, there would be no need to maintain this merely human guise, appearing to be a mortal with mortal concerns, even mortal fears, in order to make them his foils. With a disgusted grunt, Valdaimon waved his feeble hand in the air and vanished from the street.

In the next instant, he was standing in his study, high in the tower of Lundlow Keep, a modest stone castle only three miles southwest of the now ruined city of Kala. No candle or torch provided light in the dark, round tower room, for its user needed no light to see. His keen eyes saw every parchment, tome, vial, and beaker that littered the long wooden worktable in the center of the room. They took in the great white circle inscribed on the floor several feet away from that workbench—the circle where he would stand while casting the spell that would be the culmination of his existence, the fulfillment of his desire. He could read every sign and sigil inscribed around the interior of that circle, signs and sigils that would protect him from any form of attack. He glanced toward the hearth, where normally a fire would roar. The ashes were cold, but it did not matter to Valdaimon; unlike the mortal whose castle this had been until the arrival of Heilesheim's armies, Valdaimon had no need for warmth. In fact, he preferred the cold.

He studied the room a moment longer, to be certain that all was in readiness. The shelves around the walls were largely empty: he had not yet had time to have all his library shipped from Heilesheim. But all the equipment he needed was here. A cold black pot hung over the hearth, emitting a foul odor. Valdaimon shuffled over to it, scooped up a ladle full of the brackish liquid it contained, and tasted it. It was done, fully steeped. He checked the high reading stand at the end of the workbench. His most precious volume lay open there, turned already to the appropriate page.

A squawk interrupted his examination of the room—his crow. The fat bird stood in a narrow window, actually an arrow slit. Valdaimon held out his arm, and the crow flew over, shedding feathers as it loudly flapped its tattered wings.

"Are you restless, too?" Valdaimon whispered to the bird. "You need not be. There is work again for you." The mage whispered a short incantation, then spoke aloud to his black-eyed servant. "Go back to Bagsby. Seek him out. Follow him. Listen to him. Then, when his whereabouts are certain, go to Kala to the thief Nebuchar and tell him what you've learned," Valdaimon commanded.

The crow squawked loudly once, spread its wings, and beat the air noisily until it was through the narrow window and flying upward into the night sky.

Valdaimon once more circled the room, double-checking that all was in readiness. Finally satisfied, he walked to a large open area between the workbench and the circle on the floor. He reached out his hand and touched the coolness of metal.

At his touch, the Golden Eggs of Parona, at last his, became visible. They rested on a block of pure white marble. Two hollows had been carved and smoothed in the top of the stone, one to cradle each of the fabulous golden eggs.

Now Valdaimon moved very carefully. From the litter on the workbench he picked up a cup made of silver, which he filled with a portion of the vile fluid from the cold iron pot on the hearth. Moving with measured steps as he intoned a singsong chant and mentally counted each step, the wizard walked back to the eggs and, as the chant reached it vocal peak, poured the vile fluid over the tops of the eggs. When only a tiny amount of the potion remained, he concluded his chant and raised the cup to his lips, draining the last of the liquid.

Valdaimon felt a cool thrill as the power of the potion took effect. All things were more clearly visible now, in their true natures, than they had been only instants before. The eggs glowed with a brilliant red aura, an aura of stunning magical energy that swirled and pulsated in patterns five millennia old. The wizard carefully walked to the reading stand and took up the large tome. The book, too, glowed with a magic aura of black and crimson—a black so black it could almost be felt. He cradled the open book in his right arm, returned to the workbench, and took up a small silver wand. The wand, too, glowed with magical energy, as did the tiny, specially cut and fashioned black sapphire embedded in the wand's tip.

Again treading cautiously, taking care lest he trip or stumble on the uneven stones that formed the floor of the room, Valdaimon moved into the circle. He bowed to the four cardinal points of the compass, indicated by sigils. Then he turned to face the golden eggs and bowed again. He stooped down and laid the wand on the stone floor. Rising, he grasped the book in both hands.

A thrilling chill of pure cold ran through Valdaimon's body as he began the casting. It had taken almost one hundred years of study, experimentation, thought, and research to determine the appropriate magical concepts that had to

underlie the spell he now began. The precise wording of
the spell had taken over two hundred years to develop. In-
gredients in the foul potion that dripped from the eggs had
been carefully aged for decades, including a great deal of
Valdaimon's own blood.

Although his mind was focused intensely on the spell as
he read aloud the words he had so carefully crafted, his
heightened senses conveyed to him all that was transpiring
in the castle. He could hear the breathing of the two
guards posted outside the only door to the tower room. He
could hear the snoring and grunting of the garrison in the
main chamber far below, and the snorting of their horses,
some inside with them, others stabled in makeshift lean-
tos on the hillside outside the castle walls. In all, a guard
of one hundred men secured the castle, and this hour,
against any interruption. Every man of that guard knew
that no one was to enter the tower room on pain of instant
death.

As he finished the first, and simplest, portion of the
grand spell, Valdaimon noted with satisfaction that his entire body was glowing with its own magical energy. He
had successfully invoked the power of the elements, the
planets, the stars, and several beings whose names alone
were too terrifying to be spoken by mortal wizards. The
raw energy roiled around his feet and flowed up his body,
bathing his trunk, arms, and hands, blending with the aura
of the book to create a dazzling chromatic display of ever-
changing color.

Next, he began to fashion and shape the energy thus acquired. His singsong chanting became punctuated more
and more with grunts, groans, rasps, and hacking, coughing sounds as he verbalized words of a magical tongue unheard by human or elven wizards for five thousand years.
Streams of energy formed themselves, streaking out from
his lips and his fingertips, darting toward the pulsating red
aura of the eggs. Sparks like sparks of flame erupted as the
opposing energies met. The red aura of the eggs flared,
then subsided, then flared again, as the streams from
Valdaimon grew in size and intensity.

The casting went on and on, as each particular type of

magical energy was brought under control, shaped, and tested in contact with the magic of the golden treasure. The reading of this portion of the spell took fully an hour. At length the wizard, his concentration perfect now, was content that the magical energy was properly honed and shaped.

Now, at last, to channel it, he thought. Without a single pause in his incantation, the wizard stooped over and grasped the wand, laying the book open in front of him on the floor. He remained kneeling, so as to see the magical text, and aimed the wand toward the golden eggs.

But before speaking the words of power that would force the summoned, shaped energy through the wand to achieve his ultimate aim, Valdaimon spoke the words that would activate the sigils of the circle. He called upon every spirit that served him, every elemental force, every force of the dark night sky, to protect him from the explosion of magical energy that was about to occur and from the wrath of the beings it would bring forth. The white-painted sigils began to glow with a silvery, moonlight quality, indication that Valdaimon's protection was complete.

At last, all was in readiness. Valdaimon paused in the casting for an instant. It was a planned pause, for he had known that at this crucial moment he would need to summon all the force of his own will to augment every last reserve of power at his command. Valdaimon stood, extending his left arm full-length, with the silver wand pointed directly at the fabled treasure of Parona. With a great shout that woke the sleeping guards in the castle's main room a full sixty feet below him Valdaimon uttered the final word of power that he had researched and fashioned, based upon a language almost as old as the gods themselves.

Chromatic streams of magical power flowed over Valdaimon's body, down his arm, and through the wand to crash with the force of a thousand lightning bolts into the red aura of the eggs. Valdaimon reeled backward involuntarily as the resulting explosion rocked the castle. His legs pumped up and down as his feet sought solid footing, for the floor stones were loosened and several jolted upward, out of place. Beneath the roar of the blast that would have deafened any mortal man so near to it Valdaimon could hear the shouts of the garrison, now fully awake. Already he could tell many of the men were near panic, and the very stones of the castle walls continued to shake.

The great wash of magical energy filled the entire room, save for a cylinder of space whose base was Valdaimon's protective circle. The blinding flash of the explosion remained for a full ten seconds before the last of the energy was dissipated, most of it eventually seeping out the arrow slits that served the room as windows.

Valdaimon regained his balance and allowed his eyesight to readjust. On the workbench behind the eggs, several parchments smouldered, and the array of beakers and vials was a shambles. But on the slab of white marble the two Golden Eggs of Parona stood, unchanged, unscathed, untouched, still surrounded by their pulsating red aura.

Valdaimon stood motionless, stunned. For a brief moment he waited, reserving judgment; perhaps the effect would be delayed; perhaps his pure will could still prevail; perhaps the eggs would yet crack open, revealing the leathery shells he knew were inside; perhaps yet they would do what above all else he wanted them to do: hatch.

They did not. The castle guards years later would recount that the scream of rage emitted from the tower was far more frightening than the explosion had been.

7

The Battle of Clairton

Cᴜʟᴅᴜꜱ ʙᴇᴀᴍᴇᴅ ᴡɪᴛʜ satisfaction as he detailed the latest troop movements to King Ruprecht, sweeping his big hands in broad arcs over his maps, occasionally stabbing at a critical point with his thick forefinger.

"The Fifth and Sixth Legions have already crossed from the County of the Wyche into Argolia. They're making their way along the border of the Elven Preserve northward, where they'll be in position to turn eastward toward Clairton—and into the flank of any army south that city," Culdus explained. "Fortress Alban is already besieged by the first four legions. How long it will hold out I'm not sure, but the latest dispatches indicate that the enemy's morale is failing rapidly."

"Yes, yes," the bored Ruprecht replied, barely glancing at the maps. The young monarch popped another cluster of sugared nuts, sprinkled with gold dust, into his mouth, and with a wave dismissed the serving girl with her tray of delicacies. "Everything's going according to our plan. I never thought conquest could be so boring." Ruprecht rubbed his fingers together, frowned, then disdainfully wiped them on his white shirt. "Damned hard, these camp conditions," he said.

"Your Majesty will be pleased to learn," Culdus continued, as enthusiastic as ever, "that the Tower of Asbel has surrendered without prolonged siege." That ought to get the whelp's attention, he thought.

"*We* distinctly recall," Ruprecht replied, sauntering over to look at the map more carefully and emphasizing the royal plural, "your prediction that the siege of Asbel could occupy several months."

"I attribute this unexpected success to the terror inspired by our ruthlessness toward those who resist. The garrison of Asbel hoped to avoid the fate that befell Kala," Culdus explained.

"Ah, I see," the king said. "Well, go on."

"The fall of Asbel frees four legions. The Tenth we'll use to garrison Kala and guard our lines of communication and supply."

"Yes," the king interjected. "We learned the importance of these from that unfortunate incident in Argolia." Ruprecht smiled; he loved discomfiting the stodgy Culdus.

"That was militarily insignificant," Culdus insisted.

"But not politically insignificant," Ruprecht rejoined. "King Harold is whipping all of Argolia into a war frenzy, and our agents report that the remaining members of the Holy Alliance are rallying to his assistance. How soon can we seize Clairton?"

"The legions are already marching. The Seventh, Eighth, and Ninth are passing through Kala as we speak, picking up the detachments there that were charged with the sack of that city," Culdus said. "In another day they will cross the border on the main highway. I expect a battle in three to four days, somewhere south of Clairton where Harold is gathering his forces."

"Another easy victory?" the king asked, throwing himself onto his large camp bed.

"Our system has proven invincible thus far," Culdus answered carefully. He made it a policy never to promise more to the king than he was certain he could deliver.

"Except in Argolia." Ruprecht pouted. "The defeat of our detachment there, by this upstart knight, was humiliating beyond endurance. I'll not tolerate such failure again."

"I understand, Your Majesty," Culdus responded stiffly.

"To insure our victory in the upcoming battle, you will make full use of Valdaimon's assistance. The League of the Black Wing is assembling in Kala. They will join the army there. As you leave, be so kind as to send back that wench with my sugared nuts, will you?"

Culdus nodded curtly and left the king's tent. Valdaimon again, he mused. Every day his influence grew more pow-

erful. Someday, Culdus thought, for the good of the kingdom that influence would have to be ended, permanently.
Then, to his surprise, Culdus realized he had not yet seen
the wizard today. He wondered what the old crow was up
to this time.

Valdaimon sat in his circle of protection, his head held
wearily in his hands. Not even his power was great enough
to hatch the eggs of the Ancient One. His memory
stretched back through the centuries; it was some six hundred years ago that he had first realized the true nature of
the Golden Eggs of Parona. From that day to this he had
dreamed of the power he could wield as commander, ruler
of the only dragons on the earth. With the dragons under
his command, he would be invincible. Without them, he
would have to continue this charade of mortality and his
association with, even dependence on, mere men.

The failure was devastating, even more so because of
the demands made on his power. I am exhausted, he
thought. For the first time in a century, I must rest. And
yet—the secret must be hidden in some scrap of legend,
some verse or tome I've overlooked.

Then he remembered. The shaman of the desert people!
The shaman he had sought in Laga! Those verses, those
scraps of the puzzle, must contain the secret that was
needed to make the eggs hatch!

The wizard knew what he must do. He would rest here
in Lundlow Keep and guard his treasure, but at the same
time he would send a portion of himself to Laga. This
time, no thief, no Bagsby, would prevent him from obtain-
ing the information he so desperately needed.

Carefully monitoring his remaining power, the exhausted mage stood and cast a new spell of invisibility
over the marble block and the Golden Eggs. Then, with a
terse call, he summoned the guards outside the door.

"In the storeroom off the main chamber you will find a
sealed crate," Valdaimon said to the nervous men. "Bring
it up here."

The guards jumped to obey. While they were gone,

Valdaimon sorted through his vials of potions until he found the one he sought.

The two soldiers returned, lugging a heavy wooden crate, so heavy that they'd enlisted the aid of two of their comrades to carry it up the tower stairs. Valdaimon bid them bring it into the room and place it in an empty space up against an outside wall. He studied the men carefully as they lugged the crate to the position he indicated. As they left, he ordered one man to stay.

The soldier looked nervously at the old mage; Valdaimon shut the door and waited until the two extra guards had descended the stairs. He reached into the tattered shreds that passed for his robe and pulled out the vial he had selected just moments before.

"Drink this," he commanded, passing the vial to the pale soldier.

So terrified was the man that against his own judgment he obeyed. Five seconds later his corpse collapsed to the floor.

Eager for his rest, Valdaimon acted swiftly. With a bit of red powder, he inscribed magical sigils at random around the floor of the room, including one on the first stone a man would step upon when entering the door. Then, with a quick incantation, he rendered these signs invisible. He dragged the soldier's body over to the crate and laid it out carefully, with the head touching one end of the big box. Then he opened the crate.

A bed of earth awaited him inside the crate—the earth in which his body had been first interred when he had tasted death many hundreds of years ago. The mage stepped inside the box. Already he could feel rest coming upon him. He lay down, taking from within his robe a gold chain with a large diamond set in a pendant. This he clutched tightly in his right hand. Then he reached up and pulled shut the lid of the crate.

Now entombed, Valdaimon began a final incantation. As he muttered the words he'd learned so long ago, the diamond began to glow softly, as if it possessed a life of its own. Into the gem the wizard poured his soul, where, disembodied, it could at last find rest for the period of time

Valdaimon set in his spell. But he did not pour all of his soul, all of his will, intelligence, memory, knowledge, and desire, into the gem. A tiny bit he directed through the walls of the crate into the body of the dead soldier.

Moments later, the soldier's body rose. Animated now by a bit of Valdaimon, the body moved and breathed. He carefully tested the muscles, the coordination, the voice. All exceeded his expectations; he had chosen well. The soldier walked carefully to the door, opened it, and stepped outside.

"What happened in there," the guard's breathless companion asked.

"None of your business," the animated corpse replied. "No one goes in or out, Valdaimon's orders. First one in that room dies, no matter what."

The second guard nodded in dumb comprehension of the order. His former friend began the long trek down the tower stairs. He had a long way to go; it would take him at least a week of hard riding to reach Laga.

Inside the tower room, in the bowels of the crate, the body of Valdaimon the wizard turned to dust.

Bagsby shook his head in near despair. The crowded camp tent of King Harold rang with the shouts of hotly debating nobles, as it had for the past six hours as the king vainly attempted to form some type of order of battle for the slaughter that would surely occur on the following day.

"I cannot serve under Sir Thomas, for he claims rights to the estate of our cousin, the late Sir George of Loomis, to which I have a superior claim," one knight was shouting to the king.

"Your claim is by marriage; mine is by blood," Sir George retorted. "I cannot possibly accept a rank equal to or lower than yours."

Twenty or more similar debates were occurring simultaneously. Armored knights pounded the table, beat their chests, rattled their swords, clanked their armor, beat on their shields, rolled their eyes to heaven, and invoked the gods to judge the justice of their claims. Compounding the difficulty were the claims of nobles from the surrounding counties and baronies, including a scratch force hastily sent south from mighty Parona. The result was that an organization for battle was being slowly cobbled together based more on arguments about genealogy going back for four generations than on the hard facts of military necessity.

Maybe Shulana had been right, Bagsby thought. She had urged him to forget the nonsense of battle. It was obvious that the Golden Eggs were already far south, somewhere in Kala; there was no reason for Bagsby to stay to fight a battle for Clairton.

"But," Bagsby had argued, "the king made me a knight, a real knight. Now I have lands to defend, honor to uphold. By the gods, what a burden!"

"The king played you for a fool," Shulana had said coldly. "You're a symbol for the people, nothing more, Sir Bagsby. Our business lies in Kala."

Bagsby hadn't mentioned that aside from upholding his knightly honor and defending his estates, the locations of which he did not even know yet, he'd rather be flayed by a professional torturer than go to Kala, where everyone in the Thieves' Quarter would know him on sight and be happy to collect the bounty Nebuchar had declared on his person. Thus far, Shulana's magic and his nearness to the king had prevented assassins from acting, but Bagsby knew that political favor was fleeting, and he didn't know enough about magic to trust his life to its protection.

At this moment, though, Bagsby wondered if even the assassins of Kala might not be preferable to this interminable, self-important bickering. King Harold seemed resigned to accepting these arguments until the wee hours of the morning. If something wasn't done, and quickly, this entire army would be shattered by the Heilesheim tactics which Bagsby now understood only too well.

"My lords," Bagsby shouted, "your attention for a moment, please!" Gradually the bickering died down; the only hero of the war to date commanded enough respect to be heard at least briefly. "My lords, the foe we face tomorrow I have faced before. Therefore, hear me a moment for the sake of my knowledge," Bagsby began. "You debate among yourselves over the honor of position in the line of battle. But I tell you, the enemy will use a method of battle that will deny us all honor unless we counter it."

The rowdy barons grew completely silent. Bagsby saw looks of grave concern on their broad, bearded and mustached faces. Threats to their honor were to be taken seriously. Well, Bagsby thought, so far it's working.

"The enemy's knights will not come forward to meet our charge, nor will they position themselves where we can charge them," Bagsby declared. "Rather, like the dishonorable cowards they are, they will hide behind their foot soldiers!"

"What?" came the chorus of cries. "That's unthinkable," one knight declared. "No knight would hide behind common footmen," another said skeptically.

"I tell you," Bagsby went on, "that this is exactly what the enemy did in battle against me. Our knights were forced to charge footmen. Had we not won a great victory, many a knight of ours would have lost honor that day."

"There's nothing but dishonor in riding down foot soldiers, at least until the enemy's knights have been defeated. Then, of course, a certain amount of butcher's work must be done," one of the barons reasoned.

"Quite right," Bagsby said. "And so, I propose that to foil this dishonorable behavior by our foe, we also put our footmen in the front lines. Let our archers and spearmen advance against theirs, and when their footmen are defeated, their knights will be forced to fight us!"

Silence greeted Bagsby's proposal. The knights and lords looked glumly at one another and at the floor of the tent. None wanted to oppose Sir John Wolfe in open council, but his notion was near mad.

"Let our footmen attack first?" one knight finally queried. "Wouldn't that be the same as what the enemy is doing?"

"No, there is no dishonor in this for us," Bagsby declared forcefully. "For they use their footmen to avoid battle, while we would be using ours to force the knights to fight."

The king rose to his feet. "Sir John, as usual, speaks wisely," he announced. "We will adopt this plan."

"I kindly thank Your Majesty," Bagsby said quickly, before dissenting voices could be raised. "Now, as touching the order in which our knights line up for battle, I would propose that we form one mass, under the command of the king. Let every knight be positioned a distance from the king proportional to the number of men he has brought to this battle. And let the king decree that this order of battle shall have no bearing on any future disputes over land and titles."

"By the gods, an ingenious scheme," King Harold said with relish. "Assemble your forces," he commanded the lords. "We will count the men before sunset, and I shall announce the order of battle at dawn. The council of war is concluded."

There was much murmuring but no open dissent as the crowd of lords, still not certain what had happened, filed slowly out of the royal presence. Bagsby attached himself to the crowd and waited his turn to exit the royal presence. He was eager for the comforts of his own tent, and, he admitted to himself, the company of Shulana.

"Sir John Wolfe," King Harold called, "a moment."

The king waited until the tent had cleared, then quietly said to Bagsby. "You have brought to the battle only yourself."

"That is true," the little thief agreed, feigning surprise.

"Then you would take station far from us. But, as the appointed commander of our Royal Guard, you have brought to the battle the largest single force of any knight."

"Your Majesty knows full well that I have not the experience or military knowledge to command Your Majesty's Guard. Let the honor fall to another," Bagsby pleaded.

"I think not," King Harold answered. "We would have you, of all people, close to us in this battle."

"Your Majesty does not trust me?"

"On the contrary," King Harold said. "We trust you to be lucky, as always, and we would have good fortune with us in this bloody affair."

"It will take more than good fortune to defeat the legions of Heilesheim," Bagsby said. "May I speak my mind?"

"By all means. You are one knight I can trust to give me candid advice, when it suits your purpose to do so. That's another good reason to have you by my side. I know that if our royal person is threatened, you will honestly suggest what should be done."

Bagsby grinned. The king, he knew, was only partially in jest. "Your Majesty knows I do not think like a knight or a general—"

"Thank the gods for that. Few enough of them have any sense," King Harold interjected.

"I fear we shall lose this battle," Bagsby stated. "The men of the legions of Heilesheim are well trained to work together. With them, discipline is greater than pride of place."

"I fear you are correct," the king admitted. "There is more. The Heilesheim forces come in two groups. My agents report two full legions approaching Clairton from the west, while three march from the south along the great highway. Rather than divide my force to face two threats, I must fight as one unit, where at least my will can maintain order. And I would rather not face the danger of being flanked. Sound strategy would dictate a vigorous defense of the city from within its walls, then a retirement to the north. Yet I must fight to defend my greatest city. Failure to do so would bring . . . dishonor."

"Does Your Majesty think like a knight?" Bagsby asked.

"A king must think like many types of men."

"If Valdaimon is there, they will use magic against us," Bagsby cautioned.

"Our priests will stand around me—and you. They, too, have magic. But it is not magic that will decide this day, but rather cunning and the desire to win."

"Let it be as Your Majesty says," Bagsby replied. Though he had faced death countless times in his career, for the very first time, Bagsby felt afraid that he would die and sad that it might be so.

* * *

Bagsby stood on the broad open plain at the foot of the hill where King Harold's tent was pitched and gazed into the cool night down the broad highway toward the enemy camp. Three full legions of Heilesheim troops camped not three thousand yards away. Their camp fires dotted the dark landscape like gleaming, red, hostile stars. Closer in front of him, Bagsby could hear the calls of the sentries and pickets of both armies as they exchanged the night passwords and shouted taunts across the field to one another. Behind him, atop the very low rise, Argolia's forces rested for the day to come. Most of the common men were fast asleep, too weary from marching, drilling, and carrying the excessive burdens of their knightly masters to allow the fear of death to deny them rest. The knights, however, stirred; Bagsby could hear them clanking about in the camp, talking in their deep voices, spinning tales of battles lost and won, dreaming of the great ransoms they would earn for the prisoners they would take, predicting a great victory on the morrow.

Shulana stood silently beside Bagsby, the toes of her tiny bare feet wriggling happily in the low grass. She knew that Bagsby had something on his mind—he seldom asked her to walk with him alone, and when he did, it meant he wanted advice. It pleased her more than she cared to admit that he wanted to be with her now, even though she still thought him a fool for becoming committed to a battle when their real objective lay to the south and time was against them.

"Shulana," Bagsby said softly, "I fear we will lose this battle tomorrow."

"Almost certainly," she agreed. "I too have seen the Heilesheim men fight. This vast collection of knights will be no match for them, and the foot troops are not used to fighting on their own without their knights to goad them forward and protect them. The enemy will certainly use magic, which most of these men have never seen. They will panic."

"I am not a coward," Bagsby continued, not responding to her gloomy assessment of the situation.

Shulana was puzzled. "Who has said you are a coward?" she asked. She sat down in the cool, damp grass and let the green life of it touch her bare legs. Had Bagsby not needed her now, she would have communed this night. All the new green life of spring called to her elven nature, and yet she resisted because this human, who irritated her, needed her.

"No one has said I am a coward," Bagsby answered, staring into the dark distance. "At least," he added with a chuckle, "not here and not recently. What I mean is, for the first time, I feel afraid to die."

"You have faced death many times. I have never seen you afraid before," Shulana said. "Why should you fear now something you have beaten many times in the past?"

Bagsby squatted down beside her and placed his hands on the wet grass, loving the feel of it. His lungs drank in the night air, laden with spring scents. He listened intently to the sounds of insects celebrating love in the spring night. His hands happened upon a small mint plant growing in the meadow. He plucked a flat leaf, crushed it between his fingers, and popped it in his mouth. The crisp flavor exploded powerfully, bringing tears to his eyes.

"I fear it now," Bagsby said very softly, "because now I feel that life is worth living."

"Because you can gain revenge on Valdaimon?" Shulana asked.

"No, although that is one thing I would like to do."

"Then why?"

"Because . . ." Bagsby stopped his mouth and thought. Because why indeed? How could he explain that life seemed worth living partly because he now felt as though he himself had some value? How could he explain that he feared to lose that value? And how could he explain that, for some reason he still refused to face fully, he did not want to leave her?

Bagsby did not explain. Instead he leaned his face over toward Shulana's and gently brushed her cheek with his lips.

Shulana placed a slim elven hand on Bagsby's cheek

and stared, partly puzzled, partly strangely thrilled, into his eyes. "Promise me one thing," she whispered.

"What?"

"After the battle, lost or won, you will continue with our mission to steal the treasure of Parona."

Bagsby grunted. That again. "We'll have to go to Kala to do that, you know. Every thief and cutthroat in that city will be after my blood."

"I know. I will share the danger with you."

"Oh, all right. After the battle, we press on for the treasure," Bagsby said grumpily, turning away from her. "You have the word of a knight," he added sarcastically.

"Good," Shulana said merrily, leaping to her feet. "Then you need not fear death in the battle, for you have given your word to accomplish a great feat after it!"

Bagsby snorted, then joined her in laughter.

Four miles to the west, George the miller's son lay on the earth and stared up at the stars, unable to sleep. He, too, had concerns about the battle coming in the morning, even though the scuttlebutt had it that his unit, the Fifth Legion, would pounce on the enemy's flank with thunderclap surprise. But it was not the fear of death that bothered George.

"Frederick, you awake?" he whispered.

"Is 'at you, Georgie?" a weary voice muttered from only a few feet away. "Go to sleep. We've a battle to fight when we get up."

"Aye, and that's what I'm thinkin' about," George said. He raised himself up on an elbow and glanced about at the crowded camp. Men were sprawled hither and yon around their camp fires, and the stands of mighty pikes stabbed upward into the night sky. Horses snorted and neighed from somewhere nearby, but there was neither a noble nor even their own leader of a score in the immediate area. All the men within easy earshot of George were snoring. It was safe, he decided, to speak his mind.

"What I mean is, who does the fightin' and killin', really?" George said. "We do, that's who. And what do we get? A few baubles, a few women, a few night's carouse, and then it's on to the next town where we do it again."

"Right!" Frederick agreed. "Ain't soldierin' grand? It's better than sweatin' in a field all day and listenin' to my old woman grouse through the night with her cold ugly feet up agin' me, I tell you that."

"No, no," George said, exasperated. "That ain't what I mean. What I mean, is, look at them nobles, them knights. What do they do? They ride out across the field after the enemy's been beat and chop up them 'at can't fight into little bits, that's all. And what do they get? More than baubles and wenches and booze, I'll tell you that. It was the likes of me and you that conquered Dunsford, remember? And who owns Dunsford now?"

Frederick raised his face from the ground and wiped a smudge of mud from his nose. "The knights own it, of course. That's the way of things. What are you gettin' at?"

"A knight dies as easy as a common man," George said gruffly. "I ought to know; I've skewered 'em a-plenty on me pike. So why don't we get some of the good stuff—the lands, the riches, the titles, all that?"

Frederick rolled over with his back to George and dropped his head back to the ground. "You're daft," he said. "Them is noble, and we is common, and that's the way of it, that's all. Quit talkin' nonsense and let me sleep. If our leader of a score hears you sayin' things like that, it'll be a noose or an axe for both our necks."

"Aye, that's the way of it, all right," George said. "And the noose and the axe for us if we get out o' line. Well, maybe it's time the way of things was changed. Maybe it's time we showed them a noose and an axe, and took what our own sweat and blood 'as won."

Frederick made no response. George stared at his friend for a moment, then shook his head in disgust. The way of things changed right enough when the nobles wanted it to—that's what wars was about, George thought. They was about one bunch of nobles wantin' to change the way things was for another bunch of nobles. And when they wanted that to 'appen, they got a big bunch of millers'

sons and peasants' sons and other people's sons together
and made them go change it.

George lay back down and stared up at the sky. Maybe
the gods had decreed the way things was, he thought. No
matter. As far as George could tell, the gods hadn't done
much for him. They must be as bad as the nobles, he decided. With such angry thoughts keeping him awake,
George awaited the dawn.

Fat Marta waited until all were asleep in the wagons
and on the ground around her. Even then the camp was
noisy with the sounds of snoring men and women, the
muttering of small children in their dreams, and the occasional moans of lovers, secreted in the bushes off the side
of the road.

Marta had planned her move for days, ever since she realized there was to be a battle and the little tailor she now
worked for was going along with the camp to mend the
knights' tunics and cloaks and look after the thousand
other sewing chores associated with a great army. She had
gathered what she needed by a combination of barter, bar-
gaining, and theft. Now, on the eve of battle, she was
ready.

Marta raised herself up from the damp ground and
checked the area around her again carefully. No one
stirred. From the wagon came the soft sounds of the tailor's mild snores. Marta stealthily stood and hefted up the
great cloth bag in which she carried her few possessions.
She stepped over the body of an armorer's apprentice who
had passed out drunk beside her and carefully picked her
way through the bushes at the side of the road.

The night was dark and the moon had already set; the
army was more than a mile ahead on the road. Once she
was out of the area of the camp, Marta moved freely over
the grassland without fear of being seen. She made her
way to the small stream that had provided water for the
camp, then worked her way southward along its banks until it meandered into a copse.

There, in the shelter of the trees, Marta laid her bundle
on the stream bank and stripped off her clothes. She

stepped into the stream and gave herself a quick, bracing cold bath. When she came out of the water, her large folds of fat were covered with gooseflesh. She knelt by the bank. Her hands dug in the mud at the edge of the water, and she smeared it thickly on her face and hands.

That done, Marta carefully unpacked her large sack and laid out the garments she had so carefully collected. First came the tunic. It had been a tight fight, but she'd let it out at the seams and filled in the gap with a strip of bright red material that did not match. No matter, she had thought. No one will see it unless I'm dead or dying. Next she drew on the breeches she'd swiped from the tailor's stores—a pair made of soft brown cloth and big enough to fit her, for they had belonged to the fat wagon driver who did nothing all day except drive the wagon and swill down heavily malted beer. The boots she'd stolen from a soldier who'd passed out drunk two nights ago; it was not hard to find a pair that fit her well.

The mail shirt, helmet, spear, small round shield, sword, and dagger had been more difficult to obtain. She chose not to think about the compromises she had made to get these items; instead, as she donned them, she thought about her late husband, Albert. She remembered how handsome he had looked, even on the night that he died. She remembered his severed head, lying in the mud, impaled on the spike of a morning star. She remembered how much she wanted to defeat the Black Prince who'd burned his mark into her back, how she wanted to slay him with her bare hands, to rip his heart from his chest and shove it, still beating, down his throat.

At length Marta finished. Only one touch remained. Marta grabbed a hunk of her hair and with the crude dagger, not nearly sharp enough, she cut it off short. She repeated this procedure until her hair was no more than a ragged crown upon her high forehead. Satisfied, she donned the helmet and began clanking her way downstream toward the soldier's camp. One more footman had joined the army of Argolia.

* * *

King Ruprecht's skittish white stallion pranced daintily in front of the three legions of Heilesheim. Cheers broke out from the ranks as he passed by, cheers that in truth were more directed toward Culdus, the large man on the steady gray war-horse that trotted solidly behind the king's mount.

It was a perfect day for battle. The sun was up, the sky was clear, and the air was cool but not cold. There was enough of a breeze to flutter the banners and standards, making them easier to see, but not so much that the archers would have difficulty with their aim.

Culdus allowed himself a smug smile as the king in his gleaming white armor with black dragon crest emblazoned on the cuirass fought to control his skittish horse. With each loud hurrah the horse would startle, back step, and almost rear into the air, making the young rider, trying so hard to look magnificent, appear ridiculous instead.

At the risk of upstaging the king, Culdus acknowledged each round of cheers with an upraised hand. After all, he thought, it was not the king who brought them this far and who would lead them to victory today. It was he, Culdus, who designed the most magnificent military system the world of men had yet known.

Only two things were spoiling the day for Culdus. The first was this ridiculous parade-ground display. The king had demanded it, saying that his parading before the army in full array in front of the enemy lines and allowing the enemy to see him cheered by his troops would dishearten the enemy soldiers. Probably nonsense, Culdus thought, but he did not object except for the delay. The sun was up; it was time to attack.

The second cloud on Culdus's horizon was the League of the Black Wing. The wizards and their specially trained wyvern riders had joined the army on its march northward from Kala. Now, in center of each legion block, a small contingent of mages stood, their fire and lightning spells ready to sow havoc in the enemy ranks. As if those would be needed, Culdus reminded himself. For the attack, against his advice, was to open with an air assault by the wyvern riders. This alone might be enough to break the enemy and send his forces fleeing back to Clairton. Culdus opposed the move for two reasons. First, he wanted to test his system on a large scale. This would be the greatest battle of the war so far, with fully twenty thousand enemy troops from all over the Holy Alliance arrayed against Culdus's well-honed legions. It would be pleasing to see what his men could do without all the claptrap of magic. Second, Culdus did not want the enemy forces to be routed too soon. In addition to the three legions deployed in battle array on the front, two more were even now marching from the west. If the delicate timing worked correctly, these two legions would fall on the enemy's right flank at the height of the battle, insuring the destruction of the foe. If the Argolians ran away too soon, many would live to fight another day.

Culdus reined in his horse and gazed across the field. The great red and gold banner of the King of Argolia and his Royal Guard stood at the center of the enemy's deep lines of mounted horsemen. That line stretched about a thousand yards across the field, with occasional gaps between the forces of the different noble commanders. Culdus was both pleased and surprised to see that the enemy's foot soldiers, instead of being deployed behind their knights, as was normal, were thrown in clumps out in front of the enemy's main battle line. There they stood, obviously poorly organized, just awaiting an attack that could scatter them like sand in the wind.

Culdus's own three legions were deployed in their block formation, with the center legion about two hundred yards forward of the flanking legions. This triangular wedge, Culdus knew, was extremely flexible and capable of responding to a threat from any direction save the rear. But this time there would be no threat to the rear. The wagon camp was heavily garrisoned with a detachment from the reserve legion, and south of Clairton an enemy force would find nothing but waste: burned fields, ruined villages, and pillaged towns.

King Ruprecht, having completed his parade across the front, rode over to Culdus, who had already taken his place at the front of the center legion, the Eighth.

"Well, Culdus, a fine day for it, is it not?"

"Indeed, Your Majesty. Now the sun is well up. Shall we begin?"

"Very well. Give the signal."

Culdus turned and shouted to the standard bearers at the front of the Eighth Legion, "Raise the standard of the League of the Black Wing!" The youth passed the order on, and quickly a huge green banner with the black dragon crest was held aloft from the center of the Eighth Legion.

From a position to the rear of the Heilesheim forces on the crest of a small knoll, a scout saw the banner and in turn shouted the command to the wyvern riders of the league.

Malak, Orgon, and Barak leapt to their feet.

"At last!" Barak cried. "At last, the league goes into battle. Riders, to your mounts!"

The field behind the knoll was covered with two hundred of the deadly reptiles who lolled in the sun, awaiting nothing. At Barak's order their masters began the process of kicking and cajoling the giant lizards to their feet and the sometimes dangerous process of mounting them. Barak lost no time in rousing his beast and climbing into the leather-covered wooden saddle secured to the monster's back.

"As we agreed, brothers," he shouted to Malak and Orgon, "I shall lead the first attack." The two older mages were only too happy to let Barak have that honor.

Gradually the flight began to form, as the greenish-black beasts extended their leathery wings and with ferocious flapping took to the sky. Their riders were of two kinds. One hundred were mages, armed with spells they would cast upon the enemy from on high. The second hundred were men-at-arms, drawn from the ranks of those most desperate for glory, who had mastered the skills of archery, spear hurling, and even fighting with longswords while mounted on their disgusting lizards. Each rider knew that his mount, too, was a formidable weapon. The mere sight of a wyvern in flight, its body and wingspan both approaching twenty feet, would terrify many a foe. The creatures' talons were sharper than most swords, and their mouths were lined with teeth whose sole purpose was to rend flesh. Finally, the long, serpentine tail of each beast carried a poisonous stinger. Men struck by it who survived the shock of the blow would die a painful death over a period of several minutes.

With Barak guiding them with hand signals, the riders circled low in the sky until all were airborne. Once aloft, they formed into three lines, like cavalry, and mounted higher into the morning sky. There, ahead, they saw the three great legions looking like a wedge made of square blocks. And beyond, they saw the enemy lines, with his infantry out front like wheat, waiting to be threshed.

Barak raised his magic staff, a hefty piece of wood about six feet long, high over his head and then lowered it toward the enemy lines. He pulled back the reins of his wyvern, and the beast mounted higher in the sky, preparing for the moment when it would suddenly lower its head, tilt its body forward, and dive down upon the hapless enemy.

From the Argolian ranks a cry of astonishment arose as the formation of wyvern riders burst into view, rising in the sky behind the enemy's carefully formed ranks.

"Flying beasts!" went the cry along the lines. The horses of the knights in the front ranks began to whinny and paw the ground; only with difficulty could their riders hold them in their ranks.

Bagsby stared in disbelief as the winged creatures edged higher in the sky. "What in the name of thousand demons?" he shouted.

"Wyverns," Shulana answered from her position by his side. "Flying beasts distantly related to the dragons of old. Watch for their tails—the sting is poisonous."

"Your Majesty," Bagsby called, suddenly alarmed for the sovereign's life, "you should quit the field at once!"

"Nonsense," shouted the king in reply. "Have your Guard stand their ground; our priests will deal with this. Only see that the infantry doesn't panic!"

Bagsby glanced at the priests who stood directly behind the king. Already their arms and eyes were raised to the heavens, and the names of the gods of Argolia tumbled from their lips in rapid succession as divine aid was sought to repel the airborne foe.

"Be calm," Shulana counseled. "It's the footmen who are in the greatest danger. We cannot afford for them to panic."

Bagsby wheeled his mount and looked down on the plain where the infantry were already starting to slowly move back toward the line of friendly knights. Their ranks were in disarray, and the archers, rather than preparing to fire death-dealing volleys into the air, were preparing to run.

"Stand!" Bagsby shouted to the Royal Guard as he spurred his own mount, a chestnut provided by the king, and rode hell-for-leather down the front of the hill, waving his sword in the air.

He plowed into the ranks of the disordered infantry. "Form ranks!" he cried. "Form up and stand! Archers, form line and ready to fire! Stand fast! The gods themselves are coming to fight for you!"

The presence of a knight on the field reassured some of the footmen, but the mass looked upon Bagsby as though he were a madman. Then the storm of magical attack broke upon them all.

The wyverns dived earthward, gaining speed as they plunged, their wings fully extended. One hundred mages pointed their wands downward, and brilliant orange, yellow, and blue streams of magical fire shot forth ahead of them, streaking toward the Argolian foot soldiers.

"Fireballs!" Bagsby shouted. "Drop to the ground, drop to the ground!" Bagsby's mount circled about in the mass of men who, seeing flaming death dropping toward them from the heavens, began to drop their weapons and run pell-mell toward the imagined safety of their knights.

The fireballs hit only seconds later, with devastating effect. The entire one thousand yards of the Argolian front was engulfed in balls of flame to a depth of more than one hundred yards. Countless hundreds of the infantry were instantly incinerated. Thousands more fell screaming to the ground, rolling and slapping themselves in an attempt to extinguish their flaming tunics, breeches, and hair.

Bagsby's horse plunged to the earth, and the little thief felt the fall coming in time to hurl himself off the horse and land beside it rather than beneath it. In the next instant the horse was a mass of burning flesh, and Bagsby's pants were aflame beneath the scorchingly hot plate mail he wore. Like countless others, Bagsby began to roll in the grass, hoping to put out the flames, gagging and choking on the greasy smoke that roiled all around him.

"For Heilesheim!" Barak cried high in the sky as his wyvern led the mass downward. The first line of the beasts soared through the smoke, dropping within a few feet of the ground. Unfortunate men screamed as the razor-sharp talons of wyverns ripped through their body armor, pierced their sides, and, grasping them firmly about the ribs, lifted them into the sky. More men writhed and screamed as the horrid stinging tails dropped down out of the thick smoke, plunging into backs and stomachs to pour in their deadly, burning venom.

Bagsby put his head down and crawled in the direction he hoped was toward his own lines. This, he thought, was disaster.

The wyvern-mounted archers had just set their bows and were in the last portion of their dive when the Argolian gods answered the prayers of the priests.

Bagsby felt the ground shake violently; he tried to hug the soil, but his body bounced up into the air nonetheless, to land again quickly with a thud that drove the burning breath from his pain-filled lungs. Then he felt the wind.

Barak screamed aloud in terror as his wyvern, at the head of the flight, was suddenly tossed backward in the air, spinning head over tail. The roar of the wall of wind that hit him was so great that he could not even hear the cries of the riders who came behind him. The great lizards were tossed randomly in the air like dust in a whirlwind, and their riders, almost to the man, toppled from their mounts to be carried away by the air itself, until both wyverns and men were dropped to plunge to the earth far below, where many met their death.

Culdus swore a mighty oath as the helpless wyverns were smashed back toward his tightly packed legions, a few crashing down to their death right in the midst of his formations, burying men beneath them. The wind ripped through the ground forces as well, taking with it the loosely held spear or bow, and toppling Culdus's own horse and the horses of the mounted nobles in their ranks behind the great infantry wedge.

"Damn all wizards and priests!" the general shouted. "You see, you see," he cried, fighting to rise to his feet, "what comes of allowing wizardry in battles!"

"I see defeat," the king shouted back, straining his throat to make himself heard above the howl of the wind, "unless you act swiftly."

Culdus tried to gain his feet again, and once more the wind tumbled him back to the ground. A third time he tried to rise and found to his surprise that he could. The wind was dying. It had had the beneficial effect of clearing the smoke of the fireball attack, so the field of battle could now be clearly seen. A great patch of scorched earth littered with burning corpses extended across the front of the Argolian lines, but the main cavalry force was still intact. Dying wyverns and their riders screamed and bleated in pain and terror, but to these Culdus paid no heed.

He raised his right arm and shouted, "The legions will advance!" Those few drummers who still had their instruments began to beat the pace, and slowly the great block formations, still roughly in their wedge, began crawling forward, their front bristling with the deadly points and hooks of the eighteen-foot-long pikes that made them so effective.

Bagsby, meanwhile, had reached the top of the hill, where two lackeys sent by the subcommanders of the Guard to find him helped him to his feet. A great cheer erupted from the Argolian knights as the little man staggered over the top of the hill, his face and armor black with greasy soot.

King Harold still held his position at the center of the line, and before the cheering had stopped, Bagsby found himself on a fresh mount at the king's side, with Shulana discreetly taking her station on his left.

"The gods fight for us today," King Harold suggested.

"Yes, but our footmen are all but gone, and the enemy advances," Bagsby replied, coughing from the smoke he had inhaled.

"Whatever happens now, hold the Royal Guard as a reserve!" the king commanded. All around the king and Bagsby the chants of the priests rose heavenward again.

"What now?" Bagsby wondered.

"Thunderbolts from your god of war," Shulana said quietly.

"Eh?" Bagsby replied. But even as he spoke the sunlight that had drenched the field disappeared, and Bagsby shot his gaze skyward to behold thick, black thunderheads forming.

Culdus, too, saw the clouds and had some idea of what the enemy intended. Whether the attack took the form of fire or lightning, his tightly packed masses could hardly survive such a strike.

"Deploy!" he shouted. "Deploy!"

Only the Eighth Legion in the center of the wedge heard the shouted command. Their few drummers quickened their beat, and the formation began to break apart, each battle moving toward one flank or the other, as the six thousand men attempted to transform themselves from a giant block into a line three ranks deep extending across a front of nearly a thousand yards, with the archers and wizards tucked behind the front lines.

The legion was in the midst of this maneuver when the lightning fell from the sky. Thunderbolts of pure energy thicker than the most ancient trees fell from the black clouds, forked, and plunged into the moving bodies of the Heilesheim men. The earth itself rebelled against this onslaught of pure energy, spewing up great clods of mud and rock. Dozens of men were burned to death; still more stumbled and fell into the ten-foot-deep pits the bolts opened in the earth where they hit. But even worse, the legion began to lose its tightly disciplined formation. The men, blinded by the lightning flashes, deafened by the thunder, and stumbling into the pits, could not find their positions to form the battle line.

"Now! Now is the moment!" King Harold shouted over the cheers of his knights. "All but the Guard—charge!"

Culdus ran through the mass of his disorganized troops, trying to gain sight of the Seventh and Ninth legions and trying to find the contingent of wizards who marched with the Eighth. He feared that the Eighth was doomed; in their current state they could not possibly stand against the charge of twelve thousand horses that at this moment was flying across the field toward them. At last he thrust his way through the last of his pikemen. Overhead, the clouds began to slowly dissipate, and Culdus saw with relief that the Seventh and Ninth were still advancing, relatively intact, still in their block formation.

Now to save the Eighth, he thought. He whirled around, searching wildly for his wizards. For the first time in his long life, he was actually glad to see one. They were still an intact mass, and had even seen the danger descending upon them. They chanted and muttered strange sounds and waved their arms in the air in the manner Culdus had seen Valdaimon do countless times.

None too soon, Culdus realized, for he heard the mighty crash of the first line of Argolian cavalry plunging into the milling, unformed ranks of the pikemen of his center legion. Without their tight formation, the pikemen were nearly helpless against the mounted foes, for their horses could weave their way between the individual men. The knights began with relish their task of hacking down the enemy foot.

The second line followed hard upon the first at a distance of only fifty yards, but before it could tear into the front of the Eighth, the Heilesheim wizards' spell was completed. Culdus stumbled and fell as the very earth trembled. There was another deafening crash, deeper than the sound of the thunderbolts, and the earth itself began to rip open in a huge crack along the Heilesheim front. Into this widening ditch the Argolian horse galloped. Some made the leap and crashed into the enemy lines; more did not, and horses and armored riders tumbled screaming and neighing into the very bowels of the earth.

From the small rise at the center of his original line,

King Harold looked on aghast as some of his cavalry made good progress through the enemy but even more seemed to disappear, swallowed by the ground itself.

"Priests!" he shouted. "Do what you can!"

"Majesty," the high priest responded, "our power is spent. One can only tax the gods so much, and then . . ."

"Sir John Wolfe, what do you recommend?" the king demanded, his voice beginning to be edged with despair.

Bagsby looked out on the field of battle where some of the Argolian mounted knights had broken through the lines of the center legion, only to begin swirling helplessly about the great block formations of the flanking legions.

"Before you answer," Shulana whispered in his ear, "listen." The slim elf pointed beyond the far right of the Argolian's original line.

From the distance, straining, Bagsby could just hear the sounds of drumming.

"Majesty, the enemy's two legions from the west are approaching," Bagsby said. As he spoke the first banner of the enemy force became visible, protruding above a distant rise. "Our main force will be flanked and trapped. There is no way for cavalry to break those blocks without magic or bowfire."

"Then our Royal Guard will charge the flanking force," King Harold said, his eyes wide with rage, frustration, and despair.

"No, Majesty," Bagsby said quietly. "Honor has been served. Save the Guard and yourself. Retire to the north of Clairton, pray for aid from Parona, and have a force left to join with theirs when they come."

The king sat silently, not responding to Bagsby's advice, but not ordering the Guard to charge, either.

The battle raged on for another full hour, as the inevitable doom of the Argolian force was played out. The Fifth and Sixth legions closed on the Argolian flank, leaving the surviving knights no avenue of escape. Still they fought on, many dismounting and managing to dodge between and amid the spearpoints to land a blow against a foe, but their struggle was doomed. King Harold sat silently, with

Bagsby beside him, until the last Argolian banners, save those of the Guard, had fallen to the ground.

"Sir John Wolfe," the king finally said, his voice heavy as lead, "the Royal Guard will retire to Clairton."

"Your Majesty," Bagsby replied, "I have fought with you as you required. Now I must beg your leave. For there is a task I must do, and do alone, in the enemy country. If I am successful, my success will redound to your benefit. If I fail, I will be but one more knight slain in this war, which now seems will engulf the whole earth."

King Harold stared numbly at Bagsby, the color draining from his face, his spirit broken. "Go then, Sir John Wolfe, and the gods of Argolia grant you fairer days than this has been for me."

"The gods keep Your Majesty until my return," Bagsby said. With a glance at Shulana, Bagsby gently spurred his mount and began riding slowly onto the field of battle, making for the extreme left.

"Dull work, eh, Frederick?" George said as his rank of pikemen advanced behind the Argolian horse. The only opposition they had encountered was in the form of dead men and beasts strewn about the field and the crumbling edges of the great gash in the earth which the legion cautiously avoided.

"True, I've seen hotter battles than this," Frederick responded. "But say now, look there!" Frederick inclined his head to the right, where three dismounted Argolian knights stood, swords in hand, desperate resolve written on their dark, sweaty faces. They were three against thousands, but they would die as men.

"Right!" George cried, and with a shout lowered his great pike and charged forward. About a dozen other men, Frederick among them, broke ranks and followed him. In fifteen seconds the three knights were dead, one of them impaled on George's pike.

"Let's see what we got 'ere now!" George shouted with glee.

"George son of the miller get back in ranks," barked the

leader of a score. "No one gave you the order to fight at will!"

"You get back in the ranks, then," George snapped. "Nobody ordered you to come after me!"

"You there," a third voice boomed, "get those men back in their ranks."

An armored Heilesheim knight rode up, his face red with fury. "Officer, get these men back in ranks, and see they're flogged when this day is done."

"I thought we were here to kill the enemy," George shouted at the knight. "Well, I done my bit, see, and I'm takin' a bit o' this plunder." He bent over the slain foe's body and began removing the man's scabbard.

A mighty blow caught George on the back of the head and sent him sprawling facedown in the blood-soaked earth.

"Hang this one," he heard the mounted man say.

Rage rose in George's bosom even faster than the pain spread through his head and body. With a sudden great effort he pushed himself off the ground, grabbed his pike, and pulled it from the dead man's body, blood dripping from its point and hook.

"'Ang me? You goin' to 'ang me, your lordship?" he shouted. "You ain't goin' to 'ang nobody!"

With a might heave, George plunged the pike into the back of the rider. The sharp blade of the hook sliced through the man's armor and the point bit into his back so deeply that it emerged through his cuirass in the front. The man turned in his saddle, blood spurting from between his lips, as George wrestled the pike around and brought his kill to the ground. Quickly, he pulled the great spear free and whirled to face his former companions.

"Anybody else want to 'ang me?" he bellowed.

"You men go on," the leader of a score ordered Frederick and the others. He then cautiously backed away from George. "Now, as for you, George, go on about your business, and we'll settle all this back in camp after the battle."

"Aye," George said, grinning with understanding. The ranks of the Fifth continued to parade past, while George, shedding bits and pieces of his armor as he went but still clutching his great pike, wandered into the chaos of the battlefield, making his way east and south, headed for freedom.

Bagsby rode carefully, keeping a sharp eye out, as he led Shulana around the field of the lost battle. Still the conflict raged in isolated spots, even after King Harold had quit his post on the hillcrest and the Royal Guard had begun their long march back toward Clairton and ignominy. Bagsby began to shed his armor, not wanting to be taken for an Argolian by some band of wandering Heilesheim soldiers. For now the tight formations were breaking up, and bands of armed men were beginning to roam the field, stripping the dead, fighting for loot and plunder, and chasing down any Argolian unlucky enough to still be alive.

He made for the far hill, hoping that beyond it he could find a bit of woods for shelter and cover. As he rode, his cares began to evaporate, and despite the carnage within easy sight and the magnitude of the victory won by Ruprecht, Bagsby felt suddenly and strangely lighthearted. He began to whistle as he rode.

"You've not done that for a great while," Shulana called to him as she rode by his side.

"Not done what?"

"Whistled."

"I've not felt like it until now!" Bagsby gleefully shouted back. In fact, he thought, I do feel better. I don't much like being a knight and a general, but a good sneaky job—that's more my style. And with a beautiful woman by my side—elf, Bagsby reminded himself—I feel glorious. It's a wonder to be alive!

On the pair rode, past the field of battle until they came, as Bagsby had hoped, to a place where a small stream flowed out of a copse.

"Over there," Bagsby directed, and Shulana gladly agreed. The two guided their mounts in among the trees, out of any possible sight of the Heilesheim troops who were still coming and going across the field and up and down the great highway.

No sooner had Bagsby reined his steed to a halt than he thought he had made a mistake.

"Die, you Heilesheim dog!" a clearly female, though very loud, voice was screaming.

"I'll die soon enough, wench," came the laughing reply. "But give us a kiss first. Hah!"

There was a great crash in the bushes and out from between two trees tumbled a large man, his right hand still gripping a great Heilesheim pike, with an even larger, most bizarre woman riding him down. The man fell onto his back with a loud thump and an oath, while the woman, who was dressed in scorched men's clothing, clouted him about the ears with all her might.

George the miller's son got his kiss, but his left ear was bleeding by the time he finally managed to hurl fat Marta off himself. The hefty would-be warrior staggered to her feet, then her gaze took in the little man and the elf who had blundered into them.

Marta formed her fists and turned slightly, her feet spread wide apart, so she could face both George and these newcomers. "Friends or foes of Argolia?" she challenged.

"Friends," Bagsby called back, breaking into laughter despite himself. "And who might you be?"

"My name is Marta from Shallowford in Dunsford, and this is a Heilesheim beast!" she said, shaking a fist in George's direction.

"Not no more I ain't," George declared.

"How's that?" Bagsby inquired.

"I killed a Heilesheim noble and earned myself an 'anging', that's 'ow," George said.

"What?" Marta asked, her face forming a scowl.

"That's what I been tryin' to tell you," George said. "I'm a deserter. I got no more love for Heilesheim now than you do."

Bagsby had stopped laughing, for now he recognized this woman, the same one he had seen in the King Harold's council chambers on a day that already seemed long ago. Apparently she had fought in the battle alongside the Argolian footmen.

"Marta," Bagsby asked, "what are you doing here?"

"I've come to kill the Black Prince and all who serve him," the feisty woman snarled, still eyeing George with no little distrust.

"Then you'd better fall in with us," Bagsby offered. "There's no use trying to get back north now."

"And where are you going?" George asked. "Are you deserters too?"

"Of a sort," Bagsby admitted. "We're going south. We're going to strike a blow against Valdaimon, Ruprecht's wizard."

Shulana reached out and grabbed Bagsby's arm. "Are you mad?" she whispered. "You can't trust these strange people."

"There are few people I trust more than those out for revenge," Bagsby said, gesturing toward Marta, "and cutthroats and scoundrels," he added, gesturing toward George. "The former have but one purpose and can be trusted to try to carry it out. The latter may have any purpose, but it is always to serve themselves. They too, can be counted on to be most predictable." Bagsby laughed again. He was beginning, he thought, to feel like his old self.

"Will there be killing and plunder, and will I be under orders from some knight?" George asked.

"Yes to the first question, no to the second," Bagsby said. "Just a bunch of hardy thieves out to foil an enemy of all men."

"I'm no thief," Marta insisted indignantly.

"Oh no?" Bagsby said. "Then where did you get your weapons and armor?"

Marta lowered her eyes. "Sometimes a poor widow is forced to do a few things . . ."

Bagsby roared with laughter. "Look, Shulana, only twenty minutes back into the thief business, and I've a great gang already!"

In the treetops high above, a ragged black crow echoed back Bagsby's laughter.

➺8⇇

Dragonspawn

A SINGLE SHOUT from Nebuchar, who actually emerged from the tiny room, which served him as business office, eating quarters, and even sleeping quarters, stilled the commotion in his tavern. The usual band of cutthroats, thieves, and murderers quickly fell silent when the most powerful leader of all vice and crime in the Land Between the Rivers made it clear that their racket was disturbing his rest. He was even more angry to learn that the ruckus was caused by a bird that had flown into the tavern. Every vagabond and roughneck in the place had tried to kill the thing.

Nebuchar held out his arm and the scraggly feathered, fat crow landed on it at once. The big man retreated to his tiny sanctuary and placed the bird on the small table, where it cocked its head, looked at him, and cawed loudly.

"All right, enough," Nebuchar growled. "Just a minute."

From a plain wooden box that sat by the foot his chair he withdrew the vial of blue liquid that Valdaimon had given him. How badly, he wondered, did he want Bagsby dead? Badly enough to risk being poisoned by Valdaimon? He placed the vial on the table by the bird. His fingers felt cold. He stared at the bottle and rubbed them. He had not become the greatest lord of crime in the human world by not knowing when to trust and when not to trust, he told himself. Valdaimon wanted Bagsby dead as much as he did. Therefore, he probably wouldn't poison Nebuchar until that job was done.

"Bah!" the man said. He grabbed the vial, yanked out the cork, and downed the potion in a single gulp.

201

The crow cawed again, but this time Nebuchar heard his name.

"Nebuchar," the bird repeated.

"Tell me of Bagsby," Nebuchar demanded.

"He is coming here, to see you."

"When?"

"Soon."

"Is he alone?" Nebuchar asked, still hardly able to believe that Bagsby would risk coming to Kala.

"No."

Nebuchar grunted. Obviously the crow only gave the information you asked for.

"Who is with him?"

"An elf, a soldier, and a fat woman," the bird said plainly.

"What else can you tell me?" Nebuchar gruffly demanded.

"I'm hungry."

"Here, sit in my hand, and I'll feed you," Nebuchar said.

The crow obediently hopped into the man's outstretched palm. Nebuchar closed his hand and squeezed. The bird kicked and clawed and cawed, but to no avail. In seconds its insides were crushed. Nebuchar twisted its neck with his free hand to finish it off. That, he thought, would teach Valdaimon a lesson.

Far away, in another realm of reality, entered through a gemstone in this world, the slumbering soul of Valdaimon stirred uneasily. Something, his partial consciousness realized, was wrong. But what? What? Then his soul sank back into the blackness of the rest of the undead.

The journey to Kala had taken three weeks. During that time, Bagsby thought, his little band had molded together quite nicely. George, it turned out, had a strong talent for throat cutting with the dagger and goring with the pike, a talent Bagsby had occasion to make use of more than once. He also had a weakness for women, which was a weakness Bagsby could respect. That George's particular weakness was for women of stout build had caused

Bagsby and Shulana considerable relief and Marta no end
of grief, which she had voiced loudly whenever it was safe
to do so.

That had not been often. Traveling through the country-
side, avoiding the roads, hiding, stealing food when necessary, and fighting the occasional Heilesheim man-at-arms
who discovered them was a dangerous business, and there
had not been much time for careless chatter. There was
even less time now that they were in Kala.

Of course Shulana had thought Bagsby mad to head for
Kala. Valdaimon, she argued, would never leave the treasure in so obvious a place as the city. But Bagsby had
countered that the one man who would most likely know
where Valdaimon was, and therefore the location of the
treasure, was Nebuchar.

Amid the burned-out buildings of the city, scuttling
around like the few surviving citizens, the foursome had
not attracted much attention from garrison troops. These
men had lost their edge, Bagsby noticed, from their easy
duty. Penetrating the Thieves' Quarter, however, was another matter. Every protected cutthroat in the city, Bagsby
knew, would be looking for him. He would have to strike,
strike quickly and quietly, and get out.

"One thing in my favor," Bagsby had told his small
gang, "is that I know all his tricks. That tiny room he
holes up in is a secret fortress. None of the usual ruses
will work."

"What do you mean?" Shulana had asked.

"Well, for example, an invisibility potion is no good,
because he has hidden sigils in the floor that break the
spell. Nebuchar was always a master at protecting himself."

"The sigils could be seen by a wizard," Shulana had
suggested.

"But I'm not wizard," Bagsby had said.

"But I am," Shulana had answered.

Thus Bagsby found himself waiting in the street outside
Nebuchar's tavern. Shulana had almost exhausted the powers of her magic preparing for this bold strike. She had
rendered Bagsby invisible, and then silent. Not only could

he not speak, no action he took would make any sound. Next, she had cast a spell that, she said, would enable her to see magic auras of any kind, even those from Nebuchar's invisible sigils.

Now, armed with nothing more than a handful of violets and a small sack of gold, she was venturing alone inside Nebuchar's tavern. George and Marta were stationed just across the narrow alleyway outside, while Bagsby stood right by the door, close enough to touch anyone coming in or out and within easy earshot of any disturbance inside.

Shulana flung open the tavern door and strode boldly inside. Her slight feminine, elven form was clad in a short green tunic, belted at the waist. Hanging from her belt was a coin purse, and in her hand she carried a bunch of violets, nothing more.

"I seek Nebuchar," she announced loudly.

Her statement was greeted first with stunned silence, then with catcalls from the carousing vermin who frequented the place.

"He ain't here, honey, but we'll be glad to help you find what you want," one drunk bawled out.

"Me too," voiced another, and soon the room resounded with raucous laughter from would-be "suitors."

"I said, I seek Nebuchar. If you know what's good for you, you'll tell him I'm here. I have something he wants," Shulana said.

"We bet you do!" one rowdy replied.

Shulana's eyes drank in the scene; she saw the aura of magical items scattered about the room. One thief had a magic ring; one villain carried an enchanted blade; a third had an amulet that radiated powerful magic.

"I have come to bring him Bagsby," Shulana announced.

The room fell suddenly silent. Each man pondered whether to capture this elven wench and wring the secret from her or to be the first to alert Nebuchar of her presence. As it was, no decision was required. Nebuchar himself appeared in the doorway of his tiny room.

"Come in. I've been expecting you," he gruffly commanded.

What sort of treachery does she have in mind? Nebuchar wondered, as Shulana slowly and carefully, somewhat timidly, made her way through the tavern to his door.

"We must talk," Shulana said simply.

"Then sit down, close the door, and talk," Nebuchar said, taking his own chair by the plain table.

Shulana crossed the threshold. As she did, she dropped a tiny violet petal from her hand onto the sigil on the floor directly in front of the door. Other sigils were hidden beneath the table, on the seats of chairs, and in the corners of the room. Some were designed to make the invisible become visible; others had a more deadly effect—they could kill upon a word of command from the one for whose benefit they had been placed.

"Bagsby is in Kala," she said. "I can take you to him. My price is ten thousand gold crowns." She walked nervously around the room, dropping more petals as she went.

"Why should I trust you?" Nebuchar asked. "You've been traveling with him. Perhaps you're his ally."

Shulana noted that two of Nebuchar's gold rings glowed with a magical aura.

"Perhaps I am," she said, continuing her nervous pacing. "You'll have to decide."

"I've no need to pay you," Nebuchar said coolly. "I can find Bagsby for myself."

"So far you haven't."

"Maybe I will now, that I have a prisoner from his gang."

Nebuchar stood and moved quickly to the door. He thrust it open and called out, "Take this elf prisoner—and see that no harm comes to her. I may want her alive later."

Even as Nebuchar spoke, Bagsby, squeezing himself as flat as possible, slipped through the doorway. Once past Nebuchar, he jumped over the area marked by the violet petals toward the center of the room.

A group of rowdies moved to obey Nebuchar's command.

"Wait, please!" Shulana cried out. "There is more I can offer you!"

"What can you offer me that I cannot take for myself?" Nebuchar snarled.

"Close the door and I'll tell you," Shulana said, giving Nebuchar what humans called a "wink," just as Bagsby had taught her.

"A moment," Nebuchar said. He slammed the door and took his seat again. "All right. What else do you have to offer that I can't take for myself?"

"Your life," Shulana said flatly, her eyes suddenly as hard as any murderer's that Nebuchar had ever known. "Be silent or die."

As she spoke, Nebuchar felt the tickle of cold, sharp steel against his throat and a vice grip around his chest.

"What magic is this?" Nebuchar whispered, stunned.

Shulana made a slight gesture with her hand, and Nebuchar heard the voice of Bagsby whisper in his ear.

"The kind that works, unlike yours. No matter what you do, you'll die before you can harm me or her. So tell us what we want to know, and we'll go away quietly."

"Bagsby!" Nebuchar whispered. "Is that you?"

"The same."

"Then I have something you want or I'd be dead already."

"Where is Valdaimon?" Bagsby hissed, putting more pressure on the blade.

"Since I'll die whether I tell you or not, why should I tell you?" Nebuchar said softly.

"I need you alive to get the elf out of here."

"So if I don't talk, she dies."

"Do you really think that matters to me?" Bagsby asked, his voice dripping with sarcasm.

Nebuchar thought hard. He had no doubt that the Bagsby he had known couldn't care less whether the elf lived or died. And, since Bagsby was somehow invisible, despite the sigils that protected the room, he would likely escape.

"You'll kill me anyway once we're outside," Nebuchar argued.

"But it's such a long walk through your tavern. You'll think of something."

Nebuchar grinned. Bagsby was right. He would think of something. "Lundlow Keep," Nebuchar breathed.

"You may be lying," Bagsby suggested.

"Why should I? If I can't kill you, I'm only too glad to send you to a confrontation with Valdaimon."

"You're right," Bagsby said agreeably. He cut Nebuchar's throat from ear to ear. The big man looked surprised for an instant. He tried to shout, but could only gurgle. Then he slumped in the chair, clutching his throat, and felt his life force gush out onto the floor.

"Wait!" Shulana gasped as Bagsby stepped on the sigil by the door and became visible. "How do we get out of here now?"

"Simple," Bagsby said. He grabbed Nebuchar's body and threw it over the table, then drew his longsword and hacked off the head. Holding it aloft by the hair, he threw open the door and stepped into the tavern. The startled Shulana walked behind him.

"I am Bagsby!" he shouted, holding the head high in one hand and his sword in the other. "This piece of garbage is Nebuchar," he added, shaking the head for emphasis. He strode forward, eyes meeting each and every man's as walked past him. "I'm taking over, as of now. Any objections?"

As Bagsby anticipated, there were none. The crowd was too stunned to think how to react.

"Good," Bagsby said, nonchalantly tossing the head to the tavern keeper. "My second in command and I will be back in an hour. See that my room is cleaned up."

Bagsby walked out the door without glancing back. Shulana, still stunned, followed him into the narrow street. George and Marta fell in behind the new, if temporary, lord of the Kalan underworld who walked boldly through the Thieves' Quarter toward the ruins of the once great city.

"We go tonight," Bagsby announced.

George's eyes lit up with interest. The past two days had been boring. Camping in the woods about a mile from some old castle, studying it from every angle, thinking through and discarding one plan after another; none of this was to George's taste. But the thought of action and treasure interested him greatly.

Marta tossed another branch onto the tiny fire the group allowed themselves. The woods were full of camp fires, as refugees from Kala and the surrounding towns struggled to stay alive and out of the way of the brutal garrison troops. One more fire would hardly matter.

"What plan have you decided on?" she asked. So far, it seemed to Marta, they hadn't done much to hurt the Heilesheim cause. The prospect of actually encountering Valdaimon, an important servant of the king, appealed to her greatly.

"Well," Bagsby said, grinning, "we wait until dark. Then we walk in the front door, kill everyone, and steal the treasure."

"Right," George said, lying back down. "That worked once, with a lot o' magic to 'elp you. I don't think it will work again, not against a wizard like old Valdaimon. And not against a hundred some guards like we counted at that castle."

"Hmmm," Bagsby teased. "You may be right. Shulana, what magic do we have available?" While she talked, Bagsby worked on a tree limb with his dagger, pruning off tiny branches, skinning off the bark, forming a half-finished quarterstaff.

"You've seen almost everything I can do," Shulana said. "I can cause silence. I can render things invisible for a while. I can move almost undetected in this cloak of mine, and I can throw a ball of magical fire. Oh, and I can see whether things are magical or not, and I can shrink things to a tiny size. Also, I have learned to cause a certain number of foes to fall asleep. As a young elf, my magical powers are quite limited."

"You're sure the treasure will be in the tower room?" Bagsby asked for what Shulana thought must be the hundredth time.

"Of course. Any wizard would put it there, under heavy magical guards—fire traps, stones that strike you dead when you step on them, other things I may not know of."

"Good!" Bagsby exclaimed. "Then we go tonight! All we need is a length of rope."

"But 'ow? 'Ow we gonna get in and out?" George asked.

"Like I said," Bagsby taunted, "we're going to walk in the front door and take what we want."

The night was dark with little light provided by the sliver of a moon that hung on the horizon. Bagsby, George, and Shulana sneaked out of the woods into the meadow that surrounded the hill atop which Lundlow Keep was set. The tallness of the grass aided them as they approached the front of the hill. The castle itself, a small stone keep dominated by its sixty-foot round tower, loomed ahead like an indomitable fortress. George still had little understanding of the plan, and Shulana had grave doubts, but Bagsby moved forward with quiet confidence, stopping only once when he had to pinch his nose to stop a sneeze, for he had a shoot of grass up one nostril.

Stealthily the trio crept past the outer sentries, who hardly took their duties seriously. The damp earth stained their cloaks and tunics as they crawled on their bellies and inched their way slowly up the hill toward the main door. Bagsby was glad to see that their observations of the past few days were correct; the door was not locked. Men of the garrison moved freely in and out past the two guards posted at the doorway.

The thieves crawled up to within twenty yards of the door. They could hear the quiet conversation of the guards carried on the night air. George crawled up close beside Bagsby and whispered, "What now?"

"Wait for Marta," Bagsby mouthed back.

The wait was not long. From beyond the opposite side of the castle Marta ran into the open field, screaming at the top of her lungs.

"Thieves! Murderers! Cutthroats!" she shouted. "There's one, there, on the castle wall! He's going up the castle wall!"

The woman's shrill shrieks could be heard all over the

compound. The response, as Bagsby had hoped, was both swift and confused.

The outer perimeter sentries, and those posted by the stables on the far side of the keep, came running in toward the castle, not a few making directly for Marta to see what all the shouting was really about. The castle doors flew open and a soldier with some authority stood in the doorway, silhouetted by the light from the main room behind him. He barked orders back inside as he pulled on his helmet. A troop of half-armored, half-armed, half-awake men came running to the doorway behind him.

"Fan out!" he ordered. "Search the perimeter."

The men scrambled out into the darkness and quickly dissipated into disordered clumps, vainly beating the bushes and asking one another what was going on.

Marta kept up her shrieking. "There're thieves inside the castle! I saw them going up the wall, climbing it like spiders, they was," she babbled. Repeatedly she pointed to the tower room, and eventually one soldier had the brilliant idea of reporting this news to the commander inside.

"There are thieves afoot, in the tower!" the soldier shouted as he raced in through the main door. Bagsby strained to see through the doorway. The huge single room inside was in chaos. Men were running about, grabbing clothes, armor, and weapons, while others staggered to their feet, still groggy from being awakened from their deep sleep.

"Shulana, are you ready?" Bagsby asked.

The elf nodded, and Bagsby slapped George on the back. "Go!" he ordered.

George stood up suddenly, let out a roar, and charged forward with his great pike. Bagsby followed close behind, his quarterstaff in one hand, dagger in the other. George skewered the first guard before the man could react. The second managed to level his weapon to break Bagsby's charge, but Bagsby, anticipating this move, leapt high into the air and, avoiding the spear, hurled himself feet first at the man's chest. The guard crashed against the stone wall and collapsed to the ground. One quick thrust from Bagsby's dagger finished him.

"Now, Shulana!" Bagsby shouted.

The elf was already in position just inside the doorway, her hands extended toward the great hall. Swiftly she muttered the incantation for sleep, and as she completed the spell, more than thirty men in the huge room fell over as though struck dead. That left only about fifteen active— the rest of the garrison was already scattered throughout the compound.

"Follow me, George, and stay close," Bagsby said. He waded into the room full of still-startled warriors who grabbed what weapons they could to oppose him. As soon as he was inside, Bagsby began shouting toward the huge circular staircase that led upward to the tower room.

"Hurry! Hurry! We can't hold them for long!" Bagsby called.

"Yeah, hurry up! There's a bunch o' 'em down 'ere," George echoed, grasping the idea.

Bagsby's homemade quarterstaff landed a crushing blow against one man's skull, and a forward thrust jabbed it into the chest of the man behind him. George, meanwhile, had already dispatched two with his pike, one with a blow to the head with the flat of the business end and the second with sharp, stabbing thrust.

More of the men came running to oppose the pair, but several of the remainder took to the stairs, lingering, looking first up and then down at the melee below, uncertain what to do.

Bagsby swung his staff like a giant club, knocking down two more opponents. Then he ran forward and, planting the end of the staff on the stone floor, vaulted upward, landing about five feet up the stairway. One guard took the challenge and swung with his sword at Bagsby's head. Bagsby dodged the blow and somersaulted backward down the stairs, feigning a fall.

"By all the gods, hurry. We can't keep them down here much longer," he shouted.

"The tower room!" one of the guards finally yelled. "They're in the tower room. Quickly!" The cluster of guards on the stairs lost their hesitation as that man charged up the stairway, sword in hand. They turned and followed.

Shulana and George, meanwhile, had succeeded in either killing or knocking out all the remaining guards downstairs.

"Hurry," Bagsby said. "There'll be more coming from outside."

Running full tilt, Bagsby charged up the stairs behind the seven soldiers, thrusting his staff forward to entangle the legs of the rearmost man. That hapless soul toppled downward, where George grabbed him and, with a mighty heave, tossed him on down the stairwell.

"Six to go," Bagsby muttered to himself. "Better leave at least four alive."

Bagsby and George continued the chase up the stairs until the door to the tower room came into view.

"Hold them off," shouted the soldier who, in the crisis, had assumed command. Two of the guards turned and stood side by side, facing down the stairs, to ward off Bagsby, George, and Shulana.

At the top of the stairs by the door, the soldier barked at the guards. "Open it!"

"You know the rules," one guard protested. "No one goes there on pain of death."

"Hurry!" Bagsby shouted, thrusting at one of the two guards opposing him with his quarterstaff. "They're just outside the door! We can't keep them out!"

"They're already inside there, you dolt!" the would-be leader growled. "Open it!"

"We ain't got a key," the guard protested.

"Then break it down!"

Bagsby rammed the end of his quarterstaff up against the underside of his opponent's jaw, rendering the man unconscious. At the same time, George dispatched his foe, using nothing but a dagger, as the stairway was too narrow for his great pike.

Bagsby glanced up. The four men at the top of the stairs were preparing to force the door; two of them would hit it to break it down.

"Now! Duck!" he shouted.

The trio of thieves threw themselves down flat on the stone staircase and covered their heads with their hands. Bagsby heard a solid thud, followed by a loud crash. Then the explosion flashed.

Deadly magic fire flared up from the floor of the tower room, consuming the fallen door and two of the guards in the first second of its existence. The two remaining men screamed in panic and beat the flames that rose from their tunics.

"In there—let's go!" the leader still ordered. The second soldier hesitated. The first, glancing back down the stairwell, cursed and charged into the room. A second great explosion rocked the entire castle. Even with his eyes closed, Bagsby could see the flash of that second explosion, and an instant later the peculiar odor of ozone was in the air.

"Lightning trap," Shulana called.

"Right," Bagsby answered. "Let's go."

The little thief pounded up to the top of the stairs. "You!" he barked at the sole remaining soldier. "Out of my way!" The man dropped his spear and fled down the stairs past George, who tripped him, and Shulana, who watched him tumble toward the bottom of the great spiral far below.

"Shulana, hurry!" Bagsby said.

He stepped into the tower room, where everything that could burn was in flames. George was right behind Bagsby.

"Stay put until Shulana comes," Bagsby ordered.

Shulana stood in the doorway, quickly chanting the words of the spell that made the magic auras of all things visible. When the spell was completed, she reeled backward! Never had she seen such strong auras, and so many, in so small a space.

"Hurry, hurry," Bagsby urged.

Shulana forced herself to concentrate despite her shock and fear. She quickly spotted the glowing, pulsating, red egg-shaped auras in the center of the room. Next, she checked the floor. Only the magic circle glowed.

"The floor is safe," she announced. "The Golden Eggs are right here." She reached out her hand, touched one egg and then the other, and to her great relief saw them become visible. Then she located the source of the other extremely powerful aura that flooded the room.

"That crate against the wall. Don't touch it—it's enchanted," she warned.

Bagsby noticed then that the plain wooden crate had not burned, despite the fire that had consumed shelves, parchments, and books in the room, and devoured human flesh in an instant.

"Valdaimon," he breathed.

Inside the crate, in another realm reached through the gateway of a specially cut diamond, the soul of Valdaimon stirred. Intruders? Could it be?

Bagsby ran to the crate, despite Shulana's warning. "Do what you must," he said to her. "I will do what I must."

Shulana once more set herself to casting a spell, this time a spell of diminution that made whatever she chose to affect shrink to a mere one-sixth of its normal size.

Bagsby flipped open the crate and screamed.

Before his eyes he saw living dust, thousands of tiny particles, swirling and blending with one another to take on a vaguely human form. First there was the hint of the outline of a head, then a torso, then a bony arm took shape.

Shulana finished her spell. She reached out and touched each egg again. As she did so, each shrank small enough for a man to hold easily in his hand.

George, who had watched all this in astonishment, nodded dumbly as Shulana extended her hand to him. She touched him, and he shrank. She picked him up and placed him on the tiny ledge of the arrow slit in the wall.

"Bagsby!" she shouted. "The rope!"

But Bagsby could not tear his eyes from the fascinating, horrifying sight inside the crate. The head, which moments before had been a vague, smooth outline, now revealed a face—a face which after a lifetime Bagsby still recognized.

"Valdaimon!" Bagsby bellowed. "You foul, murdering . . ."

"No time!" Shulana called. Already her keen elven

hearing picked up the clank of armor coming from the bottom of the great stairway. "Get to the rope!"

"No," Bagsby shouted. "No! I have to kill him! Now's our chance!"

Shulana raced to Bagsby's side, carefully turning her head so as not to stare directly into the forming face. Instead, she peeked side-long into the crate, aiming her glance at the middle portion. She saw the smooth outline of robes forming over the shape of two, scrawny, bony legs.

"You can't kill him," she said flatly. "He's already dead."

"I must!" Bagsby proclaimed, still staring at the now plainly visible, wrathful face as an almost solid arm began to reach slowly toward him.

Desperately, Shulana glanced about the room. Bagsby was useless, he was already in the power of those rheumy, dusty eyes whose gaze was locked on his. On the floor, just a few feet away, she spied a vial that had survived the explosion. A faint, pure-white aura still glowed about it.

"Water of the human gods!" Shulana exclaimed, excitement peaking in her voice.

"What?" Bagsby asked, turning in surprise to Shulana. So unusual was the excitement in her voice that his attention was drawn from the wizard's eyes.

"Pour that vial on him—and quickly!" Shulana said. "Look out!" she added, suddenly shoving Bagsby backward, out of the grasp of the withered hand that suddenly darted from inside the crate.

Bagsby, taken by surprise and off balance, started to fall backward, and instinctively went into a back somersault. He flipped himself over twice, and rammed his head straight into the curving wall of the room. With a stunned, questioning look, he slumped over, unconscious.

Without further thought, Shulana grabbed the vial, ripped out the stopper, and poured the half contents over the bony arm. The remainder she splashed, without looking, into the crate. A piteous, wailing scream arose from within, as water blessed by the gods burned into the undead body! The arm crumbled into dust.

Shulana worked with lightning speed to complete her mission. She slammed the crate shut without looking inside, for she knew full well what was in it. Then she took the rope from around Bagsby's waist, tied it to his sword, and dropped it out the arrow slit. She placed the eggs in a cloth sack she'd brought for that purpose. Lastly, she knelt beside Bagsby and roused him.

"Huhhnn . . ." Bagsby moaned.

"Quickly, awaken," she whispered.

Bagsby's eyes fluttered open.

"We leave now or we die here," Shulana told him. The thief staggered to his feet. He was extremely dizzy but able to stand.

"Get to the rope," Shulana ordered.

The last thing Bagsby remembered was holding the rope in his hand, gazing back in confusion at the wooden crate, while the sounds of clanking armor and confused shouts drifted through the door.

"And then, after I had reduced us in size, George helped me carry you down the rope. We were so small the guards never noticed us in the dark," Shulana explained.

Bagsby raised his head and winced with the pain.

"I'm surprised we carried it off," he said, grinning broadly.

"Who was that guy who appeared in the tower window while we was runnin' across the field?" George asked. " 'E 'ad the ugliest face I ever saw!"

"Valdaimon," Shulana answered. "What you saw," she said to Bagsby, "was his body re-forming as his soul returned to it."

"Why didn't he just blast us with a fireball or something?" Bagsby wondered out loud. "He must have been able to see us, despite our size."

"He could not cast spells," Shulana answered softly. "The blessed water damaged him. His right arm was gone, and from what George said, I think his eyes and mouth may be injured as well. No human mage can cast spells without gestures and the careful forming of the words of power."

"Then he's powerless!" Bagsby said, thirst for vengeance again rising in his breast.

"No!" Shulana said. "Only until he finds a way to heal his dead flesh or, more than likely, take on a new body."

"A new body?" George said, incredulous.

"The undead, such as Valdaimon, need to preserve only a portion of their original body to maintain their existence."

"You think he knows who we are?" George asked.

"Certainly," Bagsby responded with a grimace.

"Well, then, we're in for it someday," George said cheerfully.

Bagsby gazed around at their woodland campsite. In the near distance he could hear the sound of flowing water and the splashes of a large animal.

"There's water nearby?" he asked.

"Aye," George said. "And fat Marta's about 'er bath. I think I'll go and join 'er. If I'm goin' to die by some undead thingie's 'and, I want a bit of sport before I go!" George winked at Bagsby, then got up and disappeared into the bushes.

"It's the River Rigel," Shulana explained. "We've been on the run from Heilesheim troops for two days. We have to stay in the woods The only natural route led here, to the river."

Bagsby looked at the large sacks that lay by a nearby tree.

"The Golden Eggs of Parona?"

"Yes," Shulana answered.

"So, now you kill me, eh?" Bagsby said, trying his most charming grin.

"Only if you keep me from doing what I must do."

"And what is that?"

"I must destroy them."

Bagsby stood, shakily. He walked over to the large sacks and opened first one, then the other. "Why," he asked, "would you want to destroy these?"

"You don't know what they truly are," Shulana said simply.

"And I'll not let them be destroyed until I know their secret," Bagsby stated flatly.

"Then I must kill you," Shulana answered. "For their secret I cannot reveal, even to you. It is a secret known only by Elrond, myself, and some on the Elven Council."

Bagsby leaned back, resting his weight against the two large treasures. "Go ahead."

Shulana's eyes met his in a level gaze. "You know I cannot," she said.

"Nor can you tell me the secret?"

"No."

Bagsby opened his arms and drew Shulana to him. "Then I must learn it for myself," he said. "It may be that there is one other who knows it. There is a man with the desert tribes who knows wondrous things from ancient times."

Bagsby basked in the warmth of Shulana's body pressed against his own. Only then did he notice with some surprise that there was also great warmth radiating from the Golden Eggs of Parona, and a strange vibratation, almost like a series of blows, coming from inside them—as the magical words spoken five thousand years before drifted through the web of time and came together to work their speaker's will.